Linc

COMMUNITIES & CULTURAL SERVICES

This boo

e Black Dress Reader,

r picking up this Little Black Dress book, one
at new titles from our series of fun, page–turning
novels. Lucky you — you're about to have a fantastic
read that we know you won't be able to put down!

t you make your Little Black Dress experience
r by logging on to

www.littleblackdressbooks.com

where you can:

er our **monthly competitions** to win
eous prizes

hot-off-the-press news about our latest titles

l **exclusive** preview chapters both from
favourite authors and from brilliant new
ng talent

up-and-coming books online

a up for an essential slice of romance via
fortnightly email newsletter

To renew c othing more than to curl up and indulge in an
romance, and so we're delighted to welcome you
You Little Black Dress club!

from,

The little *black dress* team

Five interesting things about Niamh Shaw:

1. I was made in Ireland and – stereotypically – have never come across a spud I didn't love.

2. My physiology is ideally suited to a diet of chocolate and coffee. For this reason, I do lots of exercise, although I'm not as bendy as I should be.

3. My best features are my feet, which are small for their size with a lovely colour and novelty toes that can perform a variety of tricks. The rest of me is pretty lame in comparison.

4. I have travelled widely, but my favourite destination is still my bed.

5. There is little photographic evidence of my existence.

To find out more about Niamh Shaw,
log on to www.niamheshaw.com

Smart Casual

Niamh Shaw

little
black
dress

First published in 2009
by LITTLE BLACK DRESS
An imprint of HEADLINE PUBLISHING GROUP

A LITTLE BLACK DRESS paperback

2

Cataloguing in Publication Data is available from the British Library

ISBN 978 0 7553 4856 5

Typeset in Transit511BT by Avon DataSet Ltd,
Bidford-on-Avon, Warwickshire

Printed and bound in Great Britain by
Clays Ltd, St Ives plc

Headline's policy is to use papers that are natural, renewable and
recyclable products and made from wood grown in sustainable forests.
The logging and manufacturing processes are expected to conform to the
environmental regulations of the country of origin.

HEADLINE PUBLISHING GROUP
An Hachette UK Company
338 Euston Road
London NW1 3BH

www.littleblackdressbooks.com
www.headline.co.uk
www.hachette.co.uk

For Andrew

Acknowledgements

Thanks a million to:

David, who always steered me back on track. I am also grateful for the encouragement, feedback and erotic ego massages; and sorry again for exterminating Bob.

Keren, who taught me about Proper Nouns, but never fully cured my wilful addiction to capital letters.

Sammy, the Ruddocks, Rosina, Penny and Carol for reading *Smart Casual* in various stages of completion with no lasting side effects.

Róisín, who always makes me laugh; also many thanks for providing focused encouragement over the years.

Since Ronan is one of the funniest people in the known universe, I robbed many of his best lines, including 'his mother knit him'. Thanks for that and for allowing some of your sense of humour to rub off on me.

Any mistakes, errors or omissions are totally someone else's fault, most likely JohnO's. However, thanks for the invaluable information on how to avoid exploding kidneys and the real reason for the brace position.

My online friends at Litopia and Bookshed, who gave hours of their valuable time, feedback and encouragement; especially John a.k.a. Moto, Rob a.k.a. Juan, Larry a.k.a. Harkrider, Priceless a.k.a. Lynn, Sonnambulista a.k.a. Carolyn, and Nick with a P.

Over the years, many people ordered me to write and threatened horrible retribution if I did not. These include: Philip 'Fatboy' Sheehan, Paul Berryman, Michelle Fraser and Mo Glover.

My agent, Peter Buckman, and my editor(s), Cat Cobain and Leah Woodburn – thanks for your belief and all your hard work on *Smart Casual*.

My parents, Vera and Alan, who have always been my biggest fans; and my brothers, Eoin and Daire.

To Husband, who not only put up with a feisty muse, excessive creative angst, reckless overstatement, tears and associated mucous, but also provided support, encouragement, counsel, and car maintenance. I am so glad I scored you and sincerely hope we never divorce.

To any bastards who provided nothing constructive, positive or even the right side of ambiguous, I don't thank you AT ALL and additionally, hope you get foot-rot, pest infestations, nasty synthetic materials, electrical surges and rising damp.

Seeing how they last and all, I was keen to make an impression.

A *good* impression, of course. The type that leaves a dent in the cranium and a bad case of tinnitus takes a rare degree of talent.

But I digress (it happens a lot: I am full of pent-up digression).

Despite it being a perverted hour of the morning, I was pretty confident of high-kicking in with my best foot forward. At that moment I, Olivia Anderson, was en route to the Director's annual strategy meeting to accept my promotion. In less than an hour, I would be the new Projects Director of Puttock Leavitt's Business Systems Services department. Bullshit Services, for short.

Soon, I would be able to claim booze on expenses. I would possess a leather wizard chair with little rubber wheels and a seat that swivelled, and a corner office with hectares of space and natural light issuing from *windows*. Most important, at the end of each month there would be significantly more salary nestling in my bank account, clamouring to be spent on executive toys and needlessly expensive designer suits and ludicrously pointy shoes.

But what mattered was the promotion itself. I took pride in being exceptionally good at my job. Being a control freak with a mild case of OCD might not be an ideal personality type for, say, a bomb disposal expert or a yoga instructor, but it was useful for a project manager.

In preparation for the sadistic breakfast meeting, I had enjoyed a decent night's sleep (defined as anything over four hours). I wore my best power underwear, under the sharpest of Armani skirt suits. My make-up triumphantly prevailed against the bitter autumn wind that scraped through London Bridge station.

Even my raging torrent of hair was behaving itself – courtesy of three gallons of product and half the remaining ozone layer. I often wondered what such disorganised hair was doing on such an organised head – although, obviously, I wouldn't have it the other way round.

Just for a change, I felt enthusiastic and positive about life. My default setting was anxious and worried, and on the rare occasions there wasn't anything to be anxious and worried about, I was anxious about not being worried. I felt almost . . . happy. Happy and successful and fulfilled and *thin*.

Catching sight of myself in a shop window, I gave myself a flirty little smile. Christ, I was foxy. My bat-coat billowed impressively as I walked. And please note that I was walking. This particular day, I was exceptionally early – even for me.

It was this that directly precipitated my downfall.

Well, I didn't want to be the first to turn up at the meeting. That might have been construed as a bit sucky, and I would probably be coerced into setting up the Director's laptop and projector. It was hardly fitting for the new Projects Director to be rolling around the floor hunting down power outlets and faulty network points with a pair of pliers waving her arse in the air.

With seven minutes and twelve seconds to slaughter, I decided to indulge myself in a little pre-business shopping. I was not practised at impulse shopping and London Bridge station would drive a shopaholic to drink, but there were some valid options. Knickerbox exercised a frilly appeal, but for someone without even a whiff of a boyfriend it was difficult to justify the purchase of frivolous knickers. There was always Tie Rack, but I already had a scarf, and a woman can only wear one at a time.

Then, across the cavernous reach of the station, I harked the gentle call of Lynott's Pharmacy. I usually avoided Lynott's, because the shop mocked my will-power. Once, I went in for a sandwich, and emerged in a daze clutching a nettle and liquorice facial scrub, enough intensive-action moisturiser to keep a baby whale moist for a decade, and three packets of travel sickness pills.

But this time I would be strong. All I wanted was lipsalve. It would be a flying visit, leaving plenty of time to pick up my low-foam extra-caff hazelnut flavour soya latte from the Coffee Spot next door.

Making a marginal adjustment to my course, I strode towards the shop.

My self-control wilted in the blast of heat as the doors smoothly ushered me in. But it prevailed, and soon I waited in line to pay for my stick of lipsalve. I was behind a woman in the process of paying for a pregnancy kit and it was there, as I took a break from gazing wistfully at the flavoured condom display, that I spotted: The Love God.

Indeed, he would have been impossible to miss, being – as he was – tall and chiselled and quite simply totally, irredeemably, unquestionably luscious. A rare (if not practically extinct) example of the alpha male of the species, prowling free and rampant in his virile prime.

My salivary ducts sprang into dribbly overtime.

I briefly checked there were no woodland creatures roaming around my head, and worked hard on projecting an air of desirability. For a while, I did a pretty good job of pretending to be entirely engrossed in a range of incontinence knickers nearby, until I realised that, on the off chance that The Love God looked across and noticed me, incontinence knickers did not broadcast the right sort of message *at all*.

Seconds earlier, I had been internally willing the potentially pregnant woman to hurry the fuck up, but now I welcomed the opportunity to surreptitiously observe The Love God.

Oh my flying nellie, he was divine. The love of my life, the inspirer of dreams, the sparkle in my eye. He had the potential to be all these things.

Or at the very least, a bloody good shag.

To be objective about it, I suppose you could say that his earlobes were on the fat side.

(Sure, nothing the love of a good woman couldn't fix.)

But otherwise . . . well, hel-lo Major Yum!

His scrumptious credentials included dull gold hair without a hint of bouff; long, narrowed ice-blue eyes (slightly on the small side, but not detracting from the overall impression of improbable dishiness); a sharp aquiline nose which flared slightly at the bottom; and the most beautiful pair of lips I've ever wanted to nibble on – large and soft and mouth-wateringly tasty-looking.

But not rubbery.

There's nothing worse than rubbery lips.

Except maybe hairy fingers.

You could've chopped logs with his jaw.

I nearly wet myself.

(I might need those incontinence knickers after all.)

In a moment of weakness, I nearly gave into the urge to clamber over the prophylactic display that cruelly separated us, and snog him senseless right there in the middle of Lynott's.

Of course, I didn't. But I did drift off in a little daydream – 'When I saw you come in the door, I knew you were the only woman who could ever satisfy me' etc. – and therefore failed to notice that The Love God had moved closer until he was practically standing next to me.

Which was when I realised that the most recent object of my devotion was trying to jump the queue. He tried to act as if he was just hanging out enjoying the view, but it was clear he was plotting to cut in.

A swell of indignation replaced my previous state of fulsome well being. The nerve of the man! It was quite obvious that I and the other shoppers were queuing. At least, I'm not sure three other shoppers standing in rough line formation constituted an ISO-certified queue, but it certainly qualified more than *no people at all*.

I considered how to convey to The Love God that he was an arrogant prick who could wait his fucking turn just like everyone else in a charming and flirty way. Hey, he might have been cute, but I wasn't about to betray a principle for any man.

Bloody tourist, I seethed. Okay, I was manufactured in Ireland, but I'd lived in London six years. I had embraced the Oyster card, hadn't visited Buckingham Palace in ages, and observed queuing structures regardless of chronological deficiencies.

While the possibly pregnant lady signed her receipt, I shifted subtly to increase territorial advantage. Seconds later, the man *rested his hand on the counter*. Oh, this was outrageous! I'm not an unreasonable person – in fact, that very morning I had given up my seat on the train to an old boy. And although I have occasionally been known to 'Tut!' people standing in the middle of the escalator, I'm not proud of it.

If he'd asked, it might have been different. You know, if he'd said: 'Excuse me, I hope you don't mind but I have to get this insulin to my sister – she's the one slumped on the ground outside – do you mind if I go first? You don't? Oh, that's lovely, thank you so much.'

Instead he was buying – I stole a peek – a packet of peppermint mouth freshener strips. I doubted his sister was slumped on the ground outside dying of halitosis.

The probably pregnant lady moved away and the man and I clashed over the counter.

'Just this, thanks,' he said to the cashier and I noticed the American twang.

'Excuse me!' I said, adrenaline rendering my voice unusually shrill. 'I was next.'

The man looked at me like I had popped fully formed out of the ground. He delivered a smile that I'm sure had brightened the lives of thousands of women. At that moment, it had quite the opposite effect on me.

'I'm sure you don't mind—' he said.

'Actually, I'm sure I do.'

'I just wanna pay for this and I'll—'

'Really? Fancy that. I just want to pay for this.' I pointed the lipsalve at him like a gun. 'And these people here' – I indicated the people behind me – 'are either Morris dancers, or standing in line for roughly the same reason.'

If I'd expected to get support from the people behind

me, I was mistaken. Suddenly the huffing and foot-tapping turned into a collective fascination with the ceiling.

The American retired the plastic smirk. 'I didn't realise there was a queue—'

'The big blue sign with "Queue Here" and an arrow wasn't enough of a clue?'

The person behind me coughed pointedly.

'I didn't see it—'

'Well, now that you do, why don't you go and join it?'

'Lady, what is your problem?'

'My problem? Generally: global warming and account managers who oversell inefficiently designed computer systems. But specifically: you. Why don't you wait your turn just like everyone else?'

'Why don't *you* back the fuck off?' said the American. His tone was conversational, but I recoiled from the words.

I was reassured when I spotted the Lynott's security guard standing by the herbal supplements. I had always got the impression that he took his role in the service of retail surveillance seriously.

'Okay, maybe . . . why don't we all just . . . just calm down, and let's just . . . let's, er, discuss this rationally.'

Well, that's what men always say in these types of situations

'Oh, I am calm,' said the American in the same quiet voice, although the pulsing vein standing out on his forehead belied it. 'This conversation is over.' Turning to the checkout assistant, he flicked some coins across the counter.

'Sir, I need to scan—'

'Keep the change.'

'Hey!' I said. 'You – I—'

'Get away from me, you uptight bitch.'

I was shocked almost speechless. 'I – you – I will then! With p-p-pleasure!'

I spun round and stalked to the exit, seething with anger. My thoughts jangled around my head. How dare he? I mean, how – how *dare* he?

I was at the automatic doors when the air was rent by an ear-splitting alarm, magnified by the hard acoustics of London Bridge station. I came to an abrupt halt, whereupon one of the doors slid to with a *crack!* on the side of my head.

As I reeled uncontrollably to the right, I felt the heel of my shoe give way. A meaty hand clamped on my shoulder arrested my abrupt descent.

It was Security.

'Please come with me, madam,' he roared over the alarm.

'What – what for?' With a flash of awful clarity, I realised I still clutched the lipsalve. Surely it couldn't be *that*?

Thankfully, the alarm deactivated before my head exploded.

'Madam, I am charging you with abducting a product and exiting the store, which is a felony,' said Security, evidently thoroughly overexcited. 'Don't try to deny it – I saw you with me own eyes. Walking out of the shop with the goods in full view—'

'Goods?' I spluttered. 'A tube of lipsalve is not goods! It's a *good*! If even that! I forgot it was in my hand—'

'Store policy is to detain shoplifters and notify the police.'

'I – I wasn't – I wasn't shoplifting!' I said, horrified.

'Madam, you can explain that to the fuzz.'

The store manager arrived at the scene of the minor misunderstanding and was no more sympathetic. I opted for an offensive strategy based on his scrofulous moustache. I suggested the police should be called to examine the faulty automatic doors that resulted in such grievous bodily harm to my person, and wondered aloud how much a court would award in damages for my split cheekbone, broken Jimmy Choo and acute emotional trauma.

We parted amicably after I paid Lynott's £3.89 for the tube of lipsalve.

Two minutes later, I lurched out of London Bridge station clutching my wayward heel. I tried to ignore it, but my mind fretted at the confrontation' with the American. Every time I thought about him, rage swarmed over me. Lucky for him he wasn't standing in front of me, or I would – I would—

I would do absolutely nothing, if my previous performance was anything to go by. Why, *why* hadn't I advised the American to take his breath freshener strips and apply them up his arse? But instead, I had just stood there displaying my imaginary backbone.

I glanced at my watch, and my intestines squirmed. God, I was so late! What if the Director decided to give the job to someone else?

Thankfully, the Puttock Leavitt offices – twenty-five floors of prime real estate – were right beside the station. I swirled through the revolving doors and pushed through the eddies of accountants.

According to Puttock Leavitt's extensive publicity material, PL is the most prestigious accounting firm in the world. I have no idea what the corporation does, apart from fight malpractice suits and employ some of the most boring individuals to roam this earth.

All that really matters is that PL has an annual turnover of £26.37 billion, give or take a pound or two. That number may have been rounded up/down to the nearest ten million, but you can bet that somewhere in the bowels of PL some wonk has a figure that is accurate to within three decimal places.

PL's corporate logo is pretty inspiring:

'Embracing the future with honour and integrity.'

Although to be entirely accurate, the word 'honour' should be 'greed', and a more appropriate word than 'integrity' would be 'sleaze'; and if you really wanted to be pedantic, you could substitute the word 'profits' for 'future'. But the word 'embracing' is good, and well worth £3.4 million, which was what PL paid their PR firm to come up with it.

In the lift, I examined myself in the chrome hand-rail. My head was furry carnage: random tendrils exploding from the hairgrip and standing to attention at right angles. Blood seeped from a cut just below my left eye.

No getting around it: an emergency pit stop was required. I punched the button for the nineteenth floor. I was pretty sure there was a hair-clogged roller brush in my desk drawer and, if my God-given quotient of Irish luck did its stuff for once, a can of hairspray that might be good for one last, tired squirt.

Erupting from the lift, I kicked off my shoes to better charge down the corridor to the Maze, the labyrinth of cubicles housing the BSS department. There was a hint of tumbleweed in the air as I crashed through the office area door, which rebounded in my face.

'Fuck!' I snarled and kicked it soundly. It was an ill-advised course of action in stockinged feet. I was thinking about hopping around the place swearing loudly, when Jed's disembodied voice made me jump anyway.

'Anderson,' he drawled, 'haven't you learned how to operate a door? It's not that difficult.'

His head appeared round the entrance to the cubicle we shared and he gave a hoot.

'What happened to you?' he cackled.

'Oh, oh, and, and . . .' I groped about for a suitably cutting riposte, but couldn't come up with anything.

Jed Marshall was my colleague of four months and the Business Systems Services Support Manager. BSS provided computer systems – or if you prefer jargon 'value-add services' – to PL's clients. My job was to manage system installation. My job description was 'ensuring client applications are built on time, within budget, with the minimum amount of resources'.

Jed's team supported and maintained the systems. His job description stated: 'sanity optional'.

My colleague was tall, lean and chiselled – although I wouldn't have said he was handsome, exactly. He was a wonderful, wonderful guy.

I wouldn't touch him with a patent-pending sterilisation system bargepole with inbuilt missile launchers.

See, Jed was still in the process of finding his inner rabbit. He had a vicious reputation for ripping your heart out via your urethra, dicing and frying it with garlic and a dash of olive oil, and eating it for dinner with some fava beans and a nice Chianti.

There were legions of bitter women who could testify to this.

However, outside his taste in cuisine, he was great. Biting sense of humour. Marvellous conversationalist. Could hold his own on a squash court. A man who – unusually – not only thought he was a bit of all right at DIY but actually was: the definitive Fix-it Man.

Most important, he was a resilient, conscientious drinking partner and regular practitioner of the fireman's lift, an occasionally useful mode of transport. He could also be counted on to steer me away from the danger zones.

Vodka: 'Makes you too frisky for me, sweet cheeks. Here, have a whiskey.'

Gin: 'You want to sit under a table and cry all night?'

Men: ('Gerroff! He's gorsheous!') 'Anderson, he's a troll. I've seen gargoyles with more sex appeal.'

'I'm sorry,' said Jed, but I could tell he wasn't because he was still smiling broadly. 'Here, have a seat. Sorry, wait a moment . . .' He removed a tangle of network cables from my chair and added them to the jumble of computer entrails, old keyboards, broken mice, pliers and soldering irons littered across his desk. 'Sit.'

'No, I can't. I'm late,' I said, plopping into the chair. Although I am strictly opposed to blubbing in the workplace, I felt my chin give a dangerous wobble and I involuntarily snorted. It was an absolutely brazen, shameless bid for sympathy.

Like many men, Jed had not half a clue what to do with an overemotional woman threatening to leak everywhere, turn red and ugly, and start talking about feelings and issuing unspoken demands for hugs.

'Shit!' he said with distaste. 'Christ, girl, get a grip.'

Briskly, he did up four buttons on my blouse.

'What happened?' he asked, extracting a packet of plasters from his rucksack.

'I wuh-wuh-was in Luh-Luh-Lynott's, and some muh-muh-mental fucker started going fucking mental at me and attacked me—'

'Attacked you?' said Jed, tensed to jump on a white horse and gallop off to avenge my honour. 'He did this?' His long fingers brushed my cheekbone.

'No. I wuh-wuh-was hit by an automatic door. And th-th-then the security guard accused me of shoplifting. Nuh-now I'm late for this stupid meeting – Christ, Jed, it's eight twenty-eight. What are you doing here?'

'Figured I'd check my e-mail before going down,' he said, gripping me by the right ear and applying a plaster to the opposite cheek. 'The first half-hour will be the usual inspirational, motivational, goal-oriented crap. Hold it. You need another one above your eye. There. You look like shit.'

'You're one to talk. Couldn't you have worn a tie?'

'What for?'

'Well, isn't the Executive Cheese coming?'

James Henderson was one of PL's partners, and a corporate superstar. Within the rarefied atmosphere of PL, he was like a rock god without the rock. Essentially, he employed all of us. Our Director, Max, reported directly to him.

Mr Henderson attended the annual strategy meeting to add an element of glamour – or menace. He always gave a speech underlain with dark threats about justifying our existence, but BSS did well for PL. He also liked to castigate Max in corporate speak, which was always entertaining.

'Henderson?' said Jed. 'So what? It's not as if I want to sleep with the man. Look, give me your shoes, and this—' Jed relieved me of my errant heel. 'Hold on.' He opened my desk drawer, rummaged around in a cloud of face powder and presented me with my hairbrush and spray. He looked doubtfully at the face powder before tossing the tub back in the drawer.

'Go to the bathroom and tidy yourself up. I'll take care of your shoes. Oh, one moment . . .'

He wheeled me towards him and stapled a rip in my skirt.

'My Armani,' I quivered.

'Good as new.' He hauled me out of my chair and gave me a little push.

Taking in the horror of my reflection in the Ladies' mirror, I moaned aloud. I applied the brush to my hair, but there would have been a better chance of running a comb over a grizzly bear's arse. I damped it down with water before giving up in despair.

Jed had gone when I limped back to the Maze, but my shoes sat primly on the desk. He had reaffixed the heel with brown packing tape, which was carefully trimmed round the edges. Not only that, but he had applied packing tape to the left shoe also – presumably to achieve some degree of symmetry – and scribbled in some tasteful polka dots.

A Coffee Spot extra-large cappuccino sat next to the shoes with a yellow Post-it note on the side.

Easy on the shoes. No twirling or jumping, instructed Jed's decisive scrawl. *You can have my coffee. Meeting room 614.*

I was so touched I nearly started blubbing again.

As I sidled into the conference room our director was spotlit in the projector's glare. Max Feshwari stood about five foot two on a good day and was exceptionally hairy, like something a giant cat had coughed up. Consequently, he inspired in everyone a chronic itch. Thirty BSS staff clustered round a table large enough to shelter an appreciation of accountants, all engaged in surreptitious scratching.

Max was in full flow, giving the odd power salute when unspeakably moved by poignant topics such as revenue and sales projections. As my eyes adjusted to the darkness, I made out James Henderson's cadaverous form at the head of the table. His hooded eyes flickered in my direction.

I saw Jed had kept a seat for me. Unfortunately, it was diametrically opposite the door and, while I was thankful the room was darkened for the presentation, it made the journey somewhat perilous. Defying the packing tape, my right heel issued a warning wobble.

Sidling around the perimeter of the room, I kicked over the waste-paper bin. Max paused in the middle of a complex Tai Chi move.

'Nice of ya ta join us, yang lidy,' he said cosily. Max's broad New Zealand accent was delivered in a nasal whine, an aural experience akin to putting your nerves through a cheese grater. 'Please, come in, sit down, make yourself comfortable. Coffee? Ah, grite, you have one already.'

Just then, I tripped over an extension cable and slopped most of it over the Commercial Director, Brenda Calburn.

'Sorry,' I mumbled. The look Brenda gave me curdled my blood, and I hurried by before she could suck it out of my neck.

'Fall out the wrong side of the bed this morning, did we?' blared Max, insistent as a foghorn. 'Look like you've been dragged backwards through the ugly tree. HAH!'

Max's laugh was a sinister thing: an explosion of mirthless noise projected directly from the diaphragm. My colleagues gave an obligatory snigger.

Two years ago, BSS was high in overheads and low in profit margins, the sum of which fell short of a lean, mean, money-making machine. PL brought in 'Max the Axe' to hack out the dead wood. Within six months, half of BSS was gone, along with most of our hardware inventory and the contents of the stationery cupboard. My friend Chanelle and I were amongst the few who survived the carnage.

Personally, I didn't disapprove of Max's 'letting people go'. After all, he got rid of Stinky Dave, which was – quite literally – a breath of fresh air. However, firing the more fragrant members of staff made Max deeply unpopular.

'Right, where were we, before we were so' – Max gave me a pointed look – 'rudely interrupted?'

'People,' he went on, turning back to his presentation, 'it is our obligation as a team to facilitate low-risk high-yield paradigms to efficiently supply quality solutions while maintaining a compelling bottom line . . .'

'Flipping hell,' I muttered to Jed. 'I've been here two minutes and already I feel like ripping off my arms and stuffing them in my ears.'

'You might have difficulty with the logistics of that plan.'

Max frowned at us, then fascinated everyone rigid with a description of last month's performance, next month's performance and achievable margins.

I stifled a yawn and glanced around the room.

Max's evil henchwoman, Brenda, a.k.a. the Poison Dwarf, sat at his right, her head going like a nodding dog over rough terrain. Brenda Calburn was small and birdlike, and so brittle it seemed as if a sudden sharp noise might snap her in two.

But that was only wishful thinking.

She was too toxic to have slept her way to the top, but Brenda could skewer a fly with a butter knife at fifty paces. She was unfailingly unflinching in her mission to steal credit where it was not due, or apportion blame to save her rancid hide.

Her two account managers, Nigel Usher and Chanelle Fyffe, sat opposite her. Chanelle was seriously beautiful and should have been legally required to erect a hazard warning sign: 'Beware: Dangerous Curves Ahead'. Many people were misdirected by Chanelle's clothes and breathless giggle, but my friend was sharp as a duck's quack. She lured her quarry into a false sense of security before impaling them on her wit and intellect.

The look on her face could have been interpreted as either spellbound fascination or terminal boredom.

Nigel's fat head was currently synchronised with

Brenda's. As always, he was slightly shiny in his purple pinstripe suit.

Nigel was a posh wide boy, resigned to working for PL until he came up with a failsafe pyramid scheme to swindle little old ladies out of their life savings. He fancied himself as a daring International Man of Mystery, irresistible to all classes of women. In reality, his definition of daring was a 'No Fear' sticker on his Peugeot. Suffice to say his back seat hadn't seen much action – although not for want of trying.

Since he was averse to anything resembling hard work, Nigel's career trod the perilous and no doubt pungent path up his manager's bottom. If Brenda had told him black was white, Nigel would have only had to work his way through a shade or two of grey before swearing he'd never seen a more fluorescent shade of pale.

Max moved on to maintaining the edge, thinking outside the box and it being time for us to 'wake up and smell the fat lady sing'.

'People,' he finally intoned. He nodded at his PA, Michelle, who flipped on the lights. 'As you are aware, BSS has been undergoing a strategic departmental reorganisation, in addition to which our client base has expanded so rapidly, and commensurately our project management team, that we have identified an urgent requirement for a projects director to coordinate activity within the group.'

I felt a swell of excitement. This was it!

'Therefore,' continued Max, 'BSS has been working in close conjunction with PL's HR department for the purpose of identifying a worthy candidate.'

Me! I clutched Jed's arm in excitement.

'The person chosen to lead our project team to new

heights of excellence is a pioneer of many years' experience with an extensive background in support and development and a thorough understanding of project management issues.'

I smoothed back my hair and prepared a discreet and gracious smile.

'People.' Max paused for dramatic effect and trotted off down the side of the conference room. 'I am proud to present', he announced portentously, 'the *new* Projects *Director* of BSS Technology – *Luke Wylie*!'

He flung back the conference room door with a flourish.

I had been about to burst into a flurry of 'Oh my *God*, I can't *believe it*!'s, but the words choked in my throat and emerged as a strangled gasp.

'Who the fuck is Luke fucking Wylie?' whispered Jed. He shot a look at my face, which had settled into a disbelieving rictus grin, and gripped my hand. 'Easy, sweetheart.'

'Luke?' said Max and poked his head out the door. '*Luke!*' he barked. 'Ah, there you are. Ladies and gentlemen . . . the new BSS Projects Director . . . Luke *Wylie*!' Putting out an arm, he grasped the large hand that appeared round the doorjamb.

And to my horror, with a great yank, Max heaved into the room . . . the American.

For several minutes, Max and the American a.k.a. Luke Wylie grappled in one of the most vicious displays of handshaking ever recorded in Puttock Leavitt history.

Swept away by a surfeit of enthusiasm, the shake Max administered would have ripped the arm off a lesser man. He had Luke Wylie in his special Genuine Double-handed Whammy normally reserved for VIPs or potential clients, leaping off the floor to give himself more leverage.

Luke Wylie hung on grimly and launched a tactical counter-offensive, gripping Max's arm like he was wringing out a wet sheet. Feeling a bit empty-handed in comparison to his opponent, he slapped away on Max's shoulder with his free hand, all snapping teeth and bouffant bonhomie.

'Luke, mate! Good to see ya!' boomed Max, giving one last wistful wrench.

'You too, man. How are you?'

'Grite, grite! Right, time to take the bull by the balls. Now ya here, ya might as well meet the team.'

Max indicated us with a flourish. I shrank back in my chair – what if Wylie saw me? This couldn't be happening.

'Everyone, this is Luke Wylie. Ya like to say a few words, mate?'

Despite being about to address some of the UK's best and brightest (at *what* PL's recruitment literature didn't specify), Luke Wylie showed no hint of nerves.

'Hi, everyone,' he said, giving an unselfconscious royal wave. 'Mr Feshwari – Max – thank you so much for the introduction. It's real nice to meet y'all.'

At this point, I had not even begun to get over the fact that not only had I been passed up for promotion, but I was also officially reporting to someone who should more appropriately be confined to a high-security psychiatric unit than adorning the Puttock Leavitt conference room. However, I had recovered the power of speech, which never deserts me for long.

'Jed!' I hissed. 'The mental fucker!'

'What?'

'The mental fucker from Lynott's! Remember? From this morning?'

'What about it?'

'*That's him!*'

'You're *joking*,' breathed Jed. He narrowed his eyes, peering through the gloom at Luke Wylie. After a minute, he whispered, 'He looks all right.'

'He does not! Whose bloody side are you on?' I hissed furiously.

But the overwhelming female consensus was that Luke Wylie did indeed look considerably all right. The levels of oestrogen in the room rose noticeably. Chanelle carefully arranged her bosom on the conference table. Michelle, Max's assistant, hiked up her skirt a couple of inches and dangled her shoe on the end of her foot. Even Brenda Calburn fluffed up her pussycat bow and adjusted her helmet of hair. They obviously failed to note the man's pointy nose; the hint of mania glinting out of those suspicious, shifty little eyes; the fat ears and rubbery lips.

Luke Wylie focused a presidential beam on the room. Michelle's shoe fell off, and Brenda nearly swallowed her shirt.

'I would like to say how very honoured I am to accept this position,' continued Wylie.

He paused a moment and I wondered whether he was about to thank his manager, his parents, his agent, and the Business Studies tutor who taught him the meaning of true love and made him the man he was today.

'Mr Feshwari – Max – told me all about the good job the PM team does. I am positive that with a little focus and direction, together we can do a *great* job. Remember, there is no "I" in team.'

'There may be no "I" in team, but there is in gobshite,' I growled at Jed.

'I suppose I'd better tell you about myself,' Wylie went on, smoothing his tie. 'Well, I'm educated to a degree. Ha ha ha,' he added, to indicate that it was a joke.

I was ashamed that the other members of my sex indulged themselves in immoderate displays of mirth. Chanelle laughed so hard she gave herself hiccups and it took some time for the excitement to abate. Luke Wylie cast her a dubious glance and Chanelle simpered, 'Oh! Oh, dear!' and flapped her eyelashes and lashings of cleavage at him.

'But seriously though, I have a broad background in the industry, and I'm very confident that in a very short space of time we can turn things around. I understand you had a very early start this morning' – he threw an ingratiating glance at Max – 'so to finish off, I look forward to meeting you all and to a very prosperous— a pros . . . er, preposterous . . . no, ah . . .'

During his speech, Luke had made eye contact with all his audience – as recommended by any good presentation techniques self-help book – and his gaze had finally fallen on me.

And I looked decidedly unfriendly.

The last thing I felt like post conference was a little tête-à-tête with Luke Wylie. I couldn't do much about the flush I felt sweeping up my neck, but I drew back my shoulders and strode to the door as deliberately as my fluctuating heel allowed. My colleagues cast darting, furtive glances that slid quickly away as I passed.

Adrenaline propelled me up ten flights of stairs before my legs gave out, and I sank abruptly on to a step. My heaving lungs felt like they might explode, and black spots tangoed across my line of vision.

So. After devoting a big chunk of the best years of my life to Puttock Leavitt, working through public holidays, occasionally neglecting my personal hygiene, it appeared that PL was not going to reward me for my years of faithful service. No promotion; no 'Thank you very much'; no 'Please accept this gold-plated monogrammed fountain pen as a token of our appreciation'.

More like: 'Want to know what a great big kick up the arse feels like? Here, try this for size.'

And Luke Wylie!

'Another? Just a sec, let me back up and take a bit of a run at it.'

I finally identified the acrid smell in my nostrils as the

bitter stench of failure. Oh, God, I'd never failed at anything in my life! I had been the neighbourhood hopscotch titleholder for five consecutive years; was in the top percentile of my class through school; boasted a first class Bachelor of Science degree. I even understood differentiation theory.

How could I face my colleagues after this? It had been widely acknowledged that I would get the job – mainly because I had told everyone. I had practically ordered business cards saying 'Projects Director Elect, BSS Technology'.

It wasn't entirely wishful thinking. Max and I had discussed the position less than two months ago, and he had practically offered me the job on the spot. At least, he had indicated the position was as good as mine. Well, he had said that BSS needed a projects director – but look, he wouldn't have mentioned it if he didn't think I was a valid candidate, would he?

It was time to pay Max a visit and give him a particularly explosive piece of my mind. I wasn't sure exactly what to say, but I had an icebreaker. See what you think.

'Now look here, Max, you fucker.'

Maybe not the most professional of greetings – but direct and relatively informative, you'd have to agree.

I got to my feet and tramped purposefully on up the stairs, rehearsing the pending confrontation.

'No Max, let *me* tell *you*. I don't know what you think you're playing at, you furry midget. You know what your problem is? Actually you have several, but I'll start at the top . . .'

'Speaking to me, yang lidy?' came a nasal bark behind me.

Giving a high-tensile shriek, I leapt about five feet up the stairs and settled in a heap on the landing.

However, rather than a bristling Max, below me lounged a smirking Jed.

'Sweet holy Mary virgin mother of the sacred Jesus,' I whispered, slumping weakly against the wall. 'What the hell? You . . . you . . . cock! Goddammit, Jed! I think you ruptured my appendix.'

'Nah,' said Jed, concertinaing his length on to a stair. 'Appendices don't generally rupture spontaneously. In fact, it's highly unlikely unless you suffer a direct blow to the area. It might be susceptible to bursting if it's diseased, but I'd say you're all right. Chewing gum?' He proffered a pack.

'No!' I glared at him.

'Suit yourself. You left your stuff in the conference room. Chanelle's got it. You all right?'

'Fine.'

'Sure. You look it. That's going to be a gorgeous shiner,' he said, touching my cheek gently. 'We should get some ice on it.'

'I'm grand. What – what happened after I left?'

'Wylie went around meeting and greeting – you missed some great eye contact. I don't think I've ever seen so many teeth. He should hire out his gums as prime advertising space.' Jed folded a stick of spearmint into his mouth and stretched out his legs. 'So have you finished giving the stairwell a good talking to?'

'Suppose,' I muttered.

'Well then,' said Jed. 'Want to come to the canteen and score some caffeine?'

'Er, no. Not right away. Got some things I need to do.'

'Like what?' he said sharply.

'I'm going to see Max.'

'I see. And what are you going to say? Apart from: "Fire Luke Wylie and give me his job"?'

'Jed.' I paused and swallowed. 'That job was *mine*. You know it.'

'Baby, you don't have the line in fake sincerity,' said Jed, his green eyes regarding me steadily. 'Essentially, you just aren't slimy enough to slither up the corporate ranks of PL.'

'You shouldn't *have* to! It should be about whether you're good at your job, not who you stab in the back or – or how much time you spend on yours.'

'Yeah,' said Jed. 'But in the great Puttock Leavitt sewage pit, only the turds rise to the top.'

I leaned my head against Jed's shoulder and he stroked my hair as we contemplated this visual.

'But I presume you're not going to share that with our esteemed leader,' said Jed presently.

'No.'

'Right then. Coffee.' He stood and offered me his hand.

'Not yet,' I said heavily, allowing him to haul me to my feet. 'I'm still going to see Max.'

'What for?'

'I'm going to resign,' I said, taking myself by surprise.

'Wha-at? Anderson—'

'Jed, I'm not going to be treated like this. I won't work for a company that disrespects me. I have principles! And integrity! I don't know why I didn't think of it before.'

'At least wait until you get another job—'

'I'll find something else. Anyway, I have enough money saved up to survive at least two months, if I subsist on a diet of baked beans and don't make outgoing phone calls. I may have to give up luxury items such as deodorant, but I can live with short-term BO.'

'Anderson, this is *such* a bad idea—'

'It's not! It's a *great* idea! Tell me I'm right.'

'Okay. It's a great idea.'

'Really? You think so?'

'*No!* It's a fucking awful idea! Come on, Livvie, please don't make this decision now. Come down to the canteen, slag off the selection of pastries, get a caffeine hit. Take a while to think things through—'

'What's there to think through?'

'Well, you have responsibilities. You have a family to support – no, that's not right. But there's the TV licence to pay, the monthly rent, your Neil Diamond CD collection to maintain . . .'

But I was not to be dissuaded.

By the time I reached Max's office, my body had declared a state of personal emergency and put me at Defcon 1. I considered kicking his door in FBI-style, but I didn't have a Smith & Wesson .357 or a conflicted partner covering my back. Also, I was concerned my packing-taped shoes wouldn't stand up to the exercise – and I doubted Max would give me a reference if I broke down his door.

So instead, I knocked. Quite loudly.

'Come in!' roared Max. I turned the doorknob and poked my head in.

'Er, hi. Er, Max. Do you have a minute? I mean, excuse me. I need to speak to you.'

So much for 'Now look here, Max, you fucker'.

'What can I do for you, yang lidy?'

I stamped across the room and thought I might as well take a chair – I still had the advantage of height. My voice did not fully reflect the courage of my convictions when I said: 'I am here to, er, to er, tender my resignation. Er, yes. Please. Thanks.'

'Well,' said Max. He pressed his stumpy fingers together and leaned back. His obscene eyebrows bristled like they were infested with lice, and made me want to scratch like a dog; and the longer he sat there in silence, the greater the itch. I was getting to the stage where I'd have to go and rub up against the corner of the table when Max said, 'This comes as a surprise.'

'I'm surprised it's a surprise,' I said.

Very smooth.

'Come, come!' said Max, sounding vaguely like a Bond villain. 'You're a valued member of BSS. Why would ya want to resign?'

'Well, Max, of course I'm resigning,' I stuttered. Unfortunately, although I had rehearsed a range of puerile insults, I hadn't given the same consideration to logical and persuasive argument. 'Now that you – and Luke Wylie – have cut off my career path, I don't see much of a future for me here.'

'But ya have a good job. Well paid—'

'Max, I have worked for PL for over five years. A position opened up for which I am exceptionally qualified – in fact, I have fulfilled the role of Projects Director for two years in everything but name. Coordinating the project management team, setting up change request procedures, drawing up product interface specs. All my projects came in on time, two of them under budget. I brought home fifteen million pounds for Puttock Leavitt last year. And yet you appointed this – this Luke Wylie without even discussing it with me—'

'We did discuss it,' said Max, rummaging around in his moustache for a tasty morsel. 'During your appraisal.'

'You gave me a glowing review! And you indicated . . . Well, I assumed . . . Well.' I paused for a moment to think through the phrasing. 'I knew a projects director was required for BSS, and given my track record I feel I should at least have been considered for the position—'

'You were considered,' said Max. 'But ultimately, it is my – no, *our* responsibility to ensure that the most qualified person is assigned to the position. I can assure ya that Luke Wylie has excellent credentials. Excellent! There were concerns about your candidacy—'

'What concerns?' I barked.

'We've been over this—'

'Max, if I weren't a consummate professional, I would use the word "bullshit" in quite a direct manner.'

'Your problem, yang lidy, is ya see everything in black and white. Right or wrong. Fush or chups.' He leaned across his desk, sincerity seeping from his pores. 'In many ways, I admire that, I really do.'

He really didn't.

'You need to get imaginative with truth, appreciate that it is a flawed concept. Someone's biased perception of fact. It's open to interpretation. One person's truth is another person's dirty laundry. Suppose I asked you to do something you disagreed with, for the greater good. Would you follow that order without question?'

'Without question? I – I suppose so. I mean, yes. If it were for the ultimate good of the client and Puttock Leavitt.'

Reading between the lines is not a talent of mine; when men offer to buy me a drink I still assume their primary motive is the purely altruistic funding of my drink habit. I got the feeling that a great paragraph of subtext had just flown right over my head. Well, it hardly mattered now.

'You know,' I said, 'much as I'd love to sit around chatting, I've got a resignation letter to draft. Excuse me.'

'Miss Anderson, ya have a bright future ahead of ya—'

'I'm sure I do, but not here,' I snapped. 'This discussion is over. It's been a privilege working for

Puttock Leavitt and I wish you every success in the future blah blah blah et cetera.'

'Hang on, hang on.' Max tugged on his jaw a moment. 'Look. You're a terrific project manager. I'd be sorry to lose ya.'

'Well, you should have thought about that before—'

'Wait. Sit down, sit down! Now look, I think you should reconsider. What if I were to offer ya a little incentive?'

'Eh?'

'A raise, to show ya how much your input is valued. What would ya say to an increase of – oh, I don't know – ten thousand?'

'Ten thousand?' I gaped at him.

In case you're wondering at my incredulity, it's not as if this were a subtle enhancement of my annual salary. While senior management pull in six figures to blow on luxury yachts and cocaine, I make barely enough to cover rent, the food chain staples and the occasional Armani. Ten thousand smackoos was roughly fifteen per cent of my annual salary.

Bearing in mind how notoriously stingy the accounting profession is (and Puttock Leavitt prides itself on being an industry leader), I was pretty close to speechless.

'All right, tell ya what,' continued Max. 'We'll say fifteen thousand. Ya drive a hard bargain! Fifteen K. What d'ya say?'

'I . . . I don't . . .'

'Take some time to consider it. You have until tomorrow morning.'

'I . . . Okay.'

7

Management was a rarity around level minus two, so the canteen did not offer frivolous extras such as edible food. The atmosphere was morose: greasy Formica tables, plastic bucket chairs, a carpet that might be beige after a professional clean. The only bright spot was the serving counter, shining like kryptonite in the far corner.

My colleagues were at their usual table overlooking the PL swimming pool.

'All right?' Chanelle mouthed to me.

I nodded, not trusting myself to speak with the squeeze at the back of my throat. If Nigel hadn't been present, sprawled chubbily across a chair, I would have welcomed the opportunity to talk to Chanelle and Jed about my meeting with Max.

Nigel's eyes lit on me. 'I say, is that a projects director? Oh exsqueeze me, my mistake—'

'Usher, why don't you spend the next minute silently considering shutting up?' said Chanelle easily.

I looked at her gratefully. Nigel would not have taken that from anyone else – except maybe Jed – but since he shared a cubicle with Chanelle he was aware of her vast potential for making his life hell.

'Hey guys,' I said. 'Nigel, your tie's in your coffee.'

'Oh, fack.' He fished it out and blotted it with a napkin.

I went to the counter to get myself a coffee. When I returned, Chanelle threw her shimmering curtain of hair over her shoulder and said: 'Just in time! Jed was about to regale everyone with a sordid account of his weekend sexcapades.'

Oh goody. I had only missed the introduction, which never varies much; it's always along the lines of: 'So I said to her, "Is it hot in here, or is it just you?" She was gorgeous. Long, wavy eyelashes. Great body. We went to the Underworld and, you know, one thing led to another and we ended up at hers . . .'

I was always rather distressed by the gay abandon with which women leapt into bed with Jed, only pausing long enough to provide their name – as if it were a relevant detail. However, I couldn't help enjoying Jed's stories. I wouldn't want to feature in one, but they were fascinating vignettes of debauchery.

He had reached the interesting part.

'So we're back at hers, and we were, um, in bed. Together.' Jed could be surprisingly coy when it came to the X-rated stuff. 'I thought I'd give her a bit of a treat and migrated south for a spot of . . .' He coughed.

'What?' said Chanelle.

'Growler chomping,' said Nigel, who was versed in the lads' lexicon.

'Sorry I asked,' said Chanelle.

'You should know better,' I agreed.

'Now, I'm snuffling around the twilight zone,' Jed continued, 'and it doesn't matter how accomplished you are, it's always uncharted terrain, you know? I locate the hot spot and there I am, beavering away, but something's not quite right. Of course, I can't see a frigging thing, but it was . . . a bit . . . kind of . . . you know?'

'No, what?'

'Well, it was sort of hard and nubbly.'

'Her . . .' I said.

'Yes.'

'Her . . .' said Nigel.

'Yes!'

'*Nubbly?*' I said.

'Yeah, nubbly. As defined in the Oxford English Dictionary.'

'What's the definition again?' I asked.

'Irregularly shaped, with a knobbly or lumpy quality about it.'

'Right.'

'And also, you know, usually there is a favourable reaction from above when . . . you know. And I was getting no feedback. No screaming, no wriggling, no hair-pulling. And the next thing I realised it was . . . it was . . .'

'What?'

'I realised I was sucking away on . . .'

'*What?*' everyone shouted, even the canteen lady who had been listening avidly while pretending to wipe down a nearby table.

'A peanut.'

'*What?*' we shrieked.

'How did you know it was a peanut?' asked the hapless Nigel.

'Knob,' said Jed in exasperation, 'peanuts are not that difficult to identify. Having spent most of my formative – and, for that matter, unformative – years in a vast array of public houses, I can accurately pinpoint any brand of nut sold in the greater London region. I can reliably report that my lady friend was concealing one of KP's finest vintage honey roasted peanuts in her nether regions.'

'But wasn't it dark?' asked Chanelle misguidedly.

'Ye-es.'

'How did you know it was honey roasted?'

'Because it tasted like one,' said Jed with a patient sigh.

'You didn't *eat* it?' we screamed in delicious outrage.

'Of course I ate it,' said Jed. 'You should never pass up grub. Never know when you might regret it. I was only sorry there weren't more – I burrowed around a bit, but there was just the one.'

'You're so mangy,' I hiccuped.

'You're a legend,' said Nigel in awe. 'Got lucky myself on Saturday. Rather odd, though. We were getting on super and she excused herself to go to the bathroom. Never came back. Couldn't find her anywhere.'

'Weird,' said Jed.

Chanelle and I exchanged surreptitious grins.

'Exsqueeze me, I'm going to make like an espresso and leave,' said Nigel.

'Call me later, okay, honey?' said Chanelle, twiddling her fingers at me before undulating after Nigel.

'Tell me about the meeting with Max,' said Jed. 'Did you resign?'

'Yes.'

'And?'

'And, okay, um, he said I was a valued member of the team, and I said: "Yeah, like you sure demonstrated that this morning, you rank tumour on the pink flesh of life." And, er, he said I had a bright future with PL. And then he . . . well, he . . . offered me a raise.'

'A raise? As in, to lift?' Jed was no doubt envisaging Max boosting me out the door.

'No, money.'

'Really?' said Jed with some level of incredulity. 'How much?'

'Jed!'

'How much?'

'Fifteen thousand.'

'Sorry. I didn't catch that.'

'You caught it.'

'Seriously?'

I nodded. 'And I could probably have negotiated five more days of annual leave as well, but I didn't think of it in time.'

'So did you tell him to stick his pay rise where the sun don't shine, flick him a birdie, and kick over the plant on the way out?'

'Well . . . yes . . . no . . . kind of not exactly.'

'What happened to principles? And . . . what was the other thing?'

'Integrity. Max offered above market value for them.'

'I see.'

'I haven't made a decision yet,' I said defensively.

In the last five years or so I had spent more time in the Maze than anywhere else. It felt more like home than, well, home, but now it was like an alien environment. On the surface nothing had changed: the squares of industrial carpet with darker patches here and there, the fluorescent lights featuring silhouettes of dead flies, the vending machine in the corner that spat out indigestible scalding liquids.

People fell silent as I passed. Of course, none of them knew about Max's offer and what a valued member of BSS I was and the bright future ahead of me. I fixed a smile on my face and greeted everyone too loudly: 'Morning, Keith. Can you send me Gragnoc's throughput report? Thanks. Any news on the restraining order, Pete? Michelle, how did the audition go? No, Nigel.'

Somehow I struggled through the rest of the day. Gragnoc, my biggest client, was allegedly about to issue a purchase order to upgrade their EnTire system.

For two months, Nigel had been saying: 'The PO will definitely be in today. Probably.' I called the Production Manager and pre-ordered the hardware, then drew up a draft project plan and system interface document. The words jumbled on the page. Never mind – nobody read past the executive summary. And it was meaningless crap anyway.

All day, I diligently avoided my new manager.

I had planned to go to the PL gym that evening and work out at 110 per cent maximum heart rate, but I couldn't work up the energy. The clock had barely registered 18:00:00 when I was out the door; clambering into my bat-coat at the elevator; fighting through the commuters in the station; propped up against a smelly armpit on the South Eastern Greenwich line. I emerged into the dank of Westcombe Park.

My flat was a five-minute tramp up Humber Road. A chill breeze whipped up a fine veneer of drizzle and by the time I reached the front door my bat-coat flapped sad and defeated. My cosy little studio conversion was on the first floor, and although the National Rail line to London Bridge thundered through the bottom of the garden, I no longer noticed the noise.

I paused automatically to check the mail on the hall table. Three bills and a catalogue addressed to Mr Lief Ericsson, who I presumed was me.

As I unlocked the apartment door, I was overwhelmed by a loneliness that was almost physical. I leaned my bag neatly against the TV, then turned on the stereo. That was better.

I couldn't remember the last time I had spent serious quality time with myself. You know, not rushing around filling every waking moment with working, eating or drinking. But that was about to change. I needed to formulate a five-year, ten-point action plan. My personal strategy for the future. Tonight, I would engage in energetic and absorbed thinking time. Mull, mull, mull.

I tried to procrastinate with a bit of compulsive

tidying, but there was nothing to tidy compulsively. The place was immaculate. My clothes were ironed and hanging in the wardrobe covered in plastic, I had dusted the day before and scrubbed the skirting board with a toothbrush over the weekend.

Dinner! I had to eat. I fixed myself a Marks & Spencer frozen low-fat meal and lit a scented candle as a treat.

Good gracious, why was sitting still so difficult? No! I would *not* turn on the telly for a while!

Shame this wasn't a movie, in which case I would have no problem curling up on a window ledge for *hours* gazing beautifully blankly at the raindrops running down the sash window. (Obviously it's just a couple of seconds in the instrumental montage, since it wouldn't be much of a movie if it consisted of the characters sitting around doing nothing for 120 minutes.) (Anyway, I didn't have a sash window.)

Nothing remained with which to postpone the evil hour, so I rustled up a pad and pencil, fixed myself a Powers Irish whiskey, and pinned myself to the table.

At the top of the page, I wrote: *Resign or sell my soul to the corporation*. I drew a box round it and added a starburst design with some lightning-bolt effects at the corners.

I couldn't believe I was actually considering Max's offer. I mean, my career was everything to me. I was nearly thirty years of age, and what else had I to show for it apart from my meteoric rise to power? Or meteoric rise to mediocrity, if you prefer.

Turning to a new sheet of paper, I wrote *Assets* at the top of the page, and underlined it twice. Underneath, I wrote:

Black & Decker VersaToast wide-slot toaster: 1 piece
Pyrex oven-proof dishes mint condition: 1 set
Panasonic 29" TV circa turn of the century: 1 piece
Panasonic DVD player: 1 piece
DVDs: 31 not including Planet of the Apes *boxed set*

Hmm. Not exactly a bristling asset portfolio.

I poured myself another Powers.

Twenty-nine and three-quarter years of life on this planet and in the event of my death from a freak bowling accident I had nothing to bequeath to my significant others. Speaking of which, I had amassed very few significant others. Apart from my parents, there was nobody who might mourn my tragic untimely passing. Mind you, if it meant skiving off work, Chanelle and Nigel would definitely turn up at the funeral. No doubt Jed would be distressed, but I couldn't imagine him throwing himself on to my coffin, wailing incoherently.

Hardly a turnout of hundreds with police struggling to hold back the hordes.

I defined myself by my job. This was admittedly sad – although not as sad as if I were an accountant or a lawyer. Yet I didn't really enjoy what I did for eight plus hours a day. As a little girl, when A. N. Adult asked: 'What do you want to be when you grow up?' I cannot ever recall responding: 'Ooh, I know! An IT project manager for an accounting firm.'

No. I had dreamt of a glittering career as a princess, or a chocolate tester. Or a pop star.

In fact, I had little interest in the great information technology revolution, or the computer industry in general. It was something I just . . . sort of . . . stumbled into.

Pass the Powers.

Whoa! Glass was shrinking.

What was the point of it all? Working for the scratchiest facets of humanity, in a company snacking on your lifeblood – talk about occupational hazard. The monthly paycheque merely bought snapshots of happiness, which were usually returned overexposed.

But after a while, having clawed your way up to a certain spot on the corporate ladder, the thought of sliding all the way down and finding another ladder gives you a severe case of vertigo.

Then, at the end of it all, having given the best years of your life to Industry, you curl up your toes and snuff it.

There it is: the Meaning of Life.

Survive.
Thrive, where possible.
Die.

Terrific.

How come the whiskey bottle was getting heavier? Surely, according to the laws of physics or liquids or whatever, it should've been getting *lighter*?

Ouch. Headache. All that headbanging stuff. Interesting experience. Thinking. Worthwhile, I felt. Although not something I would embrace on a regular basis.

By golly, who'd've thought it? The underside of my table needed a good scrub. You wouldn't think dirt would stick to the underside of a table, what with all the gravity. Might have to give it a wipe with a . . . thingy. It's not like a lot of people got to see that aspect of the table – but you never know.

The following morning, I woke up fully clothed on the floor snuggled up to a table leg. The left side of my face throbbed painfully. In the mirror, a livid red fan underscored my eye. It was surrounded by a swollen patchwork of purples, blues and occasional greenish yellows.

However, I made a phenomenal comeback after a shower, two Panadols and a glass of tomato juice.

I had also woken up resolved. I would make the Faustian deal with Max. After all, focusing on my career had not added meaning to my life. Maybe I could buy some with the extra salary; and I could always look for another job in the meantime.

At PL, my first stop was Max's office. I knocked and hesitated when there was no answer, wondering whether to knock again. Instead, I tried the door to see if it was open.

Max was sitting at his desk, staring intently at his phone with hands braced on either side of it. The phone crackled into life.

'Hello, Mantis Corporation, sorry to have kept you,' said a polished female voice over the speakerphone. 'How can I—'

Max snatched up the receiver and nestled the phone to his ear, holding up a furry finger at me.

'Yeh, yeh. Max Feshwari to speak to, ah, Ernest Thompson.'

Mantis. Where did that ring a bell? It wasn't one of our accounts. Oh yes: Mantis Corporation, primary competitor of one of our clients. In fact, my major client – Gragnoc Concretes.

I wasn't sure whether I'd been invited in or not, so I hovered just inside the door and scoped Max's office. The cringing cheese plant in the corner, the wall of filing cabinets, a framed award for – what was it? – sheep-shearing, 1981.

Beside the shredder was a photograph of Max with three other suited, slightly sweaty gentlemen. Although I'd seen the photo before, I had never really looked at it. The men stood underneath a giant logo of a phenomenally ugly phoenix thrashing around in flames. Poor creature was evidently in agony – and glorious Technicolor.

'Client,' said Max amiably as he hung up the phone and, when I looked across enquiringly, 'The photo. PL client in South America, spent a couple of years there. Great place. Cheap cigars.'

'Ah, right.'

I walked to his desk. 'I've been thinking about—'

'What happened to ya face? Look like ya've been poked in the eye with the short end of the stick. HAH!'

'Er, whatever. I've been thinking about your offer, and I will stay with BSS on condition that my salary is increased by . . . er . . . t-t-twenty thousand pounds per annum.'

'Per annum?'

'Per month, if you prefer.'

'Hah!' said Max, but half-heartedly. Around these parts, money is no laughing matter. Humour might be good for a punch line but not the bottom line.

'Eighteen,' he said.

'N-n-nineteen!' I crumble in the face of heated haggling. It's one of the reasons I never got into Sales – that and the fact that it's bad for your image. 'This is . . . it's my . . . my final offer and it's . . . it's . . . non-negotiable.'

'Call it seventeen, and we've got a deal.' Max stood up and held out a hairy paw.

I nearly got a firm handshake before I smelled the fishy reek in the air. Luckily I was familiar with Max's negotiation techniques.

'Eighteen five,' I said, pumping his arm before he had a chance to withdraw it.

'I'll have a new contract drawn up by the end of the day,' said Max. 'You made the right decision, yang lidy. You have a bright future ahead of you at Puttock Leavitt.'

That's what you reckon, I thought.

When I reached our cubicle, Jed was applying a soldering iron to a computer's innards, which emitted an acrid stench.

'Angel!' he exclaimed. He was never happier than when he waved his soldering iron around. 'Wow! That is an outrageous shiner.'

'I know. Do you find it strangely compelling?'

'Yes, now that you mention it. Can I touch it?'

'No! Step away from the puffy eye, Marshall.'

'If you look at it long enough, it changes colour,' he said, squinting.

I sat down and switched on my laptop. We had a feisty relationship, Drusilla and me. Drusilla was a contrary wench with PMT (the P in this case standing for permanent) and I suspect she had a drink problem – not unlike her owner. However, over the years she had grown on me like a virus.

'You're in early,' I observed.

'I'm trying to make partner,' said Jed. 'Takes a lot of smarming. Not a difficult job, but obviously it's quantity not quality.'

'You really think the Great Buttock would be stupid enough to make you a partner?'

Sorry – I should have mentioned before. Although Puttock Leavitt retains a ludicrously expensive PR company to tell them what shade of navy the corporate logo should be and to pick their noses, in all these years they appear to have overlooked the fact that adding another cheek to Puttock makes it Buttock.

This detail might have been overlooked by the PR consultants, but not by the 220,000 employees of Puttock Leavitt (spread over 902 offices in 150 countries). Simply saying 'Buttock Leavitt' aloud was enough to raise a communal guffaw, never mind all the cracks – excuse the pun – about the hole story, cheeky behaviour, bum raps, and once in a blue moon. Around these parts, Puttock Leavitt was the butt of all jokes.

Jed leaned back in his chair and put his hands behind his head.

'I'm developing my strategy for convincing the Brown Eye that I'm partner material. You know, take up golf. Tell bad jokes. Laugh loudly while telling them. Maybe screw a client out of a couple of million, dabble in corporate espionage, all that sort of stuff. I'm formulating a plan.'

'I think it needs more work.' I successfully keyed in my password on the third attempt.

'Well, that was just a high-level overview,' said Jed. He plonked his lean, rangy legs on my desk and crossed them at the ankles.

'D'you mind?' I pointed at his feet.

'Not at all,' said Jed. He lowered his voice. 'Glad to see you're a bit brighter this morning, Anderson. Have you decided what you're going to do?'

'I've just seen Max,' I muttered.

'Oh. And?'

'Talked him up to eighteen and a half K,' I whispered.

'So you're sticking around?'

'Shh!' I hissed.

'Nigel,' called Jed over the partition separating our cubicles. 'Are you eavesdropping?'

'No, but if you could speak a bit louder—'

'No, no, as you were. So, you're staying.'

'Not really. Well, yes and no. But yes more than no. I mean, yes, in that I'm staying for the moment. But as soon as I have another job I'll be out of here faster than Nigel after some syphilitic slapper.'

'Hey!' protested Nigel from behind the partition.

'Well, I'm glad you're staying,' said Jed. He leaned forward and made an awkward pass at my hand. 'This place would be kind of boring without you—'

My phone cut him off.

'Olivia?' It was Michelle, Max's PA. 'Mr Wylie asked if you could pop into his office when you have a moment.'

In my mental rehearsals, Luke Wylie lay broken and bleeding at my feet, pleading for his life.

'I will spare you because I am merciful and terrible in my gorgeousness,' I would say, before dismissing him and succumbing to a passionate George Clooney populated embrace.

Back in reality, I wavered outside Wylie's office – or, more accurately, my stolen office. My heart pounded painfully, and my palms were slick with sweat. After all, I hadn't counted on seeing Wylie's face ever again – except maybe staring out of a 'Most Wanted' poster.

I had still not decided on a tactical offensive. Should I kill him with kindness – or a swift blow to the nose with the heel of the hand? Cool and aloof, with overtones of condescension? Condescending and aloof, with overtones of cool?

When the door flew open, I was standing with my hand poised in mid-air. I tried to turn the gesture into an ear-scratch, which ended up more like an uncoordinated hair-slick/nose-pick.

'Olivia!' drawled Luke Wylie affably. Somehow he managed to break down the syllables of my name into chewy chunks: 'Oh-LIV-ee-aah!'

I couldn't have been more astonished had he bent

over, stuck a clarinet up his bum and played a flawless rendition of *Caro Mio Ben*.

'Thanks so much for coming by,' he said, as if I'd had a choice in the matter. Before I had a chance to cheep, I was ushered into the room in a flurry of incisors and pinstripes, and deftly steered into a chair. Luke Wylie seated himself across acres of mahogany and adjusted his tie. 'Coffee?' he asked solicitously. 'Herbal tea?'

'Coffee,' I managed.

Wylie pressed a button on the phone and picked up the receiver. 'Michelle,' he murmured in ermine-lined tones. 'Two coffees, thank you.'

I fought a nervous compulsion to check that my fly was up. Instead, I crossed my legs, wrapping one around the other.

Replacing the handset, Wylie leaned across the desk, lowered his voice intimately and said: 'I guess we didn't get off to a very good start, did we?'

'You don't say.'

He gave a rueful little pout. It was a gorgeous thing to behold. He must have spent hours practising it in front of a mirror. The greater portion of me wanted to smack his rueful little pout on to the other side of his face – or better still hire someone to do it for me and rearrange his kneecaps while they were at it. However, I am ashamed to admit that a small – definitely insignificant, bordering on infinitesimal – part of me had a passing interest in grabbing him by the lapels and snogging his rueful little pout off his face.

'I don't understand how it went so far,' Wylie said.

'Maybe your being an asshole had something to do with it,' I suggested.

'I guess.'

There was silence for a moment. Luke Wylie pressed

his fingertips together and surveyed me over the top.

'Look,' I said. 'Obviously we have a personality clash—'

'Personality clash?'

'Well, I don't like you. I was being polite.'

He gave a glimmer of a smile. 'Right.'

'I'm sure we can be civil during working hours, but I'm never going to be your best friend.'

'That's a shame,' said Luke Wylie. 'Would it make any difference if I apologised for our . . . misunderstanding yesterday?'

'Maybe,' I muttered.

'I am sorry. I guess I was nervous. I overreacted. You're right: I was a bit of an asshole.' I felt he was going easy on himself, but was gracious enough to overlook it. 'Can we can put it behind us and . . . start afresh?'

Suddenly, deep down inside, I felt something thaw. And give a little wiggle.

'Okay,' I said grudgingly.

'Luke Wylie,' he said, holding out his hand.

'Liv Anderson,' I said, and even managed to coax up a smile.

Michelle entered with the coffee and there was the palaver about whether there was any brown sugar, and how many spoons would I like, and shall I pour?, and just say when.

After she left, Luke settled himself on the corner of the desk in front of me, his cup incongruous in his big hands.

I was uncomfortably aware of his crotch looming gently in my line of sight. Surprised by an onslaught of lust, I slugged my coffee too fast and burnt my tongue.

'So, tell me about yourself,' he suggested.

While I gave him a synopsis of my résumé complete

with hobbies and interests, Luke Wylie nodded and smiled and sipped his drink and exhibited his magnificent groin. He had to have socks stuffed down there.

'You're extremely qualified,' he observed. 'Why didn't you apply for my position?'

'I did,' I said shortly.

'I see.' There was a pause. 'Will it be a problem for you? Reporting to me?'

'No, no problem. Not at all. No, I don't think so,' I said, making a mental note to add 'problem solving' to my CV.

'Great, great. I guess you wanna know about me.'

As Luke described the highlights of his dazzling career, it slowly dawned on me that I had probably not even made the starting blocks in the race for Projects Director.

He had two MBAs and a PhD in something unpronounceable – let's just call it Applied Brilliance. There was mention of Fortune 500 companies and evidence of voluminous achievements. Apparently, he had been COO of two companies and CEO of another.

I felt humbled comparing my stale crumb of a career to Luke's great golden loaf.

'That's about it,' he concluded with a self-deprecating shrug, and I barely stopped myself from breaking into spontaneous applause.

There was a protracted silence, which it eventually became my patriotic duty to resolve.

'So how did you end up in the big arse?' I said, and immediately regretted it when Luke looked bemused. 'Buttock Leavitt.'

'Oh.' Luke smiled. 'Buttock Leavitt. Very funny.' I was mortified. 'What do you mean?'

'Well, it seems a bit of a step down. You know,

Projects Director for a division of PL. Surely with your background you should be furthering your career as Prime Minister, or inflammable Superhero, or Galactical Ruler of the Universe.'

'Well, I thought a change of pace would be kinda nice. Now, before we wrap up, I'd like to spend a little time discussing the projects you're handling right now?'

'Sure. I have five projects in various stages of implementation. Most should be largely completed when the Gragnoc purchase order comes in. It's the biggest installation BSS has ever handled.'

'How much is it worth?'

'Twenty-three point eight million.'

We covered everything, down to the very nittiest of gritty – every client, project, product, management procedure, security. I was in danger of literally boring myself to death, when Luke said: 'Okay, that's great. You seem to have everything under control so I'll let you get on with it. Let me know if there's anything you need and I'll do what I can. Okay?'

'Yes, fine.'

'Olivia,' he said, standing and smoothing his tie. 'Thank you very much for your time.'

'Er, no problem. Thank you.'

'My door is always open,' said Luke. Taking my hand, he curled his fingers round mine and gave me a look that made my eyeballs blister. 'I think we're going to enjoy working together, Olivia,' he said. 'I look forward to it.'

'Me too,' I said, although I wasn't sure whether I meant it.

I predicted that within a week Luke would be goose-stepping around the Maze demanding half-hourly client reports in 3-point Braille tabular format, suggesting we address him in PowerPoint, and denying leave requests for vague and/or spurious reasons.

One day, shortly after our meeting, he called me.

'Olivia, it's Luke. Brenda wants you to go to Glasgow and conduct a project kick-off meeting for the Gragnoc account.' I rolled my eyes so vigorously there was a fair chance he heard it down the phone. 'What do you think?'

At least he made the effort to ask my opinion before embarking on whatever random act of management took his fancy, I thought.

'I think it's crap,' I said flatly. 'We're still waiting for the purchase order, so the deliverables are not defined. I cannot accurately present timeframes without clear milestones or even a start date. The kick-off meeting is not a bloody sales tool. Is that enough to be going with?'

'Absolutely,' said Luke. 'That's great. My thoughts exactly.'

'What?' I said. '*Really?*'

Luke laughed. 'Yeah, really. I just wanted to check with you first. I'll speak to her.'

Instead of issuing regular bulletins about how great

he was as per standard middle management procedure, Luke went out of his way not to draw attention to himself.

Maybe first impressions aren't all they're cracked up to be. I mean, my first impression of Luke was of an arrogant, psychotic, presumptuous, throbbing-veined, misogynistic asshole – yet as a manager he wasn't so bad.

On the other hand, I didn't want to completely disregard his behaviour the first time we met, so I tried hard not to like him that much. But it was getting harder and harder – especially when Luke was so unprofessionally foxy.

However, I rarely saw him outside our weekly meetings. After a while, I realised that when Luke said he'd let me get on with it, he meant it literally.

Unfortunately, I was struggling to 'get on with it'. I tried to be inspired by my monthly paycheque, but it didn't work; I was bored and unmotivated. I had been a project manager for so long that I could do the job with my brain in idle.

'You know, Jed, I was thinking . . .' I said one day.

Jed snorted. 'Good grief, Anderson. Haven't I warned you about the perils of thought?'

I flicked an elastic band at his head.

'No, but really, Jed. Are you happy? You know, with what you do. With where you are. With your life.'

'What are you on about?' said Jed in horror. 'Haven't you any appreciation of how superficial I am?'

'Well, sort of,' I said after a pause. 'But I always gave you the benefit of the doubt.'

'Anderson, I think you have underestimated the depths of my shallowness—'

'Jed. Seriously.'

'Baby, look around. How many people do you see that

are happy? You work for an accounting firm! Nobody's happy.'

'I always thought you got a kick out of your job.'

'Well, I get to share a cubicle with you—'

'That is undoubtedly a perk.'

'And this isn't my real job. I'm actually a secret agent—'

'Jed—'

'Livvie, do you think I'd still be here if I won the lottery tomorrow? Of course not! The best you can hope for is that you don't hate, loathe and otherwise detest your job. If you reach retirement age without paper-clipping yourself to death, you'll have done pretty damn well.'

My life did a strange time warp, where the days dragged by really quickly. I began to dread going to work. I had never been renowned for hurling myself out of bed to greet the dawn chorus, but these days prising myself from under the duvet in the mornings was a masochistic struggle.

Once I did straggle into the office, I could not muster up so much as half an iota of interest, never mind anything approaching enthusiasm. Whenever the phone rang, I had to resist the urge to hide under my desk. Phoning Gragnoc to discuss hardware insurance broke me out in green sweat.

Some days I would have seriously considered a career change shovelling the slag pits of hell. (Admittedly, I'm not sure how I'd react if Satan actually turned up waving a contract and offering benefits like air-conditioning and an annual brimstone allowance.)

Meanwhile, I half-heartedly fired off a few CVs. I had drawn up a two-page résumé:

> *PROFILE: Dedicated, conscientious, self-motivated*
> *individual. Driving ambition and will to succeed.*
> *Show-stopping presentation skills and all-round*
> *fanfriggingtastic conversationalist. Impressive*
> *ability to pick up small items with toes. Full*
> *complement of limbs. Can produce rabbits out of*
> *hats on request.*
> *<Insert other lies according to specifics of job*
> *application>*

But it didn't take long to become disillusioned with recruitment agents.

'Hi, Dave Owen here from Inept Recruitment, is that Penelope Frazer? Oh, you're not? But I have your CV here ... who? Oh, Olivia Anderson, yes of course you are, sorry about that. Now, I've just been going through your CV, and I don't think we'll have any problem placing you. In fact, I have something here that is just perfect for someone with your background. Client of mine in Cheshire is looking for a zoo keeper ... gorillas, walruses, that sort of stuff. Interested?'

Even when Dave Owen turned something up, employers seemed to want either half a century of relevant experience, or a PhD in Abstruse Mathematicised Pterylology.

I grew accustomed to adverts like:

> *The ideal candidate will be familiar with C++,*
> *Oracle, CRAP, Java (JDBC and Swing), Linux, B-*
> *LUT, and clinical context management systems*
> *based on the CCOW protocol.*
> *Fluency in Cantonese, Hindi, Aramaic required;*
> *written Czechoslovakian a distinct advantage.*

Ability to perform backflips with 2½ twist punch front pike turn essential.

When my head was churning, I tried to distract Jed.

'Hey, Marshall! Listen to this. Sounds like my ideal job: "Bright Ideas Manager". I could be good at that – I have at least one bright idea a day, and often several dull ones that might come right with a polish. What d'you reckon?'

I had visions of myself with my feet on the desk, stabbing the air with my finger, going: 'Oops! Quick! Take a memo. Idea number 3082a. Avoid paper cuts by using scissors to cut off the sharp edge of the paper before handling.'

Jed kicked off his desk and whizzed his chair over to look at my screen.

'Ah, Livvie,' he said. 'If you read the job description, it says "to manage an employee Bright Ideas Scheme".'

'Oh, knickers.'

'Where?'

One afternoon, I was so demotivated I started scandalmongering. My rumour mill was soon in gainful production, unlike me. Colleagues clogged the corridors of the Maze furtively discussing the unexpectedness of Nigel's being Max's secret love-child, how they had always suspected Max was a closet cross-dresser and – my personal favourite – the likelihood of Brenda's being a giant lizard disguised in human form.

Another day, I spent an industrious morning dialling Nigel's number and hanging up before he could answer.

Apart from torturing Nigel, all this was totally out of character. I was racked with thwarted ambition and wasted potential. Every Thursday morning I engaged in a flurry of activity, sending out project reports and drawing up summaries for my weekly meeting with Luke.

He was always encouraging and supportive – which somehow made me feel worse.

Chanelle and I often talked about getting together for some quality girlie gossip, but something always postponed it: demanding clients, conference calls, business trips, emergency facials. We were finally on for lunch after the fourth reschedule, braving the November rain to try a new restaurant half a mile down Southwark Street.

Chanelle's hair trailed behind her in a shiny, sinuous wave. Sometimes I didn't know why I liked Chanelle so much; she presented fierce competition. It may have had something to do with the fact that she was a genuinely sweet person with no idea quite how attractive she was. Or maybe I was just awaiting the opportunity to subtly maim her – accidentally catch her head in a door, or chip her manicured fingernails.

'How's Bill these days?' I screamed above the wind.

'He's a *prat*!' shrieked Chanelle in response.

This was quite true. Bill – often fondly referred to as Uncle Bill – had little going for him except the size of his wallet, a Porsche, and an impressive mid-life crisis.

He also had a wife and one or more kids.

'He's not going to leave them,' I often told Chanelle.

'I know, I know. But he says—'

'He's lying.'

'You're right, I know, I know.'

Sometimes I worried about Chanelle. She always went for the wrong type of guy. Put her in a room with a group of men ranging from 1 to 10 on the moron scale (where 1 = displaying rare hints of moronic behaviour and 10 = irretrievable moron), and Chanelle unerringly sniffed out the mutant who ran right off the high end of the scale.

Every one of them left with a little piece of Chanelle. Underneath the veneer of self-confidence, I suspected her reserves were finite. I hoped she would one day make an exception for someone who scored less than 5.

Inside the restaurant door, Chanelle ran a hand through her hair and could have just stepped out of a three-hour session at Toni & Guy. In comparison, I knew my head looked as if it had been vigorously tousled with an electric cattle prod.

'What's he done now?' I asked, settling myself at a table. Chanelle rolled her eyes as she unfurled her scarf.

'Well, you know last Friday was our anniversary?'

I nodded. 'Three months, right?'

'Well,' said Chanelle, pausing for dramatic effect. 'He. Forgot.'

'No way!' I breathed.

'Yes! He turns up on my doorstep next morning, like nothing has happened, all "Hi babe, how's it going?" I go, "Where. The *fuck*. Were you. Last night?" '

I winced.

'He says, "I was out with the lads." The lads!' she said scathingly. 'I totally lost it. We had a huge argument. I set fire to the Agent Provocateur balcony bra he gave me for my birthday as, like, a statement – but it just melted a big hole in one of the cups. So I threw that porcelain elephant at him – the one we picked up in Thailand? –

and it hit him in the ear. I said, "Take your toothbrush and Grecian 2000 and get out." '

'Ouch.'

A taciturn waiter approached our table.

'Yeah?' he growled and tapped his foot impatiently while we fiddled with our menus. He got a bit crispy when I ordered a Waldorf salad without apple, celery, raisins or walnuts, dressing on the side.

'Could he be any more unpleasant?' I whispered as the waiter stamped off muttering to himself.

'Only if he pulled a gun,' said Chanelle, and we giggled.

'So Uncle Bill is history then?' I asked.

'Oh, he's been ringing and sending flowers, but we are *soooo* over.'

'At least until the BSS Christmas party,' I pointed out.

'True. Speaking of which . . . who are you bringing?'

'No one. Last time I took a date, he got plastered and threw Brussels sprouts at Max across the table.'

Chanelle laughed. 'God, I remember that. It was funny, though.'

'Yeah, but not great as far as career prospects are concerned.'

'You're not seeing anyone at the moment, then?'

'No. At least, there was that guy a couple of months ago . . . but I think he mistakenly fell on my face rather than willingly engaged in mutually consensual snogging.'

'You're just waiting for the right person,' Chanelle soothed me.

'I've gone through most of the wrong ones.'

'Remember that guy, what was his name? The one that e-mailed you porn?'

'Dan Game. Shit, I'd forgotten about him.'

We'd only been going out for a fortnight when Dan

sent the sort of pictures you might find in raunchier numbers of the German edition of *Penthouse* to my e-mail address *at work*. Jed's predecessor had threatened to report me for peddling smut. Even now, I sometimes wondered whether I came across as That Type of Girl: did I have a perverse, voyeuristic look about me?

'Remember Gay Gavin?' said Chanelle. 'He was lovely.'

'Yes, but *gay*,' I reminded her.

'Oh, I don't know. Couldn't you have overlooked that?'

'Knowing Gavin, he's probably still camped out in the closet. He'll be happily married for forty years until his wife comes home unexpectedly to find him stuffing a gerbil up the milkman's bottom.'

Chanelle grimaced.

Our lunch arrived and I picked up my fork.

'D'you know, Chan, the other night Nigel made a pass at me. I said to him, "Nigel, do I look like I'm desperate?" and he said, "I say yes. I would hardly have wasted my time if you didn't." '

'He's such a trier. What about your new manager? Luke Wylie.'

'He's my boss,' I pointed out shortly.

'But he's delicious,' said Chanelle, giving a huge sigh around a dainty mouthful of prosciutto. 'Like an intelligent rugby player. And very . . . decisive. He must be loaded as well . . . I think you could make an exception.'

I shook my head. 'Fishing off the company pier – never a good idea.'

In fact, I suspected the company pier was shut for maintenance. In the office, Luke kept a professional distance. There was an occasional frisson of excitement but I'm sorry to report that most of the friss was mine. I didn't think there was much danger of his ravishing me up against a filing cabinet.

'What about Jed?' asked Chanelle slyly.

'Who?'

'You know, the bloke you share your cubicle with? Support Manager, about six foot two, sex on legs . . .'

I stared at Chanelle in disbelief. 'You're *joking*, aren't you?'

'What? Oh, come on, Liv: he's gorgeous, or haven't you noticed? Those intense green eyes, the Heathcliff hair, the sexy cheekbones – and he's a real man. Strong, silent, brooding—'

'Rude, thoughtless, total mongrel. Do you *fancy* him?' I asked incredulously.

Chanelle shrugged and twisted a strand of hair round her finger.

'Aren't you worried about the fact that he can't keep his zip up?'

'Oh, he's just working off excess testosterone.'

'Well, sooner you than me, girl. Knock yourself out.'

'Maybe I will,' said Chanelle.

On a standard Friday evening, you could bet your healthy liver function on finding most of the BSS department in Spinker's celebrating the official opening of the weekend. The pub was close to the PL office and served alcohol, which was sufficient for Jed; and where Jed went, BSS followed.

Spinker's was not the trendiest watering hole in the capital: no barstools suspended from the ceiling or drinks served in test tubes. To my knowledge, none of the staff were failed actors – although tonight there was a barman on duty who would not have been out of place smouldering up a billboard. He was thrown into sharp relief by the herds of accountants braying into beer glasses – and the trusty pair of whiskey goggles clamped to my head.

After Chanelle and I finished cataloguing the talent on the ground – which didn't take long – she abandoned us to transplant Bill with another asshole.

Jed, Nigel and I remained at the table, squinting at each other across a glittering mass of empty bottles and beer glasses. My vocal cords were well lubricated and twanging away at full throttle.

'I mean, as bosses go, Luke's all right,' I said, waving around a glass of melting ice cubes. 'I mean, he's a political animal. I mean, once you appreciate that, he's all right . . .'

'Anderson, why don't you say what you mean?' said Jed. The only intimation that Jed might have more alcohol than red corpuscles swilling around his veins was his eyes, which were opaque and alive with the potential for malice.

'That's what I've been—'

'Man's shallower than a puddle of piss,' interjected Jed.

'Oh, come on, Marshall, that's a bit harsh.'

'He's absolutely tedious. Not unlike you at the moment.'

I forgot to mention that drink makes me more monotonous – and Jed crueller.

'He's got great dress sense. And he—'

'Dammit, woman!' snapped Jed. 'You have not stopped bleating on about Wylie since we arrived. Except for taking time out to leer at Mr Muscle behind the bar there—'

'I have *not!*' I sprang hotly to my own defence. Well, nobody else was about to.

'Indeed you have, and it's pretty grisly.'

'Wasn't leering,' I said sulkily. 'Although . . . he's pretty . . . snacky, isn't he?' I gave a giggle inspired by lustful thoughts of licking peanut butter off the barman.

'Livvie,' said Jed wearily, 'he's a ghoul.'

'He's my destiny,' I sighed. 'My soulmate.'

'And you picked up that from "That'll be fifteen seventy"?' snapped Jed.

'Jed, will you stop that guy? Please?' Distracted, I pointed at Nigel, who was busy trying to bite the top off a bottle of Bacardi Breezer. He was failing dismally in this demonstration of manliness, and chips of enamel were starting to fly.

'Hand it over, Usher.' Jed held out a hand.

'Almosht got it,' slurred Nigel, jabbing ineffectually at his gums.

'Give it here,' demanded Jed, confiscating the bottle.

'Let Mad-dog Marshall show you how it's done,' I said. 'Teeth like steel-reinforced pliers.'

'I'm not going to *chew* it off,' said Jed, placing the edge of the bottleneck against the bench. 'You can lose a molar with that kind of carry-on.' He gave the bottle a smart whack with the palm of his hand, the top flew off with a *pop!*, and Jed handed the bottle back to Nigel.

'Spank you very much, Oddjob,' said Nigel, and belched.

'You're welcome,' said Jed easily.

'Jesus – what the fuck is it with accountants that they feel compelled to wear their tie on their head after two pints?' I asked, as three specimens stumbled past.

'It's to hold their brains in. Who's up for another drink?' asked Jed, unfolding himself from his chair. 'Same again?'

Nigel and I serenaded him to the bar with a chorus of 'Hell, yes!'

'I say,' said Nigel, lowering his voice an octave. He was shiny, obnoxious and randy. 'See that girl over there? *Don't look!*' he hissed. 'Think she's got the hots for me, if you know what I mean.'

'Nigel, you are a master of the single entendre. Of course I know what you mean.'

I glanced at the attractive woman in a purple suit leaning against the wall. Unless she was deranged or had a ferocious squint, she had not been eyeing up Nigel.

'Know what I think?' said Nigel, screwing up his eyes

and taking another swig of Lemon Light Bacardi Breezer. 'That girl wants an introduction to the hungry elephant.'

'Oh, Nigel, please don't. Look – she's surrounded by a group of people, which rules out the possibility of damage limitation. You're going to get brutally rejected, which means you're going to sulk for the rest of the evening, before catching a cab home and throwing up in a flowerbed. Why not jusht shave yourself the hassle and cut shtraight to the flowerbed?'

'Rubbish!' shouted Nigel with the supreme arrogance afforded by eight bottles of alcopop. 'Look at her! She's facking *gagging* for it!'

Jed loped back with armfuls of grog. 'What's up?' he asked, distributing the drinks.

I sighed, and necked back half my Powers. 'Nigel thinks the woman in the purple dress ish keen.'

'On who?'

'Me!' said Nigel, affronted.

'Fantastic!' exclaimed Jed. 'Yeah, she's up for it all right. Really, mate, you should chat her up. Off you go.' He leaned over and gave Nigel an avuncular pat on the shoulder.

'Jed, tha'sh evil,' I said, as Nigel lurched off in the general direction of his shag-interest.

'Oh, come on, he was going to do it anyway,' Jed argued. 'I just speeded things up.'

'But he's gon' be *'nihilated.'*

'Yeah,' said Jed gleefully, practically rubbing his hands together. 'Look! Watch this.'

Shag-interest's face was a study in slowly dawning horror. She drew back her hand and bestowed a great slap about the chops upon the hapless Nigel, who beat a hasty retreat.

'That facking slapper!' said Nigel bitterly, not to mention literally. 'Wasted my best chat-up line on her too.'

'What was that then?' I asked, wincing in anticipation.

' "That suit is very becoming on you. If I was on you, I'd be coming too".'

Jed and I looked at each other and I snorted into my glass.

'I'm gong to th' bar,' I said, standing up carefully.

'What for?' said Jed sharply. 'You've got a full drink.'

'Not any more.' I picked up my drink and swallowed it in one go. 'I'm jush' gonna ge' packet of crishps. You wan' packet of crishps?'

'No thanks,' sighed Jed wearily. 'I'm good.'

Chairs skittered across the floor and grown men blanched in fear as I barrelled across the room, sights firmly set on the barman, a.k.a. My Destiny.

I hadn't realised how drunk I was; I shouldn't have knocked back that last whiskey. Never mind. All I needed to do was hang on to my cool, and chances were he wouldn't even notice my lack of leg.

As I approached the bar, I slowed to a deliberate tread.

Yes! There he was. Right . . . on . . . target. So far so good.

Throwing myself on to a bar stool, I promptly toppled off the other side.

Darn. How could I have forgotten there are a full 360 degrees you can fall off a bar stool?

I crouched on the floor a moment, eyes closed, in the futile hope that My Destiny hadn't noticed my abrupt plummet floorwards, despite my having leapfrogged the stool right in front of him.

His head appeared over the edge of the bar, putting paid to that notion.

'All right?' he asked, smiling broadly.

'Great!' I exclaimed, springing up like kangaroo on a pogo stick. I lowered my voice and whispered confidentially: 'Fell off th' bar stool there.'

My Destiny nodded slowly. 'I saw that,' he whispered back.

Wonderful.

Okay, no problem. Could've been worse. For example, I could've been wearing a low-cut top and had one of my tits pop out. I glanced down for a quick spot check.

Shit!

It had.

Turning my back on My Destiny, I scooped up the runaway mammary and tried to coax it back into my bra. It was a bit like trying to get toothpaste back in the tube, but I succeeded after several minutes of concentrated squishing.

It was only after I had finished – and received a scattered round of applause along with a few lusty cries of 'Encore!' – that I realised I had flashed the entire bar.

At this point, had I not been three-quarters legless and wholly desperate, I would have heeded my cue to slink home and sleep it off. But no: flashing my bosom seemed a minor setback and I was determined to press my disadvantage. All I needed to do was radiate poise.

Po. Ise.

Fixing My Destiny with a sexy smile – think lecherous leer – I draped myself across the bar and ran my tongue lasciviously round my lips. It appeared to have expanded, because I drooled all over the counter.

After a beat, My Destiny fished a bar towel out of the sink and wiped down the surface.

'What can I get you?' he asked.

'Shurprishe the heck outta me,' I purred winningly.

'You what?'

'Er, y'know. Shurprishe me. You' – I wiggled a finger at him – 'are the reshident beveraghe conshultant. Sho . . .' I leaned in close, and he recoiled slightly from the blast of whiskey fumes. 'Shurprishe me. Baby,' I added for good measure.

My Destiny gave a long sigh and my heart sang. Fear not, my love! Soon we will be together!

'How about a beer?'

I was discouraged by his lack of imagination – but only momentarily.

'Don' dring k beer.'

'All right. Gin? Tequila? Vodka? Wine? Amaretto? Port? Baileys? Absinthe? How about a cocktail?'

Three minutes later, My Destiny had adopted the air of a fugitive from justice hearing the hounds baying downriver.

'All right,' he said. 'I have an idea.'

He took out a glass and an array of bottles, mixed up a petrol-blue concoction and slid it across the bar to me.

'Wha' the frig'sh thish?' I poked it dubiously.

'My special recipe,' said My Destiny, striking a match with a flourish. He applied it to the surface of the drink. 'It's a variation on a Flaming Lamborghini. I guarantee you've never had this before.' He handed me the shortest straw I had ever seen.

'Yesh, but, it'sh on fire,' I said, staring at the thin blue flame weaving on the surface. 'How . . . ?'

'Put in the straw and drink it.'

I was still doubtful, but didn't want to disappoint My

Destiny – or the small group of hardened patrons who'd gathered to watch. Bending to the level of the countertop, I introduced the straw into the glass.

It melted.

'It melted!' I announced.

My God: three sheets to the wind but my mind was still sharp as a razor.

My Destiny relit the drink.

'You need to drink it quickly,' explained a man in a pinstripe suit.

Right. This time, I would place the straw in my mouth *before* approaching the drink. Arms braced on either side of the glass, I dived in. As soon as the straw was in contact with the liquid, I started sucking like blazes. There was definitely something happening. What a cocktail! It was a taste sensation! This man was a *genius*!

Next thing I knew, My Destiny *attacked* me. It felt as if he had one hand round the back of my head while with the other he mashed a bar towel into my face.

Valiantly I tried to fight him off, but My Destiny had his grungy old beer mat grafted on to my face. It was sopping – it reeked of lager and cigarette ash, and – more worryingly – it was seriously curtailing my air supply.

When he abruptly released me, I heaved a gasp of fresh air into my lungs and reeled into the pinstriped man.

Propping myself up on Pinstripe's paunch, I tried to speak, but the words were coming out as unintelligible little screaks.

'Wha . . . wha . . . wha?' I panted.

The barman casually tossed the bar towel into the sink. 'You set your eyebrows on fire,' he said – as if that went any way towards clarifying the farce of the last thirty seconds.

I put a trembling hand to my forehead.

To my horror, instead of nice, warm, furry eyebrows there were wiry, prickly wisps of stubble emitting – I sniffed warily – a noxious burnt odour.

For a long moment, I looked at the barman and realised that really, even had I been able to persuade the cat to liberate my tongue, there was nothing to say.

14

Back at the table, Jed sprawled in his chair helpless with laughter. I slid on to a banquette opposite and glared at him.

'Aw, Livvie!' Jed wiped his eyes with the heel of his hand. 'That was . . . that was . . . *top*! When you fell off the barstool . . . and then . . . I didn't realise your destiny was going to be that entertaining!'

'Are you quite finished?'

'What are you talking about? I haven't even started yet!'

Apart from the room, which was still swooping and gliding, I had been afflicted by a chronic case of sobriety.

Nigel was staring intently at a bottle of alcopop. Now he rolled forward on to the table emitting gentle snores.

'Fucking Usher,' said Jed. 'Give him a sniff of lemon-flavoured vodka and the man is lopsided.'

'Look on the bright side. He was due to liberate diced carrots on the world around about now, wasn't he?'

'Five minutes ago, in fact.'

Braver taxi drivers hit the central-lock button when Nigel came within thirty paces; the more sensible tore off in a cloud of exhaust fumes.

'Suppose I'd better get him home and check his vital signs,' said Jed, uncoiling himself from the chair and pulling on his leather jacket. 'He can sleep on my sofa if needs be.' Gripping Nigel's shoulders, he manoeuvred him into a sitting position and hoicked him easily on to a shoulder.

'Let's go, Fatso,' he said, patting Nigel's bottom affectionately. 'You coming?'

'No, I think I'll stay a bit longer.'

'Okay. Have a good weekend.' He kissed me on the forehead.

'You too.'

I watched him stride away, Nigel's arms dangling down his back.

I was sitting alone, fingering my travesties of eyebrows, when I sensed someone standing by the table. I looked up.

It was Luke Wylie.

I squeezed my eyes shut and jammed my fingers into the sockets. If I kept them closed for long enough, he might be gone when I opened them.

I tentatively aired an eyeball. No such luck.

'Oh, fuck, not you,' I said with feeling.

Luke threw back his head and laughed. 'Gee, thanks!'

'Shit, did I say that out loud?'

'I'm gonna assume it was the drink talking. Can I sit down?'

'Oh, ah. Of course, please.' I waved a rubbery arm and he slid on to the banquette alongside me. 'What are you doing here?'

Luke rested his arm along the back of the seat, his hand millimetres away from my hair, which was in the process of staging a violent coup. 'Same as you, I guess, but with more coordination. I come here often.'

That sounded familiar – was it a chat-up line? No, only if phrased as a question.

'When did you arrive?' I asked, wondering how much he'd seen. I found that if I closed one eye I could focus on him better, although I wished he would stop twirling around.

'A while ago.'

'Oh. Really?'

'Yeah,' he drawled. 'Would it be inappropriate to say: great tits?'

'Yes,' I said. 'Although since I flashed them at the entire bar, it would probably be rude not to compliment them. So . . . you . . . saw?'

'Kinda hard to miss.'

'I'm very embarrassed,' I said earnestly.

Luke shook his head. 'There's no need—'

'No.' I held up a hand. 'I will feel terribly embarrassed for the rest of the weekend. Possibly the entire month. Don't laugh; I'm serious. You don't think . . . do you think carnal knowledge of my mammaries will . . . adversely affect our working relationship?'

'No, I think it's gonna improve it. Is something wrong with your eye?'

'No. Why? Is there something wrong with yours?'

He grinned. 'How about I get you a cab?'

15

While my eyebrows grew back, Christmas crept insidiously into the air. All of a sudden carols played everywhere, shops did a roaring trade in tinsel, and PL erected a three-storey-high Norwegian spruce in the lobby.

It was barely November.

Luke never referred to the incident in Spinker's, but sometimes in a meeting I caught him contemplating me with a knowing look. Our eyes would catch and hold a fraction too long.

We were spending more time together now that the Gragnoc project was under way. Nigel had finally squeezed the purchase order out of Graeme, Gragnoc's CEO.

Like most of us, I put up with Nigel because he provided unsurpassed entertainment value – and was impossible to avoid. However, our working relationship was strained, largely because Nigel was crap at his job. I kept trying to encourage him in a direction more suited to his particular skill set – like selling bathroom accessories, or inheriting the family pile – but for the moment I was stuck with him.

One day I received a polite but terse phone call from Graeme.

'Nigel,' I called conversationally across the partition. 'Graeme says we sent him the wrong hardware. But it's the same equipment listed in your contract spec.' I flapped it over the cubicle partition for his inspection. 'What's the story?'

It turned out that Nigel had given me an old version of the contract.

'Christ, Usher!' I snapped. 'I've just sent Graeme a hundred and seventy thousand pound's worth – three hundred thousand after mark-up – of the wrong equipment! What the hell am I supposed to do now?'

'One: take a chill pill. Two: tell him Santa came early and we sent them better servers—'

'But they're *not* better servers!' I roared. 'There's less memory on these v280Rs than the ones Graeme signed off and paid for. Not to mention slower processing speed, no RAID control—'

'Graeme doesn't know that.'

'Usher, of *course* Graeme knows. He has about twenty times more brain matter to fiddle around with than you. The v280Rs are industry standard machines: the specifications are publicly available on the Internet—'

'Keep your facking knickers on,' said Nigel. 'The system will still run on that hardware, won't it?'

'Yes, *but*,' I gritted my teeth and fought the temptation to leap over the partition and strangle him with my thong, 'it's not what you *agreed*. It's like Graeme bought a Ferrari, and we deliver a Nissan Micra, and say: "Well, it still gets you from A to B; what are you complaining about?"'

'I don't think—'

'For once we agree.' I took a deep breath. 'This is your bloody mess, Usher. You'll have to call Graeme and offer to knock a few thousand off the price.'

'I can't do that!'

'You can, and you bloody will.'

Nigel refused to take my word for it, so Luke called an emergency meeting with Nigel and his manager, Brenda Calburn.

After some persuasive rhetoric on my part, Brenda reluctantly agreed that Nigel would renegotiate the contract with Graeme. There was no alternative apart from replacing the hardware, which would take weeks and leave BSS with a pile of obsolete servers to dust.

Then Luke surprised me.

'Ms Calburn,' he said coolly, 'I would appreciate it if you ensured your staff conducts proper handover. Why didn't Olivia receive the final contract with correct hardware specifications from Nigel? We're all professionals here.'

Wahey! Take *that*!

'Additionally – *additionally*,' he raised his voice over Brenda, who had gone an interesting shade of neon puce, 'as a matter of course, Nigel should check scheduling and deliverable dates with the relevant project manager before agreeing them with the client.'

'Well, if your team—' sputtered Brenda.

'I understand Nigel committed an unrealistic deadline to our biggest client.'

'Who – what—'

'Gragnoc's EnTire system. While Nigel addresses the server issue, perhaps he can also tell the client he underestimated the delivery time. It's not fair to expect Olivia to deal with his screw-up.'

'Well, if you—'

'I hope I've made myself clear,' barked Luke. There was just a hint of the arrogant Lynott's maniac, but when not directed at me accompanied by flecks of spit and bile, it was quite inspiring.

'I have no intention—'

'Excuse me,' said my new manager abruptly, and pushed back his chair. 'I'm very busy.'

He swept out of the room like a tsunami in reverse.

All right, Luke may not have been aware that Brenda Calburn was distilled evil personified – in fact, I'm pretty sure she put a hex on him at the door – but how terrifically rude! How quintessentially un-English! How loin-squeezingly manly!

Luke Wylie was edging up the ranks in my estimation league tables.

16

The day of the Puttock Leavitt BSS Christmas party, Max stalked the Maze in a Santa suit, issuing menacing directives to lighten up and get with the holiday spirit, goddammit.

'I say, did you know Santa's an anagram of Satan?' said Nigel darkly.

For the first time in living memory, Nigel was disobeying a direct order: he was actively *not* happy. The previous week, attempting to photocopy his arse from thirty different angles, he zoomed in for a close-up sphincter detail and broke through the glass. He had ended up in St Thomas's A&E, where the long-suffering staff – in between extracting holly leaves from retinas and flick knives from eardrums – tweezed shards of glass out of his bum.

After work, Chanelle and I twittered off to the PL health club to get changed and compliment each other on how gorgeous we looked. Then Chanelle charmed a suit into surrendering his black cab to convey us to the London Aquarium.

'Fashionably late,' agreed Chanelle as we paused for effect in the doorway. She ran a hand over her airtight kingfisher-blue ensemble.

Making An Entrance with Chanelle was always an

occasion. Conversation lulled. Men choked on their drinks. Green-eyed monsters preyed on unwary women.

Chanelle spotted—

'Bill!'

She had given him a day pass from the doghouse. I had no idea what she saw in him. Bill might have been lovably rich, but he had a distasteful line in toilet humour and blow-dried his hair into a mad bouff.

Oh, thank goodness!

'Jed!'

'Hey, angel.' Jed kissed me on the cheek.

'Wow!' I said involuntarily. 'You look *good*, Marshall.'

'I made a special effort.'

'Brushed your hair?'

'Nope, I shaved. Feel.' He stuck out his jaw.

'Attractive offer, but no thanks.'

'Don't wait for an invite, you can feel me any time. Hey, I like this,' he said, running a hand down my bare back.

'Haven't you got a date to grope?' I asked.

'No. Here, come with me.' He grabbed my hand and dragged me away. 'I had to switch your placing. You were sitting between the Poison Dwarf and That Git Wylie on the bobblehead table.'

'Oh, er, thanks.'

Our table was a froth of white linen, origami napkins and crystal. Chanelle and Bill joined us, the set of Chanelle's jaw suggesting their reunion had fallen short of merry.

'Who're we waiting on?' I asked, indicating two empty seats next to Jed.

'Let me see . . . that's Nigel, and the other place says "Amber".'

'Nigel's bringing a *date*?' I said incredulously.

'Must be.' Jed sounded doubtful.

'Amber. Sounds like a character in a daytime soap,' said Chanelle. 'Married to Falcon, who turns out to be her half-brother.'

'Let me guess,' I said. 'She divorces Falcon and marries his twin, but is devastated when she finds out he's her half-brother too.'

Out of the corner of my eye, I saw Luke take a seat beside Max at the next table. He glanced in my direction and without any reasonable warning unleashed a devastating smile. My stomach flipped and I experienced an orgasmic twang.

'What's that plonker smirking at?' growled Jed.

Me! I thought with a thrill.

Just then Nigel arrived with a woman who was quite obviously a prostitute. I was not normally proficient at detecting such things, but in this case it was unmistakable. The giveaway was the dress slit to the crotch – in both directions. There was silence around the table as everyone tried to work out how it stayed on.

Chanelle shot me a 'holy crap!' look.

'Greetings, earthlings,' said Nigel smugly. 'I'd like you all to meet Amber.' He put a protective arm round her. 'Amber, this is everyone.'

'Hi, Amber,' said Jed with a huge grin. 'Jed.'

Amber may have come across lots of men, but even she was not impervious to Jed's charm. She gave him a wet look, and ran her tongue lusciously over her lips.

I managed to close my own gob long enough to introduce myself.

Nigel pulled out Amber's chair and fussed around pouring water, buttering bread rolls and unfolding her napkin.

I nudged Jed. 'Is she . . . Amber . . . a . . . ?' I murmured from behind a menu.

'What?'

'You *know*. A *prostitute*.'

'Well, she had an ad in the back of *FHM* last month. I'm pretty sure it's her, although it's difficult to tell when she's not simulating pleasure. As far as I can recall, her areas of speciality are tit wanks and spanking.'

'Do you think Nigel *knows*?' I whispered.

'I'd say probably not.' Jed grinned.

Just then, James Henderson glided past us like a hungry vampire.

'What's Henderson doing here?' I asked the table generally. 'It's not as if he needs a free meal.'

'He's a friend of Max's,' said Jed. 'They go way back. According to the grapevine archives, Henderson and Max joined PL at the same time.'

At the next table, Max pounded James Henderson between the shoulder blades. 'Good to see ya, good to see ya, mate!' he roared around a cigar.

'I heard', said Nigel importantly, 'Puttock Leavitt is being investigated for corruption.'

'There's a surprise,' said Chanelle. 'There's always rumour of book-cooking somewhere or other.'

'Daddy was at the Club last week, and met up with a chum whose chum's chum is Chief Commissioner of Scotland Yard. He said they've got someone undercover—'

'Oh, come on,' said Jed witheringly. 'You really think the Chief Commissioner of Scotland Yard is going to tell a chum of a chum of Daddy's about an undercover officer?'

'I wonder how it came up in conversation,' I mused. ' "My word, this salmon is delicious and we have an undercover agent at Puttock Leavitt"?'

'Daddy has connections,' said Nigel sulkily.

At Luke's table, Max rose to his feet and cleared his throat.

'I hope he keeps this short,' said Jed.

'Unless he stands on a chair, you can count on it,' giggled Chanelle.

I stole another glance at Luke and – oh! He was looking at me!

'Ahem, ahem,' said Max.

'How in hell can one man be so hairy?' I muttered from behind a bread roll.

'I think his mother *knitted* him,' said Jed. 'Did you know he has a part down his back?'

'How the hell do *you* know?'

'I once found him clogging up the drain in the gym shower.'

'Hello, hello,' said Max into the microphone. He made a noise like a barking walrus. 'Testing, testing. This bladdy thing isn't working,' he informed everyone in a deep basso.

A harassed technician assured him it was.

'Er, right then, ah,' announced Max impressively. 'Can I have a bit of quiet, please. QUIET! Now, I know everybody's hungry, so I won't keep ya. HAH!'

While Max contradicted himself at length, Luke gave me another lazy smile.

I wondered whether what I felt was dread or anticipation.

17

Much later, I sat alone at our brandy-butter-spotted table surrounded by shredded Christmas crackers and empty wine glasses. The band mangled Slade, Band Aid, the Pogues. Nearly everyone was dancing – even Nigel, who humped Amber's leg around the dance floor. Jed was nowhere in evidence, but I suspected he was hot on the tail of Janine Clifford, one of BSS's marketing managers.

Luke negotiated his way towards me through stray balloons and discarded chairs. He defied several laws of attraction in that dinner suit.

'Hello, Olivia,' he said formally, pulling up in front of me. Then he leaned down and kissed me on the cheek. 'Is this seat taken?' he asked.

'It is now.'

Oh, God, was that too presumptuous? Too wanton?

Not wanton enough?

Luke drew a chair sociably close. 'Great band,' he said, smoothing his cummerbund as he sat. 'Lots of energy.'

'Shame you can't say the same about the timbre or pitch,' I said, taking a slug from a flute of warm champagne.

'You look great,' said Luke.

'You're not looking bad yourself.'

In fact, Luke was illicitly dishy. Just looking at him, my heart had to work a little harder.

'Maybe we should set up a mutual fan club,' suggested Luke.

'Actually, I've got one. It's called the Liv Anderson Fan Club.'

'Really? How do I join?'

'There's an aptitude test and a questionnaire. If you're a suitable fan, you're in. You know: general devotion, regular donations, attendance at the meetings. There's an AGM twice a year.'

'Membership fee?'

'Of course. It's a quality club – we don't let any old dodger in. You get a T-shirt and all.'

Luke laughed. 'What about a privilege card?'

'Maybe.' I swallowed. 'For you.'

'Well, sign me up,' said Luke. Putting his hand on my leg, he applied subtle pressure to the inside of my knee, where all my nerve endings relocated.

'You didn't come with anyone tonight,' he stated softly.

I flushed. 'No.' After a loaded pause, I said: 'Neither did you.'

Luke shook his head.

'Listen,' I said, 'would you excuse me for one moment?' Since I wanted to dazzle Luke with my witty repartee rather than the shine off my forehead, a bathroom check was required before this face-to-face heart-to-heart went any further. 'But I don't want you going away.'

'I won't.'

'You sure?'

'As long as it's not longer than a single moment.'

Five minutes later, fully lipsticked and discharging surplus face powder, I was on my way back when I bumped into Jed lurking behind a pillar.

'Hey.' He nodded grimly, arms crossed. 'See you're getting on well with the Great Smarmy Lick.'

'Hi, Jed,' I responded equally coolly. What was wedged in his craw? 'How are Janine Clifford's saliva samples?'

'Satisfactory. She's not incubating any deadly diseases.'

'That you know of,' I corrected.

Jed followed me to the table. 'Wylie,' he nodded.

'Hello, Jed,' said Luke warily.

When I tried to sit, both men moved to pull out my chair, but Jed elbowed Luke out of the way. I was still smoothing my dress when he wedged the chair into my legs so vigorously I thumped on to the cushion.

'Er, thanks,' I said a bit breathlessly.

Jed seated himself on my other side and slung a casual arm round my shoulder.

Taking his hand, I threw his arm back at him. 'Don't you have any women to harass?' I asked icily.

'Not at the moment. So, Wylie, how are things?' asked Jed solicitously. 'How's the brown-nosing industry these days? I've heard it's a filthy business—'

'Jed!' I hissed. Luke's cheek quilted with tension. He looked chillier than a dead yeti. 'Excuse me.' I smiled tersely at Luke. Pulling Jed to his feet, I prodded him over to a fish tank. 'Jed, I have just one word for you: fuck off!'

'But—' said Jed.

'No! What are you *doing*? I like this guy.'

'Livvie, I've got a really bad feeling about Wylie. I mean, I don't like him much – that's no secret – but it goes beyond that. He's bad news—'

'Just a moment, excuse me,' I interrupted. 'Let me get this clear. The man with the morals of a horny stockbroker is passing judgement on *Luke*?'

'Oh, come on. You're not falling for it, are you?'

'Falling for *what*, Jed?' I said furiously. 'Attention from a gorgeous bloke? Why wouldn't I fall for it? Or is it so difficult for you to imagine that someone finds me attractive?'

'No! But why *him*? Livvie, you could do so much better.'

He took my face in his hands, but I shook him off.

'Jed! *Go away!*'

Jed opened his mouth for another assault, but I put my hand on his chest and pushed firmly.

'*Go.*'

Jed turned to storm off, but whirled round mid-squall and thrust his face into mine.

'Know what, Anderson?' he said savagely. 'If I'd known you were that *easy*, I would have fucked you myself.'

I opened my mouth to gasp with horror, but he was gone.

Swallowing the lump in my throat, I uncurled my hands, which were balled into fists by my side. If I hadn't been so blisteringly angry, I would have considered crying.

When I returned to Luke, I tried the gracious approach.

'Sorry about that,' I said. 'Jed can be a bit of a shit.'

'You don't say?' said Luke, tight-lipped.

'Please, just – just forget him. Can't we take up where we left off?'

Thankfully, he was amenable to that suggestion.

He fashioned a flower out of a cracker hat and tucked it behind my ear and we talked for hours. The details of the conversation are a bit hazy, but I remember random snatches. Luke told me about his cat, Benjy. I demonstrated my double-jointed elbows. Luke told me about the time he and his mate liberated a penguin from Austin Zoo. I got up on the table and gave a rendition of 'Santa Baby' (I accidentally kicked him in the head during a spirited cancan, but he was kind enough to overlook it).

Much later, the lights blared on and I realised how late it was. The band was packing up and only an occasional limp straggler remained – some half-heartedly snogging under tables, others collapsed across chairs. Keith, a BSS engineer, was earnestly addressing a large potted plant.

It looked like a rather one-sided conversation.

The very married James Henderson had his hand up

Janine Clifford's corset. He must have been very dexterous, since there was not a lot of room for manoeuvre.

'Shall we go?' Luke suggested.

Outside, the night air was crisp. Frost glistened on the pavement and goose bumps prickled to attention beneath my flimsy chiffon wrap.

'Never a cab when you need one,' murmured Luke. 'Come here.'

He drew me to him and I realised he was about to kiss me and then he did and I completely forgot the arctic chill, except when I slipped my cold hands under his shirt and Luke gave a bit of a yelp. He pulled me against him, enfolding me in his woollen overcoat.

By gum, he knew how to operate those lips. Unlike many men, he kept his tongue roughly where it belonged instead of sending it off on the grand tonsillary tour. I was also impressed that, despite having a hint of five o'clock shadow, Luke managed to kiss me undeniably thoroughly without making my face feel like a chopped liver patty. I mean, apart from the odd prick (no, not that one; get your mind out of the gutter there), I didn't feel a thing.

Further south, however, I was feeling all sorts of things. A moan that would have made a porn star proud escaped me.

Then, having officially reduced my legs to jelly, Luke . . . well . . . he *stopped*.

'Taxi!' he cried. 'Hey! Taxi!'

There, like a ghostly apparition, was a black cab. Staggering after Luke, my frostbitten toes contrasted with the furnace raging through my reproductive system.

The taxi pulled to a stop with a groan, and Luke bundled me into the back.

'I'll call you,' he said, solicitously tucking my wrap around me.

'Oh! You – you – What?'

He dropped a kiss on my cheek.

'But—'

Luke slammed the door and patted the roof, and before my head had even *started* spinning the taxi roared off in a cloud of fumes.

'Where to, luv?' said the cabbie.

But I was so bewildered I could barely even remember my address.

19

The following morning was a long, slow swim towards consciousness. My head was trying to tunnel its way to Australia through the pillow and a family of stoats appeared to have hibernated in my mouth.

Hmm, rough night then. What...? Ah yes, the Christmas party. I vaguely remembered shadow-boxing around my manager in a fug of lust. The details were sketchy at best, but – oh! A Technicolor flashback of The Kiss hit me like a punch in the gut.

I sent out an exploratory leg, but Luke was not present, correct or otherwise. So I hadn't dreamt him drop-kicking me into a taxi.

I unglued my eyelashes and carefully eased out of bed. Why was everything blurry? In the bathroom, I found one of my contact lenses stuck to the mirror. From the prickly burning sensation, I suspected the other was doing the backstroke around the nether regions of my socket. After fishing it out, I brushed my teeth and scoured my face.

Back in the kitchen, I paused to suck down three glasses of water and a tomato juice. Then I slunk back to bed to ponder the question: why was I *alone*?

Now, let me clarify: it's not that I expected to have

rampant sex with Luke after one night swapping saliva. Really. I'm not the type of woman who, five minutes after meeting a guy, wrestles him to the floor and reverses into him on all fours demanding that he executes positions 1 to 162 of the Kama Sutra. I'm shamefully untrendy in requiring that I'm reasonably well acquainted with the donor before accepting any form of sperm deposit.

Since I couldn't claim to be well acquainted with Luke, it's unlikely I would have declared my vagina open for visitation.

But he could at least have *tried*.

After all, we had got on so well. There was definitely chemistry − not to mention physics and biology and all-round *hot sauciness* (if that doesn't already fall under the given scientific categories). Between us we had generated more pheromones than a perfume plant.

Hadn't we?

I hoped I had shown enough enthusiasm when Luke had said he'd call. Maybe I should have subtly indicated that I would be pleased if he decided to give me a ring sometime: 'You'll call? *Really?* That's terrific! I'd *love* to hear from you! I'll wait by the phone! Can you give me an indication of when? Just roughly, like. Tomorrow? The day after? How about Tuesday? Maybe you'd better give me your home number just in case . . .'

Or perhaps I should have been more offhand: 'You'll what? Oh, you'll *call*. Well, whatever. It's not like I care. I mean, I might answer as long as I'm not exfoliating. Or if I can be bothered to walk halfway across the room to pick up the phone − which I probably won't.'

Since we worked together, technically Luke would be unable to avoid phoning me, but I rather hoped he'd be calling as a precursor to foreplay rather than to discuss Gragnoc's system performance stats.

It looked like a long weekend of post-snog analysis.

Just then, my heart backfired as the phone rang. Luke! I couldn't believe he was calling this soon! He must be keen.

I dived across the room and rugby-tackled the phone almost before the second ring. Hold it! Couldn't answer right away; that smacked of desperation. I'd better wait a moment – but what if he rang off?

And how would I answer? I needed to sound wanton, yet simultaneously hard to get. Inviting, but darkly mysterious.

I picked up the receiver.

'Hello,' I croaked.

Well, it worked for Jerry Maguire.

'Is that your husky phone voice?'

It was Jed. I crumpled with disappointment. I had forgotten our argument, but now it came back to me with a rush of white-hot rage.

'I'm not talking to you,' I said coldly.

'Stop – don't hang up!'

'Why not? There doesn't seem much point if I'm not talking to you.'

'How about I talk?'

'Okay, you've got ten seconds.'

'Twenty.'

'It's just gone down to seven.'

'All right. Look, I'm sorry about last night. I was drunk and Janine Clifford had halitosis, which I was quite cut up about . . .'

I didn't say anything.

'Actually, there's no excuse for what I said. I was out of order.'

'I don't understand why – why you would say something like that. You're supposed to be my friend.'

'Livvie, I am. And I don't know why I said it, but I do know I was an arse.'

'You were.'

'I was.'

'A particularly fat hairy arse with pimples and dangleberries.'

'Yes. Will you forgive me?'

'I'm not sure. Maybe.' I wound the telephone cord round my little finger.

'How about if I buy you coffee for the next week?'

'Fortnight. And croissants – no, make that pastries.'

'You don't eat pastries.'

'Let's say snacks of choice.'

'Done. And I'll tell everyone you're *not* easy.'

'That's all right,' I said graciously.

'So we're okay?' said Jed after a pause.

'Yes, we're okay.'

We *were* okay; and I was relieved that we were okay; and I smiled as I hung up.

I heard nothing from Luke all weekend.

On Monday morning, when he burst into the office and took the Maze at a fast clip, my stomach churned like a washing machine on heavy-soil cycle. Was my hair all right? Should I say hello? Or hide behind my monitor and pretend not to notice him? Or . . .

'Olivia and Wylie, up a tree,' sniggered Nigel behind the partition. 'K-I-S-S—'

Jed handed me a chunky pad of Post-it notes and I lobbed it into the adjacent cubicle.

'FACK!' yowled Nigel. 'I *say*! That *hurt*!'

'You'd think he'd have learned to duck by now,' observed Jed.

Looking neither left nor right, Luke disappeared into his office. I felt a deep flush suffuse my face as a babble of noise erupted in his wake.

Given the high quantum of boredom sustained by PL, gossip was the primary currency of the average company employee, with minor details like hard evidence/fact never getting in the way of a good story. The hot topic of the moment was the speculated relationship between Luke and me, running second only to Brenda the Giant Alien Lizard theory. Luke's snub was duly noted and conjecture flashed around the Maze at hypersonic speed.

The only way to handle the situation was to keep my head down and avoid getting napalm in my hair.

All day long, my stomach simmered with sickly excitement. Every time one of the office doors opened, my heart performed cartwheels around my chest cavity.

When Luke finally did ring, it was only to discuss the Gragnoc system performance stats. Late in the afternoon, we bumped into each other in the corridor and it was *excruciating*. Spines plastered against the opposing walls, both parties aggressively polite: 'Oh, pardon me.'

'No, no, not at all. Please, go ahead.'

'No really, after you.'

'Absolutely not, I insist . . .'

The anticipation Luke had inspired at the Christmas party slowly ebbed away. By the end of the day, I was as grumpy as a bag of bears.

'Anderson, you seem to be struggling with the "goodwill to all men" concept,' observed Jed after I chewed his head off for asking to borrow a biro. 'What's up?'

'Nothing.'

'You're exhibiting classic symptoms of acute sexual frustration,' he announced sagely. 'Irritability, tendency towards distraction, and a slight twitching effect. How are your bowel movements? Infrequent and erratic?'

'Drop dead, Marshall,' I snarled, in support of his first behavioural diagnosis.

'She's been like a premenstrual antichrist all day,' came Chanelle's muffled voice from the other side of the partition. She was sulking because I hadn't complimented her on her new suede miniskirt.

'I take it that minging crap-artist Wylie was unable to get it up?' Jed asked solicitously.

'Christ, Marshall, keep it down!' I hissed furiously.

Jed swivelled round in his chair and watched me with eyebrows raised. I cracked after five minutes.

'Actually, I have no fucking idea whether he's able to crank it up,' I said with dignity.

'Hah so.' Jed nodded sagely. 'He's a fanny-dodger. The male equivalent of a prick-tease,' he said in response to my look of bemusement. 'Oh yes, you'd be surprised how many of them there are around. They give us dedicated fanny-foragers a bad name.'

'Really,' I said, injecting more than your average dose of scepticism into the comment.

'Let's see . . . might be a performance issue.'

'That's very common nowadays.' Chanelle's voice floated over the partition.

'Or – and this is my guess – he might be afraid you'll laugh at his tiny cock.'

'You don't like him much, do you?' I said through clenched teeth.

'What's to like about him?' said Jed, looking like he'd just taken a great suck on a sour lemon. 'He's a shiny-arse Kermit—'

'Is it alpha male syndrome? You're threatened by him – is that it?'

Jed gave a mirthless snort. 'Threatened? By what, exactly? He's so boring he could strip paint just by talking to it.'

'Hey, watch it,' I snarled. 'That's my boyfriend you're talking about.'

'Boyfriend? Well, I guess congratulations are in order. That must be why you're in great form today. Floating on air, singing in the rain et cetera.'

'Oh, drop dead, Marshall.'

21

Perhaps it would have been better had Luke's and my story ended with The Kiss. Then you could assume that we lived happily ever after, in a life full of sunshine and laughter, gorgeous gap-toothed children, wrinkle-free clothes and vigorous yet tender sex twice a night except on Saturdays, when it was five.

But just when I thought it was never going to happen, Luke finally rang and, after a prolonged debate about whether Gragnoc's EnTire system required an external RAID storage unit, asked me on a date.

Of course, I refused. He obviously hadn't had to gnaw his own arm off to stop himself calling – at least, I had seen no evidence of teeth marks when he had passed the cubicle earlier – but I was mollified by his persistence, and when he finally suggested that Saturday night I graciously accepted.

On D-Day, standing in the middle of the flat in my underwear, I would have despaired had there been the time. However, Luke was arriving any minute to sweep me off my feet so it was necessary to focus on the job at hand, which was identifying clothes that would inspire him to do just that.

Mingled with the excitement was a measure of refined terror. I really wanted this to work. I had spent the whole day preparing. I was bathed, conditioned, plucked, cleansed, toned (regrettably restricted to the open pores sense), moisturised, perfumed and subtly shaded – and all since 14:37 hours.

I spent the rest of the afternoon compiling a shortlist of potential outfits, the exercise only serving to make me wonder how I managed to attire myself on a daily basis at all. Everything was too small (lots of those); too large (not so many of those); too loud; too frumpy; not nearly frumpy enough; or a tragic combination of all the above.

It was horribly clear that whatever I chose would involve a trade-off of assets. This sweater made my waist look small, but probably only in comparison with my gigantic, burgeoning, wool-ribbed bosom. These pants flattered my backside but gave me a saggy snatch, which was hardly the look I was going for.

The door buzzer forced me into a snap decision and I grabbed the dress off the shortlist heap. It was a little too trollop-in-distress for my taste: no stinting on cleavage and it didn't reveal a hint of thigh so much as broadcast it.

'Hello!' I shouted at the intercom, pulling the dress over my head and trying not to wipe off half my make-up at the same time.

'I come bearing gifts!' said Luke's voice.

'Well, what are you waiting for? Come on up!'

Smoothing the fabric over my hips before the mirror, I had to admit that the dress did the trick. My waist suggested that I needed a bloody good feed – or at least had skipped breakfast. I swivelled round and, yes, my arse looked small and almost bordering on perky. The only exception were my boobs, rising up like a pair of humpbacked whales. Never mind. As a man, Luke was bound to appreciate that.

I threw myself on the floor to haul on my knee-high boots and yelped as the zip snagged my calf. There was a gentle knock on the door and Luke pushed it open.

Unlike me, he obviously hadn't suffered any sartorial dilemma. He wore a fawn suit with a brown shirt and a bold print tie. It might come across as poncy in print, but please believe me when I tell you that in person it was as close to manly perfection as I'd ever borne witness.

He was also carrying about a hectare's worth of flowers.

Eyeing me wriggling around the carpet, he unleashed the 300-megawatt Luke special. 'Anything I can assist you with, ma'am?'

'No, thanks,' I gasped. Last thing I wanted was Luke getting too close to my sausage-like calves and exposed to a load of flashing gusset. He attempted to kiss me as I struggled off the floor and caught me on the ear.

'You look gorgeous,' he said, and I melted. It's a positive sign when a bloke makes the effort to come up with blatant flattery. 'For you.' He proffered the flowers.

I wondered whether Luke really might be the perfect man – although he had overlooked a small but crucial point. Chocolates. The perfect man arrives armed with both flowers *and* chocolates.

'Where are we going?' I asked as we made our way downstairs.

'It's a surprise.'

Outside, a powder-blue BMW blipped and flashed its tail-lights.

'Wow!' I said. 'Nice car!'

'Isn't it?' Luke smirked. 'It's a 630i Sport. Nearly brand new too – only seven Ks on the clock. Got it for practically nothing.'

'Really? How's that?'

'Bought her from a buddy who left the country. Mind the seat!' he said sharply as I slid into the passenger side. He was obviously confusing me with some supermodel ex-girlfriend, concerned I might lacerate the leather with my razor-sharp buttocks.

'Should I hover?' I asked sarcastically.

If Luke had driven any slower, he would have been in reverse. He straddled the centre line, while opposing cars came at us flashing their lights and honking their horns. Occasionally, Luke would shout: 'Get on to your own side of the road, prick!' and crunch gears at them. He availed himself of maybe twelve of the several thousand horsepower at his command. All in all, it was depressingly unsexy.

We crossed the Thames on Waterloo Bridge, negotiated Trafalgar Square and jerked down Pall Mall. The city's restless energy gave me a familiar thrill.

'It's great to be above ground for a change,' I observed. 'I usually navigate by tube stops.'

'You like London?'

'Oh yes, I love it. Although,' I amended, 'I wouldn't want to live here too long. It gets your priorities out of whack.'

'Yeah?'

'Well, take the Big Arse. Have you ever met an accountant who loves what they do?'

'Only once.'

'And?'

'He was kinda strange.'

'Exactly. Most of the accountants I've met hate, loathe and otherwise detest their job. They do it for the money. During the financial year-end, they work eighteen-hour days and sleep under their desks and don't see their families. I mean, what is the point?'

'The point is, to paraphrase Madonna: we are all spinning in a material whirl and I am a cereal girl.'

'Madonna made a living waggling her armpits around. That's pretty screwed up in itself.'

Luke brought me to a small, exclusive restaurant – the type of place where prices don't feature on the menu. We were shown to a table, and Luke waited until I was seated before taking his chair. The waiters frisked around recommending dishes and tucking our napkins neatly into our groins.

Then Luke and I suffered an Awkward Moment. It was painful. Silence roared like the clang of doom – or it might have been my nerves all jangling at once. After what felt like three hours rearranging the cutlery, 'Shall we order drinks?' suggested Luke.

A waiter materialised as if by the power of suggestion. When he had swished off, Luke reached across the table and took my hand – a move you have to be pretty accomplished to pull off in this day and age.

'I'm so pleased to be here,' he said, playing with my fingers.

'Well, yes, it's a lovely restaurant,' I agreed.

'No, I meant, here with *you*.'

I goggled. Frankly, I couldn't understand it. In London, the ratio of average men to gorgeous women was roughly one to ten. Luke, who could have fallen out of the pages of a Mills & Boon novel fresh from pressing a gorgeous, feisty but fragile heroine to his manly chest, was pleased to be here. With *me*.

It slipped out before I could stop myself. 'Why?'

Oh, I've read enough *Cosmopolitan*s in my time to know that men as a species are not turned on by self-doubt. Take cunnilingus, for example. Is it a turn-on to lie there going: 'Is it a bit smelly down there? Sorry if it's like licking a gamey mackerel.' Of course not. Rather, one should recline beautifully as one's partner toils away down below, occasionally reminding him that he is privileged to worship at the hairy altar.

This being a direct question, Luke froze for an instant.

'Why?' he stalled. 'Why . . . there are lots of reasons. You're smart. You're clever. You're . . . er . . .'

'Nice?'

'Yes, nice . . .'

At least he wasn't after me for my looks.

'You're . . . ah . . .'

'Interesting?'

'I'm not sure that's the word I was looking for.'

'You seemed to be struggling a bit.'

'You don't accept compliments, do you?'

'I'm better with gifts and booze.'

'Look,' said Luke. 'I think you're great. Really, I do. I want to get to know you better.' He gave an intense smoulder. 'Much better. You know, I don't usually do this. Go out with colleagues, I mean. It can be . . .'

'Awkward.'

'Exactly. But . . . I think this could be the start of something special and I'm willing to take a chance.'

'You've talked me into it.' I beamed. 'Let's live on the edge. Fly by the seat of our pants. Nibble the heads off chickens.'

'I'm not sure about the last bit. I'm scared of fowl and geese.'

'Well, you should face your fear.'

'And then bite its head off?'

We grinned at each other in soft focus.

Dinner proceeded without a hitch and the conversation flowed like a fine vintage.

'By the way, if it's okay with you,' said Luke, 'I'd prefer that nobody knows about this. About us. At Puttock Leavitt.'

'Sure. We'll have a secret affair. Clandestine meetings in the janitor's closet, stolen glances across the conference table. Although you'd better steer clear of sending me raunchy e-mails. There are content filters on the mail server that check for porn or filthy language.'

'Really?'

'Oh, yes. It's part of PL's employee policy. Nobody reads the PL handbook, though, so I'm not sure how many staff actually know their mail is monitored.'

'You know,' said Luke just before dessert, 'the other day I was thinking about how we met. Wasn't it awful? At least it'll be a good story to tell our grandchildren.'

As the female, it was really my prerogative to be terrifying Luke with heavy hints about Commitment and talk of The Future. But I was encouraged by the fact that Luke was implying that this was no one-night stand.

When Luke pulled up outside my flat, I swallowed a lump in my throat.

'Would you like to come – like to – ah, would you like a cup of . . . er . . . coffee?'

I might as well just have said, 'Sex?'

Luke leant across me. If I had leant forward an inch, my lips would have brushed against his cheekbone.

'Sure,' he said, and opened my car door. 'Oh, wait up!' He rummaged around under his seat and produced a box of Hershey's Kisses. 'These are for you.'

22

I was so nervous my hands were shaking, and it took me a while to get my key in the lock. It had been a while since I'd entertained a trouser snake – so long that I feared my hymen had grown back. What if – like waxing – it had grown back twice as thick? Luke might need a machete.

What if I'd forgotten how to . . . you know?

If I recalled correctly, there wasn't much to it. Mainly a lot of up-down pelvic thrust action, with maybe a bit of spinning thrown in for variation.

I hoped to goodness he wasn't into anything kinky. I might leave my boots on, but only if Luke was persistent. Just as well I'd been involuntarily celibate during the whole anal sex fad a couple of years ago when it was all the rage; I wasn't up for any of that carry-on. Luke wouldn't be getting anywhere near my arse.

After we got into the flat, I fussed around busily – taking Luke's coat, lighting the table lamp, turning on the stereo, straightening pictures.

'Make yourself comfortable,' I instructed over a shoulder, trotting into the kitchen.

'Have you read this?' called Luke from the living room.

'What?' I stuffed a filter in the coffee machine.

'A *Brief History of Time*.'

'God no, I only have it there so people will think I'm clever. Just a moment.' I whizzed beans in the grinder. 'How do you like your coffee?' I shouted after the machine gave a final steam-fuelled burp.

'White, thanks.'

Shite! No milk.

'How about a toot of Baileys instead?' I suggested cunningly.

'Sounds great.'

When I brought the drinks into the living room, Luke had installed himself on my tiny sofa bed, one arm draped across the back. I sat down gingerly beside him.

'Mmm! Very nice,' said Luke. He'd just taken a sip of coffee, so I presumed he was referring to that. 'Great place.'

'Sure, it's grand. At least I don't have to share.' I was speaking too fast. 'And it keeps the rain out.'

Luke contemplated me lazily as he wrenched loose his tie and undid a couple of shirt buttons. Gazing mesmerised, I experienced the sort of panicky surge you get when you realise you've lost your wallet or locked yourself out of the house in the nip.

Luke put his drink down and closed in purposefully. When his nose was practically touching mine, he paused for a tension-charged moment, then kissed me.

He started off light and teasing, delivering feathery kisses along my jaw line; nibbling on my lower lip; flicking his tongue gently against mine.

Unfortunately, I was still holding my coffee. I was desperately trying to set it on the floor without alerting Luke, who settled in for some concentrated foreplay. He pressed me into the sofa until I was holding the mug by the rim. It was particularly hot, and I felt it sliding out of my sweaty grip.

I didn't want to say, 'One minute. Hold that thought, will you?' I would have done, except that I thought I could put the mug down before it slipped. Right up until the moment I dropped it.

'Forget it,' murmured Luke, running his hand over my left breast.

All right for him to say. He wasn't the one who'd have to clean it up later. And I tried to move on and achieve closure with the spilt coffee, I really did, but as Luke massaged my earlobe (bizarrely erotic, in case you were wondering) I couldn't help thinking about it soaking into the carpet; and when he drew a line of kisses down my throat I was entertaining fantasies of Stain Devil.

'Sorry, sorry, sorry.' I interrupted Luke mid-pucker. 'Just a moment. Won't be a sec.' Before he could protest, I was off like a cartoon cat.

Luke confiscated the J-cloth after I had spent ten minutes dabbing the carpet.

'Oh, we should – we should unfold the sofa bed.' I jabbered.

'How does it work?' said Luke.

'You pull this and – oh, here, I'll do it.'

'Baby, relax,' he whispered, and gave me a kiss that I felt all the way down to my toes.

'By the way, the bed collapses if you sit on the end of it,' I gasped.

'Duly noted,' said Luke against my mouth. He slowly unzipped my dress and slid it off my shoulders.

'Feel good?'

'Mmm-hmm,' I sighed.

And then he showed me his grand big willy, and I felt *really* good.

After due consideration, I decided I was madly in love with Luke. He hit nearly all the criteria on my wish list: well versed in the correct response to 'Does this make me look fat?'; generous with gifts and lavish evenings out on the town; thoughtful; well presented; pleasantly fragranced. Also, I could tell he would be a really good-looking older man.

It was difficult keeping our relationship a secret in the office, because I wanted to tell everyone. Of course Jed knew; and I told Chanelle so that we could discuss stamina, girth and centilitres. One day, I accidentally called Luke 'Sex on a Cracker' in a meeting. Convincing everyone I had actually said 'change request procedure' took some doing.

On Christmas Eve, Luke took me to the Ritz, where he had reserved a room for the night. Since I'd already shown him the pooty, it wasn't too presumptuous – although it might have been a different story had he booked the Holiday Inn.

Just before New Year, he turned up on my doorstep and told me to pack a bag with warm clothes and my passport. I had no idea where we were going, until we landed in Gstaad. It was almost the most romantic thing that had ever happened to me except that in the rush to pack I forgot my toothbrush, perfume and selection of bras. Also, since I'd never been skiing before, I spent most of the days with my face stuck in a snowdrift. But the evenings were much better.

In January, everyone returned to work on a diet. The PL gym was on twenty-four-hour alert.

Nigel had taken Amber to meet the family in Sussex, where she received a mixed reception. His father thought she was a 'fine filly'. His mother, who, it was rumoured, trod a similar career path to Amber's before marrying the Earl of Derby, did not share his enthusiasm. After catching Amber nicking some cutlery ('It was only a couple of forks!' protested Nigel hotly) she pronounced her a 'vile dolly bird' – which probably fell significantly short of conveying her true feelings towards her son's new girlfriend.

During a romantic Christmas Eve dinner, Bill had presented Chanelle with a diamond Tiffany necklace, a Louis Vuitton handbag and matching wallet, and an Issey Miyake gift set.

She gave him a pair of slippers.

He left before dessert.

'She offered to return his presents,' I told Jed between gasps. He was teaching me to play squash, which addressed three New Year resolutions in one go: 3.1) Get fit, 3.1.2) Exercise twice a week and 5.6.2.2 (b) Take up a new hobby.

Jed stood in the middle of the court lazily pucking at the ball while I charged around wheezing. 'What did he say?'

'Told her – argh! – to keep them. Said they were – huh! – presents.'

'Give it a couple of months and she'll be hearing from his lawyers. Ready? Seven love.'

'No ... stop ... stop ...' I bent over and tried to heave air into my flaming lungs. A stitch skewered my right side.

'Come on, look lively. Seven love.' Jed served the ball, and I flailed wildly at it, overbalanced and careered into the wall.

Jed stuck out a hand and hauled me to my feet. 'How's Chanelle taking it?'

Chanelle was getting over Bill just fine, judging by the monotonous parade of rich, age-challenged men escorting her around her social circle. All favoured pin-stripe suits, SUVs and bright gold cufflinks, and seemed incapable of walking if they weren't simultaneously braying into a mobile.

I didn't have enough puff left to fully communicate this, but hoped I got the point across adequately: 'I think I'm going to barf.'

Jed was restless and irritable, probably because Max had slashed his support team budget for the year. He blew off steam by subscribing Max to masses of porn sites.

'Spending money on his employees might impact his chauffeur allowance,' he said grimly, adding Max's details to *www.sexwithdonkeys.com*.

We also found a great site that *faxed* porn for a small subscription fee. In rare agreement that this was a constructive use of our salary, Jed and I registered Max for the daily PornFax. Every morning, Max's phone gave a sharp *brill!* and churned out the Position of the day 'For the attention of Max Feshwari'.

I was relieved that my relationship appeared to have injected me with fresh motivation for my job. At least, I was not motivated to explain to my new boyfriend that I was seeking alternative employment; so I decided I wasn't after all. There was certainly enough to keep me occupied, with seven demanding project implementations all in various stages of excretion. I was also maintaining a crippling schedule of coffee breaks three times daily.

I was observing my New Year resolution number 1.4.2) to not kill and/or physically maim Nigel, but it took huge reserves of willpower – especially when he came round to our cubicle to spend hours telling us how busy he was. To be fair, he was busy avoiding Gragnoc's increasingly panicked phone calls about when the EnTire system would be ready.

Within a matter of weeks, I wanted to spend every moment of every second of every minute of every hour with Luke, but unfortunately our schedules did not allow it. Going on a date in the City had to be planned days – even weeks – in advance. Occasionally we had dinner after work, and Luke conveyed me home. He preferred to come to my place; I suspect he was compelled by my *Planet of the Apes* DVD set.

But the course of true love never did run smooth – or so Shakespeare would have you believe and who am I to question such venerable wisdom? Luke's and my course was about to encounter a kink – or kinkiness might be more accurate.

Okay, look. I'd better start at the beginning. Or rather, what I hoped was the *end* – of a nightmare day. A sewer rat might have had a crappier day, but it would have been a photo finish.

It started with a bang, when my train broke down en route to London Bridge, which made me late for my eight o'clock meeting where, nibbling on my pen, I accidentally scribbled a moustache on my upper lip – and nobody told me until lunchtime. In the canteen, the accountant in front of me stole the last hummus and roast pine nut panini.

That afternoon, Gary Newbit the HR manager phoned about my January expenses claim. There was rumour that Newbit wore PL underpants, although nobody had ever confirmed it.

'Miss Anderson,' he said without preamble, 'in January's expenses you include an amount for eighty pounds: a taxi fare from Heathrow to Greenwich. Claim number 00024. As you should be aware, Puttock Leavitt limits reimbursement of travel expenses to public transport, as outlined in Section 3.3.1 paragraph 2D of the PL staff handbook.'

'It was three o'clock in the morning, and I had just come off a seven-hour flight!' I protested. 'I'm not going to risk my life getting a bus from Heathrow to Greenwich at that hour – not for love nor money nor Puttock Leavitt.'

'PL will not recognise the claim,' he droned. 'Additionally . . .' I heard rustling in the background, 'you have included three bottles of water from the hotel mini-bar.'

'I was *thirsty*!' I exclaimed. 'I wasn't getting plastered at company expense—'

'Were there no taps,' he said. Apart from the grammatical structure, there was nothing about his tone to indicate it was a question. 'As outlined in Section 3.3.0 paragraph 13A: mini-bar consumables are not covered under the expense plan and will therefore not be reimbursed by the company.'

I slammed down the phone, whereupon it rang again almost immediately.

'You should be aware,' said my nemesis pleasantly, 'that you are liable to the company for wilful vandalism of company property—'

This time, I slammed down the phone more gently.

The only thing to look forward to in the whole world, possibly for the rest of my life, was my date with Luke after work. I looked forward to settling into some cosy little restaurant where I would bemoan my various travails over a flagon of wine. Luke would take my hand and assure me that I looked great even with an ink moustache and that Gary Newbit was a pencil shagger and if I wanted him taken care of he knew someone who knew someone who could fracture a kneecap or two no questions asked.

Late in the afternoon Luke called and cancelled. It was the third time in as many days.

'I'm sorry. I have so much work to do,' he said. 'I'll make it up to you, I promise.'

We were still at that tentative stage where I was trying to demonstrate quiet understanding, my admirable unclinginess; in summary, my generic girlfriendly perfection.

Therefore, when Luke cancelled, I clucked things like 'Gosh, no, of course it's okay' and 'No problem, I've been meaning to fumigate the flat for ages' when what I really wanted to do was screech at him like a psychotic banshee. In this case, I said: 'I fully understand. Really, I have things I need to do this evening, too. It's, ah . . . stuff. Lots of stuff.'

I couldn't wait to get out of the office. When 17:59:57 dragged round, I was poised for the off – ankles flexed, feet in the starting blocks – when my phone rang.

Jed grinned at me as he pulled on his jacket.

'Sounds like overtime.'

Grimacing, I picked up the receiver. 'Olivia Anderson speaking.'

O God, let it be a wrong number.

It wasn't. My Luck of the Irish reservoir appeared to

have run dry – again. I was seriously thinking about lodging a complaint with the Irish government. I mean, I might no longer be a full-time Irish resident, but I was still a citizen of the RoI, a daughter of Erin; so what the bejaysus was going on with my patriotic quotient of Irish luck?

It was Keith, the engineer in Glasgow. I'd sent him there the previous week to install the Gragnoc hardware and thereby create the illusion that the upgrade was under way. From what I could make out, one of the servers was missing.

Losing, say, earrings; a lottery ticket; car keys – that's understandable. However, misplacing £170,000 worth of throbbing computer – that was just careless. It was another story entirely, and one that wasn't likely to feature a happy ending.

And the blame would fall on me, regardless of what had happened. Accountability: one of the side effects of project management.

'Okay, hang on,' I said. I pressed the heel of my hand against my forehead, trying to rub out the hard knot of panic. 'Let me get this straight. A server. Is missing. How the blithering hell have we managed to lose a server?'

What I really wanted to say was, 'It's pretty *large*, you know, a v280R. It's not like losing a needle in a haystack – it's like losing the whole fucking *barn* in the haystack!'

Instead, I took a deep breath.

'Sorry, Keith,' I said after I'd got my self-control in a firm headlock. 'Bad day. All right, let's work back. There were two servers to deliver. Primary and secondary, for redundancy. According to your checklist here, both of them arrived, right? Okay. Has the client noticed the server is missing? Good . . . My shite no, don't tell them for the love of Jaysus.'

While Keith went off to recheck Gragnoc's server room, I tried to track down the shipping company and/or insurance company to verify what had actually been delivered. They were all closed. Two hours later, I was waiting to hear from any of the above when Luke materialised in the cubicle.

'Excuse me, Olivia,' he said formally. 'Come to my office when you have a moment, will you?'

By this stage I had a thumping great headache – either from the AWOL server, or hunger related to our thwarted dinner date, or pent-up screeching, or a combination of all three. I was about to tell him he should consider getting stuffed – and if he needed any assistance he should feel free to ask – when my phone burst into life. Directing a crushing glare in Luke's direction, I pointedly swivelled round and picked up the receiver.

It was Keith.

'You found it,' I repeated. 'Where' – subtext: the fucking hell – 'was it?'

'Down the corridor.'

'Why didn't you notice it before?'

'Er, it was concealed,' said Keith uneasily.

'Like camouflaged? Disguised? As what? A leafy shrub? A doughnut?'

'Well, not exactly. It was kind of . . . covered. With, er . . . bubble wrap.'

'And you didn't notice it sitting there disguised as a thumping great hairy-arsed machine covered in bubble wrap?' I often use sarcasm when I'm under pressure; it's not an attractive quality.

'Well,' said Keith defensively, 'it wasn't where it was supposed to be. It looks like it was moved.'

I took a moment to process this information. 'By who?'

'I don't know.'

'They didn't woggle it, did they?'

'What?'

'You know – jar it or jiggle it or drop-kick it . . .'

'I'm not sure.'

'Has it booted up properly?'

'I haven't tried yet. I need to find a trolley, and get it back to the server room to install it.'

'Okay. If you wouldn't mind, Keith, can you do that first thing tomorrow? Say a little prayer, power it up and hope it boots.'

'Sure,' muttered Keith. 'Look . . . sorry.'

'Don't worry.' I blew out my cheeks. 'These things happen. At least you found the damn thing. Why don't you go back to the hotel and go wild on your per diem? Talk to you later – and thanks, Keith.'

After replacing the receiver, I heaved a sigh. Recalling Luke's summons, I heaved another.

I didn't want to canter down the Maze in immediate response to Luke's beck and call, so I played Killer Sudoku Extreme for half an hour. Then I punched into my coat and swung my handbag on to a shoulder. I grabbed the printouts of the weekly reports. One moment – I checked my reflection in Jed's monitor. Blasted hair. Various tufts were making separate bids for freedom; when I pressed down on one, another sprang up. Using my hands, I smoothed the writhing mass as best I could and skewered it with a stray biro.

Right. All set.

The Maze was drenched in grungy darkness. During the day it was like working in the depths of a huge beast (probably the lower intestine). Now it was slumbering, silent but for the distant hum of a Hoover. Knocking briefly on Luke's door, I entered without waiting for an invitation.

'Here are the weekly client reports,' I said frostily and threw the printouts on his desk, narrowly resisting the urge to tear them into little pieces and hurl them overarm in his face. 'I presume that's what you were looking for. Good evening.'

'Hey!' said Luke to my glacial pirouette. 'Wait a minute. Wait! Is something wrong?'

'No,' I snarled. 'I'm *fine*!'

'Come on, there's something wrong. What is it?'

'Nothing. I'm grand. Dandier than a doodled Yankee.'

At least that's what I meant to say, but I had worked up such a frenzy of rage that it came out as 'Dandier than a yoodledankee'.

Then, in what I should have recognised as a doomed attempt to correct my blistering witticism, I said: 'I mean, wankier than an eedled doodle.'

'Excuse me?' said Luke.

'Actually no, if you'll excuse *me* . . .' I went for another heel-anchored twirl.

'Olivia! Hold on a minute. Here, sit down.' He came round his desk and tried to coax me into a chair but I was having none of it. I adopted a modified crash brace position and folded my arms.

'No thank you.'

A coffee cup on his desk had a torrent of dark dribbles down the side, which for some reason enraged me further. It smacked of sloppiness. It's not that difficult to form a seal about the rim of a mug.

'Tell me,' he said. 'What's wrong?'

As if he didn't know.

'As if you didn't know!'

'Actually, I don't,' said Luke. In fairness, if he wasn't bemused he looked like he was wondering whether he'd locked the keys in the car.

'Well, let me refresh your memory. One minute you're all over me like a critical case of the pox, and the next it's like your personal gravity field has failed and you've fallen off the face of the planet. You've cancelled our last three dates—'

'You know how busy I am—'

'Why? I do most of your work. And can I say whatever—'

'Olivia.' Luke adopted a caring, concerned, metrosexual expression. 'It's that time of the month, isn't it?'

'Oh. My. God. Luke, that is so beside the point, it's behind the point or under the point, or – or not even in the vicinity of the same galaxy as the point! Just because I may or may not have PMT doesn't make my argument less valid!'

In retrospect, punctuating the sentence by stamping my foot probably did.

'And what's with the "I hereby issue you with a directive to present yourself in my office, Ms Anderson" routine? Who are you trying to impress? After ignoring me all day—'

'Olivia,' said Luke reasonably, 'we talked about this. Remember? We agreed that in the office, it's business as usual—'

'And then you come prancing into the Maze—'

'Hey!' interjected Luke hotly. 'I don't prance!'

'Luke.' I seemed unable to stem the vocal onslaught. 'I thought we had something. I mean, obviously I was misinformed. I really don't know why you bothered in the first place. So screw that. And while I'm at it, screw you.'

Luke put his hand on my arm. 'Olivia, I'm sorry—'

'Oh, sure! You obviously don't give a shit—'

'Olivia, I do! I'm really sorry – honestly I am. I really do care for you. Very much. *Very* much.'

Just to fully demonstrate how much, he kissed me. Something told me . . . he wanted me. The throbbing great stiffy jabbing me in the thigh, to be precise.

In fact, I think Luke's erection was cutting off my blood supply, because I couldn't feel my legs.

Assailed by an amorous swell, an involuntary squeak emerged from somewhere deep inside me. Before I knew what was happening, Luke picked me up and threw me across his desk. It was pretty impressive, while also being really quite painful. My shirt detached itself from my skirt band and Luke placed his splayed hands on my – in this position – relatively concave flesh. (In this context I mean relative to convex.)

Then he, er . . . ahem. Right. He, er . . . Okay, there's no other way of putting this.

He ripped off my knickers.

Unfortunately, he first attempted the manoeuvre with his teeth. A bold move – but if there are any men out there, do not try this at home and you might want to think about easing up on the porn. For successful execution a bloke would need choppers like a piranha; and even if the knicker elastic were on its last legs he'd still have to spend a not insignificant amount of time gnawing away, which rather kills spontaneity.

As it was, Luke's rugged method of divesting me of my underwear gave me a ferocious wedgie. I was picking cotton fibres out of my crack for weeks afterwards.

All of a sudden, I realised I had no recollection of the sign that read: *Welcome to Point of No Return*. Luke undid his flies with the hand that wasn't, er, otherwise engaged and, flashing by far too fast for comfort, I belatedly spotted the sign saying *You are now leaving Point Of No Return. We hope you have enjoyed your trip.*

I had the presence of mind to squeak, 'Condom!'

Being mildly to severely prudish, I was getting increasingly anxious about the merits of getting down to it on Luke's desk. What if someone saw us, or walked in on top of us, or made a secret videotape of us? But at the same time, Luke's extensive throes of passion were immensely reassuring.

Now, up to this point, things had followed a fairly standard seduction routine, albeit atop an office desk. But events were about to take a turn for the bizarre. Because next thing, Luke started passionately licking my face.

This was a new one for me. For a while I was prepared to go with the flow, as it were, but it didn't take long to realise I did not appreciate Luke's slobbery ministrations *at all*. I kept hoping he might stop, but he didn't, and after a while it became impossible to say, 'Excuse me, would you mind taking a rain check on the sputum shower?' (You might be interested to learn that the aforementioned sputum shower was having a largely similar effect to the proverbial cold shower.)

With the gradual departure of lust came the abrupt arrival of sanity – assisted by the fact that I was lying on a hole-punch which, despite being cushioned by my coat and several supplementary layers of cotton and wool, was digging painfully into the small of my back.

I looked at the gaping black windows surrounding Luke's office and suddenly realised how exposed I was with my skirt crumpled about my waist, bra wrapped around my ears and shredded knickers AWOL.

What was I *doing*? Was I *mad*?

As you can probably tell, I had just screeched to a violent halt outside the Point of No Return Saloon. However, one look at Luke thrashing around between my legs with gnashing teeth and throbbing veins and slavering tongue told me that he was far, far beyond me. Galloping across the prairie with the wind in his face and the sun at his back – although getting nowhere fast, if you know what I mean.

There was no happy alternative. I was going to have to fake it.

Generally speaking, I prefer not to broadcast that I'm enjoying nookie, so genuine fake orgasms do not come naturally to me. But I'd give it my best shot.

So I wiggled around the desk, and threw in some pretty dynamic bucking and heaving, allied with an 'oh, oh, oh, oh, oh' effect gradually increasing in tempo, although not too loud because who knew what sort of unwelcome attention that might attract? At one point, I even moaned: 'Sauce me with your sticky love juice, big boy,' although talking dirty always makes me feel like a bit of an arse and to be quite honest I felt there was quite enough of Luke's sticky juices all over my face. I'm sorry to report that he was still slurping away in the general vicinity of my jawbone.

'You're so *nasty!*' groaned Luke, and I wondered whom he was referring to. I am many things; but by no hyper-extended stretch of imagination could I be described as 'nasty' (although I sometimes picked my nose in the privacy of my flat).

I was starting to despair that Luke might chug away all night when there was a loud THUMP! at the window and I let out an almighty screech and tried to kick Luke off me. Fortunately, Luke misinterpreted this as the height of passion and finally brought things to a conclusion, happy in the belief that we had attained that mythical moment: the Simultaneous Orgasm.

Thank goodness that's over, I thought, sitting up slowly and adjusting my skirt.

On the windowsill was a ruffled-looking pigeon, shaking its head in a rather dazed fashion.

A bit like me, really.

T he incident shook me. I realised I didn't know Luke as well as I thought.

Chanelle was generally an outspoken advocate of sexual adventure, so I checked it out with her.

'He licked your . . .'

'Yeah.'

'Not . . .' She flicked her little finger delicately.

'No.'

'Weird,' she confirmed. At least she didn't say it was perverted, although I think she was considering it.

Thankfully, during the weeks that followed, Luke reverted to more traditional romping with less drool and more bed-based missionary position. He also spent more time doing so, which made me happier.

It was mid-March, and Jed, Chanelle, Nigel and I were in the PL canteen trying to digest some of the matter optimistically described as 'food'. For Jed Marshall, lustful thoughts were a perennial affair; and why stop at thinking about it? After the requisite social pleasantries and a heated discussion as to why Donald Duck never saw fit to wear a pair of underpants, he segued smoothly into his latest bonkbuster.

'It must've been about one in the morning, pretty slow for a Saturday. So I'm in the Underworld when, across a crowded dance floor, our eyes meet. Pretty girl. Terrific forehead. Anyway, one thing leads to another and we end up in a taxi outside her place. And she says, "Would you like to come in for a cup of tea?" And I think, Oho, I know what that means, and I'd *love* a cup of tea.'

'I didn't know you liked tea,' said Nigel.

'Bear with me, Knob. We're barely in the door when she pushes me on to a beanbag in the living room and starts shredding the clothes off me. Next thing, this bloke walks in. And she says, "Oh right, this is my husband. Charles, this is . . . what was your name again?" '

'No way!' I breathed.

'Oh yes. And I'm standing there with my trousers down around my ankles . . .'

'Superb!' said Nigel.

'Well, not really,' said Jed. 'Obviously an awkward situation. But I remembered my manners. So I pulled my hand out of her knickers and shook his hand—'

'Aw, man!' I grimaced.

'Hey – I wiped it on my backside first! Then she says, "Charles likes to watch. Is that okay?" That's a first for me, and I've seen a few things.'

'Peanuts in unexpected places,' giggled Chanelle.

'That's only the tip of the iceberg, angel face,' said Jed. 'Now, you guys know I'm up for most things' – I wondered what Jed would make of face-licking – 'but I wasn't at all sure about this. But I think, what the hell? Let's give it a twirl. So this guy, Charles, settles himself on the sofa with a can of Amstel Light and a packet of crisps. I was a bit worried he might take his old fella out – I'm not sure I could've coped with that. But then I figured, well, I can always ask him to put it away; and anyway, eating crisps is a full-hand job.'

'Hand-job,' sniggered Nigel.

'And sure enough, he's sitting next to us on the sofa . . . just . . . watching. So I'm getting into it, and this girl is lying in the beanbag giving it loads, growling and squealing, but I can still hear the husband in the background going scrunch, scrunch, scrunch . . .'

We all howled.

'It was putting me right off my stroke and *Retreat of the Trouser Snake* was the late-night feature. Next thing, she rakes her nails across my back, and I give a roar and leap off her, and she's going, "What's wrong?" And I'm going, "That fucking hurt!" and she's going, "Come back here!" and I'm going, "Where're my God-blasted jeans?" And then this guy, her husband, Charles . . . he says . . . "Would you like a jam sandwich?"'

'A what?'

'Oh yes. I have no idea what sort of dodginess was on offer there, but I'm a traditional type of guy and I wasn't sticking around to find out. I'm backing out the door with two feet down one leg of my jeans and my shoe in my mouth, and I say, "Mate, I think you need to give your wife a good seeing to," and he's going, "Do you want to watch a bit of telly? I think there might be cricket on."'

'Now there's a dysfunctional relationship,' I said.

25

Luke and I had been seeing each other for three months, two weeks, six days and nine hours.

Roughly.

Things were going swimmingly. We had settled into what could safely be called a Relationship. We had passed all the important milestones: the weekend in Stratford-upon-Avon, the takeaway in front of the rented DVD, Luke's toothbrush swapping saliva with mine in the bathroom.

We were getting on so well that our first argument came as a shock.

It was Friday evening and I was cooking Luke dinner.

It was rare that I forayed into the kitchen for anything other than pressing the kettle into service. I didn't often have time to do much other than boil the occasional egg and lob it on to some toast. Anyway, cooking for one always seemed a bit sad. I was hardly going to be whipping myself up five-course meals with homemade blueberry sorbet every night.

However, when I got the chance, I loved cooking. It was the order of it. I often thought there should be a recipe book for life: a precise ingredient list with specific instructions for every occasion.

Earlier in the week, I had fired up the oven for a

quick trial run. The only action it had seen in a year was drying a pair of knickers when I was stuck (not a resounding success; eventually I ironed them dry and wore them with strips of shiny chicken grease streaking up the gusset).

This evening, I wondered whether I had been overambitious. The herb-crusted beef tenderloin had been finger-twistingly fiddly, and I bitterly regretted the decision to show off with soufflé for dessert. I was already seven minutes behind the schedule outlined on my spreadsheet. You could say it was not going according to plan, unless the plan involved lots of char and gristle.

Yet by the time the door buzzer sounded, the herb-crusted tenderloin was spitting away in the oven and the roast potatoes were well on their way to a golden brown. The wine was chilling. Elsewhere, all was under control including the seduction inventory:

Sexy underwear ✓
That matches ✓
Kenzo Flower, liberal application thereof ✓
Fresh bedlinen ✓
Candles, twelve of ✓
James Taylor Greatest Hits CD ✓

That just left me. I checked my appearance in the mirror en route to the intercom. Hmm, flushed and a bit shinier than desirable. Yet what else could one expect of a domestic goddess?

'Come on up!' I pressed the release button. Luke was bang on time.

Oh! The soufflé!

'Door's open!' I roared at Luke's knock.

As I opened the cooker, a solid wall of heat roiled out. My hair prickled at the roots.

'In the kitchen!' I bellowed, picking up the soufflé and sliding it into the bottom of the stove. I closed the door with relief.

'I'd have found you eventually.' Luke grinned, appearing at the kitchen entrance. 'It's only a studio flat.'

He brandished two bottles of wine. Now I don't know much about wine – I'll approve any alcohol that doesn't result in excessive choking – but there was no doubt that Luke's was a superior vintage.

'Great! D'you want to put them in the fridge?'

'Smells good.' Luke sniffed appreciatively. 'What are we having?'

'Roast tenderloin with herbed crust and honey-roast vegetables. And port jus for the beef – I'm just getting started on that, but it should only take a few minutes.'

'Sounds great.' Luke disengaged me from the saucepan and port, and kissed me lingeringly.

As you can see, everything was on track for a resoundingly successful evening. The scent of tenderloin and roast potatoes infusing the air and the weekend stretching ahead of us. What could possibly go wrong? I wasn't about to undercook the tenderloin and give Luke food poisoning, or accuse him of seeing another woman, or another man (in the City, those last two are not necessarily mutually exclusive).

Nor, I would like to hastily point out, had I any plans to do so.

Luke poured two glasses of wine and repaired to the living room so that I could concentrate on the port jus. The recipe hinted darkly at lumpiness, without detailing how to avoid this terrible fate. I was entering the realms of Extreme Cookery, and was apprehensive.

'Hey, is this your laptop?' came Luke's voice from the sitting room.

'As opposed to some computer I boosted from an electronics store?'

'Wiseass.'

'Yes, it's mine.' I added flour to the pan juices and stirred savagely. 'Meet Drusilla. I sometimes bring her home at weekends if a project is at a critical point. Then I can log on remotely if there are any problems on site.'

God, the kitchen was sweltering. I threw open the window and took a welcome draught of air.

'Do you mind if I check my e-mail?' called Luke.

'Knock yourself out.'

'The computer's locked.'

'Oh yes, sorry. It locks automatically after five minutes' inactivity. Mind you, if Jed had his way, work-tops would automatically lock after five seconds of disuse, and the minimum password length would be three hundred characters.'

I enjoyed teasing Jed a.k.a. CyberCop about his security neuroses. However, I took it seriously since I had access to many of my clients' information databases and system directories.

'Give me a sec and I'll come and unlock it,' I shouted. The port jus was at a critical juncture; it could go either way. One being lumpy and inedible and suit-able only for filling cracks in the wall, or straight to ambrosially rapturous and earning me a bloody good seeing to.

'Why don't you give me your password,' suggested Luke.

'Just a moment and I'll be with you.' I whisked the jus briskly.

There was a moment of silence before Luke appeared in the kitchen entrance. 'Don't you trust me?' he said, hyper-casual.

I pushed a hank of damp hair out of my eyes and smiled at him. 'Of course.'

'Then why won't you tell me your password?' asked Luke, an edge to his voice. 'It's not as if I don't have the same access levels as you do.'

'Well yes, I know, but that's not the point.'

'What *is* the point?' said Luke icily.

'Well, you'd be logging on as me—'

'I only want to check my e-mail!' barked Luke.

'I know! That's no problem—'

'Obviously you have a problem!'

'Oh, come on, Luke, this is ridiculous—'

'So now I'm ridiculous?'

The situation was deteriorating rapidly. Could it have been only five minutes ago that Luke had been nuzzling me in the kitchen?

'I didn't *say* that!' I said desperately. 'Look, I'll come and key in my password and you can check your e-mail—'

'Don't bother,' snapped Luke. 'I'll go home and use my own computer. Enjoy your dinner.'

I followed him as he swept out to the living room. 'Luke, you're more than welcome to use my laptop! Please don't – come on, Luke!'

It was a hissy fit any A-list diva could be proud of. Luke shrugged on his coat. Then he turned and stamped past me into the kitchen.

He was going to stay!

No, he was retrieving his wine from the fridge.

'By the way,' he said, hand on the door.

'Yes?' I felt a spark of hope.

'Your oven's on fire.'

And with a flap of his coat tail, he was gone.

26

It was then I noticed smoke billowing gently into the living room. Just to underline the point, the fire alarm went off with an ear-piercing shriek. Too late, I realised that the delectable whiff of roasting cow had been supplanted by a scorched stench.

Galloping to the kitchen entrance, I waved my hand in front of my face. Through the smoky haze I saw bright orange flames licking out of the oven door.

Fuck! Fuck! I clutched at my head. Fuck! Fuh-fire extinguisher!

Where the hell was it? Yes! Living room, far cupboard. I dashed over and tugged it out from under a wheelie bag, two battered tennis rackets and the Hoover. There was smoke everywhere now. I was trying to navigate my way back to the kitchen by smell when all of a sudden a shadowy figure loomed in front of me.

Not only was my flat on fire, I was being burgled as well?

This evening was really starting to *suck*.

Looking on the bright side, at least I had a weapon. Channelling Bruce Lee for inspiration, I gave a ferocious howl and fecked the extinguisher at the intruder.

'Jesus Christ!' screamed Luke.

'Luke!' I gasped. 'I thought you were a robber!'

'No I'm not a damn robber!' snapped Luke. '*Give* me that! Come on, let's put this out.'

Dashing into the kitchen, we tried to decipher the instructions on the extinguisher.

'Remove safety pin,' coughed Luke.

Safety pin? What fucking safety pin? Jesus, you'd think they'd make these things fairly foolproof; there was no time to – oh, this must be it. I pulled the silver pin.

'Direct horn at base of fire,' read Luke.

I went to pull open the door of the stove.

'Aargh!'

There went my finger pads.

Luke threw the extinguisher at me, grabbed a towel and wrestled the door open. Smoke billowed out.

'Squeeze handle to discharge,' I read.

Handle. Locating the only squeezy-looking thing on the extinguisher, I duly squeezed it. Unfortunately, I had forgotten step two – the one regarding the horn and the directing thereof. The horn writhed around like a black mamba, giving me a mouthful of chemical. Better enjoy it – looked as if that and port jus was all we'd be having for dinner.

Ten minutes later, flames duly extinguished, windows open and fire alarm smashed to a pile of plastic shards, I felt it safe to burst into tears.

'Are you all right?' Luke put his arms round me.

'I'm sorry!' I blubbered. 'Thank you for coming back!'

'Of course I came back,' said Luke, stroking my hair. 'I wouldn't leave you with your kitchen on fire.'

I didn't point out that he *had*, if temporarily.

'My fuh-fuh-flat! It's ruined!'

'Wait until the smoke clears. It's not as bad as you think. The damage was contained. You might wanna get your cooker serviced.'

'And earlier,' I wept. 'I duh-duh-do trust you! Of course I'll tell you my password. I'm sorry!' At this point, I was crying so hard I was jerking around the place like a faulty android.

'It's okay,' Luke soothed. 'I overreacted. Tell you what, why don't we blow this joint? Let's go out for dinner.'

The following Tuesday, there was a problem with the Gragnoc software integration at Gragnoc. The resolution and post-mortem with Luke lasted until late in the evening.

'You wanna get a drink?' he asked. Things had reverted to normal, although every time I looked at my scorched kitchen ceiling I thought about Luke and not necessarily in a good way.

'I'd love to,' I said, largely truthfully, 'but I should really write up this delay report.' I pulled a face.

'I could wait.'

'Oh, no, that's okay. Really. It could take a while.'

'Okay,' said Luke, shuffling papers into his briefcase. 'Guess I'll see you tomorrow.'

He held the door for me as I left his office.

It took me another couple of hours to finish my report. Jed and I were the only ones left in the Maze.

'Aren't we a right pair of feckin' eejits?' I said to Jed, then sighed and stretched my arms over my head. I groaned as my shoulders flexed.

'Speak for yourself. But I think it's time to call it a day. How about you?'

'Well, if you insist, I will call it a day. Although technically speaking you could call it an hour . . . or a minute.'

'Theoretically you could argue that these are one and the same thing, or at the very least related. Any which way you look at it, we are talking about a linear measurement of time.'

'You're talking shite,' I corrected.

Jed powered down his monitor and yawned. 'What are you up to this evening?'

'No plans.'

'How about a bite to eat?'

'What a novel plan, Mr Marshall,' I cried. 'I like the way you're thinking; it's truly innovative. Oh, Chanelle's latest applicant tried to go Dutch on the first date so she gave him his P45. She might be around.'

I started to dial her mobile and was surprised when Jed gripped my wrist. 'How about just you and me?' he said casually, although the tension in his fingers belied the tone.

'Sure,' I said, retrieving my arm.

We pulled on our coats and hit the door.

'Spinker's?' suggested Jed as we followed the scent of alcohol wafting on a ripping headwind. Although Jed still frequented the place, I hadn't returned since I had flambéed my face medium-rare with Flaming Lamborghini.

'Er . . .' I was rattling my brain for an excuse when I saw Jed grin. 'Git.' I punched him in the arm.

'How about the Wine Cellar?' he amended.

'New place? Sure, let's check it out.'

The pavement was slick with rain. The iron steps descending to the Wine Cellar were slippery and if it hadn't been for Jed hanging on to the scruff of my neck I would probably have navigated them on my bottom. Five minutes later, we were ensconced in a promising-looking cranny. It was gorgeous – cosy and intimate with lashings of wood and leather and candles flickering in wax-encrusted bottles.

'This place would be great for a first date,' I said, looking around. 'Guaranteed shag venue.'

'You think?' said Jed, raising his eyebrows.

'Absolutely. I actually felt my knickers loosen as I walked in the door.'

'Really? What's their status now, as a matter of interest?'

'Hanging on by the finest of threads, my friend.' I batted my eyelashes at him campily and picked up one of the menus.

'Leather,' I said, waving it at Jed. 'So how come you didn't want Chanelle coming along? You two fallen out?'

'Not at all. I just thought it's been a while since we went out together. We used to do it all the time, remember? Where's Luke this evening?'

'No idea,' I muttered.

'Okay, then. Actually,' he said after a beat, 'I wanted to talk to you.'

'Really? What about? Oh look, nibbles. Let's get the . . . steam-fried lemon-scented tiger prawns in a crispy coconut coriander crust,' I read, drooling a bit. 'Yum!'

'Whatever,' said Jed. 'Listen, this is important—'

'And what about mushrooms stuffed with herbs served with a spicy garlic sauce?'

'Olivia!' snapped Jed. 'Can you stop thinking about your stomach for one second? I've something to tell you.'

'Oooooooh shiiiiiiiite!' I breathed in horror.

'It's not that bad,' said Jed, surprised. 'In fact . . .' he faltered, and this would have astounded me had my attention not been firmly directed elsewhere, 'I hope you'll think it's *good*.'

'Oh, holy Mary mother of Joseph blessed virgin of the sweet baby Jesus!' I whispered.

Unlike men who tend to rediscover religion during sex, I always found it in moments of extreme terror.

'What are you on about?' said Jed. Then, following my rabbit-in-car-headlights-style gawp: 'Oh, I see.'

Because there, bearing down on us as inexorably as a charging rhino, was My Destiny. Or My Ex-Destiny, if you prefer; or even the Man Who Set My Face on Fire.

'What the fuck is *he* doing here?' I hissed at Jed, hiding behind the menu. 'Were there not enough people to inflame back in Spinker's? Make him go away!'

My Ex-Destiny pulled up beside us and expertly flipped two glasses on to the table.

'Greetings,' he said importantly, rather in the manner of a Chief Alien considering the annihilation of a tribe of Earthlings. 'My name is Brian and I will be your wine waiter this evening. I can recommend the Australian Chardonnay, or the Chilean Cabernet Sauvignon. Would you like to place your order?'

'Absolutely,' said Jed. 'I'll have a pint of Murphy's, and my companion here . . .' He whipped away the menu to reveal me in all my cowering glory. 'Olivia?' he said solicitously. 'What'll you have?'

There was a fair chance Brian would not recall my impromptu variety show at Spinker's. In my professional guise, I bore little resemblance to the smouldering mess I'd been when he last clapped eyes on me. I was concentrating hard on projecting an image of incombustible bushy-browedness (although regrettably my eyebrows had never fully regained their former lustrous appeal). Also, Brian had not struck me as that bright at any point in our traumatic short-lived acquaintance. Yet as I whispered: 'I'll have the Sauvignon, thanks,' Brian frowned and I almost heard the *crunch!* as the mental gears ground into motion.

'Would you like a bottle, or a glass?' he asked, staring at me intently.

'What do you think, my *fiery* little friend?' said Jed. 'She's more a *cocktail* girl, really,' he confided to Brian.

Recognition spread across Brian's face from the forehead down. 'You're the—' he cried, and stopped himself with a chortle.

'Bottle, please. If you don't mind, we'll also have some prawns and stuffed mushrooms,' I said with dignity and jabbed the menu into his ribs. 'That will be all, *Brian.*'

'Thanks a million, Marshall,' I growled after Brian had gone to point me out to the other waiters. He said something that involved lots of hand gestures and guffawing. 'How did I ever think he was good-looking? *How?* Why didn't you *stop* me?'

'I tried, but at the time you had other things on your mind. Like defogging your beer-goggles.'

We lapsed into silence as Brian returned with the wine, which he presented with an unnecessary flourish, holding the bottle as if it were made of glass (I mean it is and all, but come on! It's not like he was juggling a baby).

'What did you want to talk about?' I said irritably when Brian receded once more.

'Forget it. We can do it some other time.'

'*Tell* me,' I pressed. I'm really bad at intrigue. When it comes to gossip I have to know every last gasping detail, and right now.

Jed regarded me with a curious, coiled stillness. 'All right,' he said slowly, rubbing his forehead. 'Thing is, Livvie, I like you.'

'Well, of course you do,' I said in some surprise. 'Except when you alerted Brian there as to my true identity. That was seriously unfriendly.' I wiggled my formerly lush eyebrows at him.

'No, that's not what I mean,' said Jed, and he did the most unexpected thing. He reached across the table and took my hand in his and caressed the back of it with his thumb. Very lightly. My whole stomach yawed in – what? Excitement? Trepidation?

Hunger?

'I *really* like you,' said Jed so quietly I barely heard him.

'What – what does that mean, exactly?' I said. I couldn't move. In fact, I was finding it difficult to breathe. 'You like me as a friend? You fancy a ride? Or' – and I choked on my wine – 'you *love* me? What?'

'Well, I . . . I don't know, exactly,' said Jed hesitantly.

He turned my hand over and pressed his thumb into my palm. Although on the surface a pedestrian action, if a more erotic activity had ever been perpetrated on my person I couldn't for the life of me remember it. *This* was electricity. $E = mc^2/0$.

'Okay, well let's run with "like", then. Big deal. Lots of guys *like* me . . .' the only one springing to mind being the bald tax specialist with a rather striking olfactory presence who habitually leered at me across the shredder – and somehow, I didn't think he strengthened my argument.

'It's more than that,' said Jed.

'Then what?'

'I don't know. I mean, what is love anyway?'

'You're not making a great case for yourself here.'

'Look. I'm not sure what love is or whether it exists. Personally, I think it's just a romantic notion, a myth perpetrated by the movies to make people feel better about themselves. Like . . . like religion.'

'And this is you trying to talk me into it? Truly, Jed, you are emotionally stunted,' I said. Good gracious, was that disappointment kicking me in the crotch? I snatched my hand back.

'Perhaps,' said Jed slowly. 'But what I'm trying to say – obviously not very well – is that I really care for you.'

'That's it? You really care for me?' A complex mix of emotions vied for attention, but all of a sudden I felt a surge of what I could finally identify as anger. Placing the source of it was a different matter – but I'd consult Sigmund later. 'That's nice.'

'You can't deny there's something between us—'

'Apart from friendly revulsion and a mutual appreciation of alcohol?'

'I'm saying I want to be with you,' said Jed simply.

'Right. So you're offering me the opportunity to become one of the husband–hampered, peanut-infested swarms who star oh-so-briefly in the famous sex annals of Jed Marshall? I'm flattered – I hear the competition is fierce at the auditions. But I'm going to have to pass.'

'Is that really what you think of me?' said Jed, looking appalled.

'Well, what do you reckon, Jed?'

'Livvie, I'm not like that, not really. It would be different with us. You're special—'

'I'm pretty sure that's a copyrighted Jed Marshall line, isn't it?'

Jed stared at me mutely.

'And had you forgotten the fact that I'm going out with Luke?' I snarled, actually quite horrified that I had only remembered that minor detail at this belated stage in the proceedings.

'Oh yes, the Great White Hope,' snapped Jed. 'He's not right for you, Livvie. He won't make you happy—'

'And you will? The man who defines a long-term relationship as anything up to twenty-four hours?'

'It wouldn't *be* like that.'

'So you keep saying.'

My stomach, unaware of the high drama of the moment, gave a ferocious growl as the food was delivered to our table.

As Jed and I ate our prawns and stuffed mushrooms in silence, my anger abated and was replaced by something more tangible.

Fear.

Somewhere deep down in a place without words, I knew this conversation had changed things between us for ever. In the space of just twenty short minutes, I had lost my best friend. For the first time in living memory, Jed and I had run out of things to say.

For the next couple of weeks, Jed and I prowled cautiously around each other like a pair of hormonal teens.

Where once Jed would have wheeled me away from the desk to pinch my stapler, now – from a safe distance – he said: 'Olivia, would you mind if I borrowed your stapler, please?'

Then, when I gave it to him, he said things like: 'Thanks', or 'I'll give it back in a minute'. And when he took it, he was careful not to let so much as half a skin cell brush against mine.

In fact, where once Jed had been a frequent guest in my personal space, now he never visited. It was quite a feat in two square metres of cubicle.

He didn't call me 'Livvie' or 'babycakes' any more.

I ached for the easy familiarity we once shared.

Deteriorating relations with Jed were not all that was cause for concern. Early one morning – I mean technically morning but really deadest, blackest night – I'd jolted suddenly awake. For a while I squeezed my eyes shut and tried to persuade myself that I was still half to three-quarters asleep. There was no fooling my brain, though, which was on full, sniffer-dog alert. Something had woken me. What?

I rolled over to prod Luke, but my subconscious had already inferred he wasn't there from the surrounding silence. Swivelling my head to the right, I noticed a dull luminescent glow issuing from a chink in the bathroom door.

I blinked stupidly. Had aliens landed in my bathroom and abducted Luke? For a moment I wondered whether I was dreaming and, if so, why it didn't involve bitter men and hot chocolate. Oops, sorry: I meant hot men and bitter chocolate (I wasn't fully with it yet).

Or even better: hot men *in* bitter chocolate.

Mmm . . .

A faint clicking noise emanated from the bathroom.

When I pushed myself out of bed, a party of disorderly goosebumps stood out on my skin so I shrugged on my dressing gown. I padded to the bathroom and pushed the door.

Luke was sitting on the lavatory with my computer on his knees, face gleaming ghostly grey in the reflection from the screen.

'Hey, baby,' I said softly.

Luke looked up with a start. 'Olivia!'

'Who did you think it was?' Going to him, I wound my arms round his neck. My bathroom was so small I had to drape myself over the sink to do so, nudging the cold tap with my ribs. 'What are you doing?' On the screen, I saw him deftly closing windows.

'Couldn't sleep. Thought I'd check my mail.'

He clicked an ⊠.

'In the bathroom?' I giggled indulgently.

Another ⊠.

'I didn't want to wake you.'

'Will you don't be mad. Are you coming back to bed?'

'Soon.'

But afterwards, long after Luke had started snoring lustily, sleep evaded my grasp. I kept recalling Luke's face as the bathroom door swung open, cast in an expression of shock.

Something told me he wasn't checking his e-mail, and there was only one other explanation.

Online porn.

He had closed the windows too fast for me to get a good look at the teenage nuns in thongs, but that was the only thing that could justify his frantic scramble for all those ⊠s.

Now, if Luke wanted to get grunty with extra-curricular stimulation, then all power to him, but I wasn't overly keen on his using Drusilla to do so. Quite apart from the fact that I didn't fancy rancid sperm on my keyboard (I suspected it would make the keys quite sticky) PL had a strict policy concerning the viewing or downloading of porn and equally strict repercussions should you do so – i.e. instant dismissal.

Should I talk to him? I fretted. Maybe I'd check Drusilla first to see whether there was incriminating evidence. It was unlikely to happen again, since I usually left Drusilla at work when I was seeing Luke.

I turned it over for the rest of the night, and what little sleep came my way was fitful and accompanied by disturbing dreams – none of which involved hot men and bitter chocolate.

The following day, I spent three hours fruitlessly auditing my computer. I was baffled and frustrated, because my browser history listed no teenage nuns in thongs websites. The cache from 03:40 that morning was clear. There was nothing in the cookies. In other words, if Luke had been cruising, he had covered his tracks well.

Normally, I would have asked Jed to scan my computer, but at the moment that was more communication than either of us could handle.

Since Jed's subversive activity on his behalf, Max's mailbox had been swamped with spam. According to Jed, Max was receiving up to 150 messages per day, of the 'Naked girls!!!!! With hairy nipples!!!!!' variety. I had also added Max's details to the alt.sex.org discussion group in an act of solidarity.

As the Support Manager/general IT lackey, Jed was subjected to regular diatribes condemning the state of Max's flesh-toned Inbox, and demanding to know what measures was he taking to address the situation.

Never renowned for his patience, Max was even more tetchy than usual. Jed and I liked to take credit for snipping at least an inch off the end of his fuse.

Speaking of short fuses, Gragnoc's CEO, Graeme – normally my favourite client – was snapping at my heels. The hardware installation had deflected him for a while, but now I was receiving a number of increasingly irate phone calls enquiring about the state of the EnTire system, which Nigel had sworn on his commission plan would be delivered to Gragnoc by the end of February. Just this morning, Graeme had sent an e-mail threatening legal action for the delay.

I felt really bad about the situation because I knew Gragnoc needed the system update. Also, I liked

Graeme. He was a big, blustery Glaswegian who said exactly what was on his mind without pausing to apply censorship. I liked knowing precisely where I stood – even when where I stood was up to the nostril-line in sewage.

Which was roughly my position at that moment.

'This is unaicceptaible!' Graeme's voice exploded out of the phone. 'Cain ye even teill me when the system will be reidy?'

'Officially—'

'No. Noat officeilly.'

'Off the record—'

'Cut oot the twinkle talk, lass.'

I gripped my pen a little tighter. 'Realistically, it is unlikely that the new release will be ready until early May.'

Graeme let out a deep breath. 'Waill, that's no' guid enough.'

'I'm so sorry—'

'Och, Ah knaw it's not yehr fault, lassie. It's tha' rubbery-gub schemey – wha's his name again?'

'Er, are you thinking of Nigel?'

'Tha's him. Ah'll crack open his heid next time Ah see him. Ah'm beelin' scunnered, Olivia. Ah need that system upgrade. The current system cannae handle the traffic.'

'I know.' I winced. 'Thing is, Graeme, the development team is already flat out. I don't think we can deliver the system any sooner. But I tell you what.' I'd just had an idea. 'Leave this with me a while. I've just thought of something.'

Luke was away on unspecified business for the next couple of days, so I went to consult Max. On my way to his office I noticed his daily PornFax sitting in the machine, and couldn't resist collecting it.

'Max.' I poked my head round the door after knocking. 'Er . . .'

'Down here!'

A movement to the side of his desk caught my eye.

'Ah, I was hoping to have a word . . .'

'Cam in, cam in.'

Max was face down on the floor.

'What are you doing?' I said, perplexed.

'Push-ups!' puffed Max. 'Seventeen . . . eighteen . . .'

I took a seat. Max's head bobbed in and out of view behind his desk.

'Huff! Huff! Huff!' went Max.

I knew what would get his attention.

'You've got a fax,' I said. 'Looks like . . . is that a—'

'Give it here!' barked Max, leaping off the floor. Adding a bonus lunge to his exercise regime, he snatched it out of my hands.

'What do ya want?' he said, collapsing into his chair and stuffing the sheet in a drawer.

'Well, we've got a bit of a problem—'

'I don't want to hear about problems – give me solutions!'

'Electric cars.'

'What?'

'Also, a better education system, identifying a viable alternative to gas, and I suppose we could all embrace vegetarianism.'

I think Max's eyes narrowed; at least, there was some movement under the explosive fuzz of eyebrow.

'No need to get lippy, yang lidy,' he said. 'What do you want?'

I carefully crossed my legs. 'All right. We've just got an e-mail from Graeme. He's threatening legal action because the EnTire system upgrade has been delayed.'

'Isn't it your bladdy job to make sure the system is delivered on time?' thundered Max.

'Well, with all due respect, it would help if the bladdy – er, bloody system was developed. Release 2.3 was only scheduled for completion by the first week in May. Unfortunately, Graeme is under the impression that it should have been ready for installation by the end of February. I never agreed to that timeframe,' I added defensively.

Max glared at me, his moustache performing an impromptu Mexican wave. 'Then who did?'

I stayed silent – Max could answer his own question.

'Bladdy Usher. Man's not the sharpest spoon in the frying pan, is he?' Max knew the answer to that one too. 'Ya think he's serious about legal action?'

'Graeme? He is pretty upset.'

Just then Max's phone rang and he raised a furry digit at me to indicate I should stay put.

'Yeah,' he barked. 'Why are ya asking me? That's what I pay ya for – to show some bladdy initiative!' I hoped he'd get the aggression out of his system with whoever was on the end of the line.

There was a pile of papers on the desk in front of me and I started to read upside-down. I was pretty good at it, although this one was in a tiny, cramped font. It looked like a letter. To . . . Max Feshwari . . . From . . . Mantis Corporation.

Mantis. Where had I heard that name before? Oh yes. Gragnoc and Mantis were the two giants of the concrete industry and by all accounts it was a cut-throat business. There were multimillion-dollar government contracts, patented cement mix solutions, and the CEOs had been known to trade subtle insults in *Concrete Weekly*.

The next word was trickier. C-O-N-F . . . ah, confirmation . . . of . . . S-H-A-R-E-H-O . . . Confirmation of shareholding.

'How should I know?' Max howled, then hung up the phone and glowered at me. 'Where were we?'

'Gragnoc. EnTire system,' I prompted. 'Now my thinking is, it wouldn't be in Graeme's interests to litigate if we helped him out a bit.'

'How are we supposed to do that? Flog the development team?'

Since he seemed to be seriously considering this, I hurried on.

'Well, what if we deliver the system in two phases? The hardware was delivered to Gragnoc last November, and Development has already completed and tested the core modules of the new release. It's the bells and whistles that are taking time. We could install the core apps now, so Graeme has an interim solution to handle the increased traffic.'

God, I was good.

'Ya think Dewar will go for this?'

'I think so. They're really struggling – the Gragnoc system had two outages last week.'

'Okay, let's do it!' shouted Max excitedly. 'Talk to Dewar. If it gets him off our tail, do it.'

In the midst of all the drama, I was actually looking forward to Gragnoc's Project Kick-off Meeting.

I hated corporate travel. Hauling myself out of bed at antisocial hours. Humping my standard-issue XL PL briefcase through acres of resounding airports. The only reason Gary Newbit featured in my life was to harass me about travel expenses, and I bitterly resented it.

Long ago, I entertained romantic notions of wiggling briskly through airports with natty slingbacks on foot, slimline briefcase in hand and *FT* under arm. I'd come a long way since then, both metaphorically and literally.

And another thing that made me froth up a spume: PL always acted as if business trips were a little jolly on company expense. As if I couldn't *wait* to visit tourist traps such as Liberia, Azerbaijan or Sweden. As if I were greasing myself up on a sunlounger and quaffing back Sex on the Beaches, instead of spending hours appeasing an irate client before retiring to an identikit hotel room to establish a dial-up modem connection at 2 a.m.

But this trip was shaping up to be different. For a start, I was looking forward to seeing Graeme again. The flight was at a sensible hour of the morning, affording me a rare opportunity to observe Heathrow in daylight. And I'd been upgraded to business class by my boyfriend-slash-manager, who was accompanying me to the kick-off meeting followed by a weekend of R&R.

(That's Raunch and Recreation, in case you were wondering.)

Glasgow may not be an obvious choice for a weekend love-fest. Personally, I thought there were better places for a holiday, for example . . . well, anywhere else except Liberia, Azerbaijan or Sweden. However, Luke had been encouragingly enthusiastic about the idea.

At least, he had said: 'I think we can claim Friday night on expenses.'

Luke and I, we . . . It's like this. Luke and I had not been getting on great. Little things about him had started to niggle. Nothing serious, just minor details. For example, the way he hogged the bathroom for hours on end and had six different types of moisturiser – which he actually *used*. And his unfortunate habit of randomly clearing his throat with a deep-gullet honk effect. And he seemed to *moult* pubic hair. The man left curly little calling cards all over the show – wiry filaments furring up the shower drain, strewn about the sheets, nestled in the butter.

Actually there were quite a lot of things, now that I thought about it. Sorry, I should probably have used bullet points.

Also, our sex life had been a bit spasmodic recently. I finally diagnosed Luke as suffering from Looker Syndrome, the major symptom of which is lying inert on the assumption that his partner will be so ecstatically gratified by his mere presence that any further effort on his part is superfluous.

Sometimes our lovemaking felt as if Luke was referring to a manual, or commanding a military operation:

TIME (minutes)	OPERATION
T–20:00	Deploy reconnaissance squadron Five Finger Foxtrot along western flanks
T–17:00	Engage rhythmic rotational manoeuvre moving northeast at rate of 0.07 knots
T–13:00	Rotate left nipple clockwise 42°39′55″
T–12:55	Rotate right nipple counter-clockwise 42°39′55″
T–12:00	Apply full oral artillery to both nippular extremities
T–09:32	Five Finger Foxtrot undercover operations in Erogenous Zone Mufti
T–08:50	Insert space probe in launch pad
T–00:10	Commence countdown
T–00:00	Blast off

When he got to T minus 09:32 and engaged in – let's call it foreplay – it was as if he was polishing a doorbell ever so precisely – whilst taking the greatest care not to ring the damn thing.

Sometimes I climaxed out of sheer boredom.

But the best self-help books will tell you that a relationship isn't all about sex; that you can't reasonably expect to click into the groove right away; that it takes time to learn about each other's bodies and what turns the other on. Shagging isn't the be-all and end-all, you know? Rather than focusing on the physical, it is more important that you are first and foremost friends, with a relationship built on the principles of trust and honesty and a firm foundation of communication and understanding in a mutually respectful environment.

God, I hoped our sex life would improve.

Other than that, things were fine, fabulous, ab-so-lute-ly cracking. This weekend would be an opportunity to escape from the daily pressures. A chance to reconnect, rediscover each other and reclaim the magic.

It didn't start off well when Luke rolled up to the airport, looking like he had all the time in the world, a scant *hour* before the flight. I'm the type of person who likes to arrive half a day before the flight in order to compulsively check and recheck the departures screen and contemplate the distance in milliseconds from Duty Free to the boarding gate.

But I was determinedly cheerful. Even if I had to kill him, this weekend would be a success.

'I was born to fly business class,' I said, wiggling further into the vast leather seat. 'I just missed my vocation somewhere along the way.'

The flight attendants, looking spectacularly bored, were miming the manual demo.

'You know,' I whispered to Luke, 'I feel very strongly that people needing instruction on how to fasten seat belts shouldn't really be out in public unsupervised.'

'Mm-hmm,' said Luke, picking up the in-flight entertainment guide.

'Flight to Glasgow's too short for a movie, so it's just TV. Did you know that if your plane's about to crash-land you should piss yourself? Otherwise the seat belt can make your bladder explode on impact. It's a horrible way to go, I hear. Death by widdle.' My kidney winced thinking about it.

The flight attendants passed the lifejackets over their heads and pulled sharply on the toggles.

'Apparently you're three times more likely to die in a plane crash than be crushed by a tractor.'

'Really?' said Luke distractedly, flicking through the magazine.

I thought he could have been more interested. Have you any idea how many farmers are crushed by tractors every day?

The crew was demonstrating the brace position for an emergency landing.

'Know why they tell you to take that position?' I continued. 'It's so that if the plane crashes, your neck will break instantly. Like a twig.' I snapped my fingers for emphasis. 'Because, since you're pretty unlikely to survive a plane crash, it's better to go fast and painless, instead of burning to death, or choking to death, or being trampled to death.'

I sighed, discouraged. Luke wasn't listening.

Now, let me be the first to step on to the podium and admit that I often talk a lot of shite, ladies and gentlemen. It's a combination of nerves and my Irish disposition to slather blather over every lull in conversation.

However, even on the random occasions I tried to initiate meaningful topics of conversation – like politics or religion or survival tips for horrific plane crashes – Luke rarely tuned in. Except . . .

The plane was nearing cruising altitude when he said: 'Tell me about this meeting.'

He never seemed to tire of discussing work.

'It's just a standard kick-off meeting,' I said. 'You want that packet of peanuts? Thanks. You know, project overview, timeframes, milestones, critical path, communication plan. The usual.' I shrugged.

'And Graeme Dewar, Gragnoc's CEO – what's he like?'

'Graeme? You'll like him. Tough but fair. His bark is worse than his bite.'

I didn't mention that Graeme's bark frequently necessitated twenty stitches and a tetanus shot.

'Tough?' said Luke.

'Well, he founded Gragnoc sixteen years ago. It was just Graeme, a secretary and a pot plant. And now it's a publicly listed company with six hundred employees and an annual turnover of five hundred and seventy million pounds. So Graeme's pretty gnarly. Tough as a boiled boot, I'd say. Still thinks of the company as his, although he only owns about twenty per cent of it now. But he's devoted to Gragnoc – works twenty-five hours a day.'

'Hmm,' said Luke distractedly.

I'd lost him again.

At that moment, with the sun bouncing off fluffed-up clouds and a flight attendant plying me with caviar, little did I suspect that I would be leaving Glasgow alone and in rather different style.

Things accelerated swiftly downhill shortly after the plane wheels screeched along the runway at Glasgow airport.

First, Luke insisted on stopping at the hotel to drop off our bags, even though my presentation was due to start in twenty minutes. Then, while I paced up and down the lobby checking my watch on a secondly basis, Luke disappeared up to his room to fix his hair and take an inventory of the mini-bar and check whether Discovery Channel was available on the TV. At about the time I should have been connecting my laptop to the projector and introducing Luke and myself to a less than enthusiastic audience, he rang my mobile.

'Go ahead without me,' he said. 'I'll be along later.'

'You're fucking joking me! I've been waiting seventeen minutes!'

'Well, I'm tied up in something here,' said Luke in his upper management voice.

'The hairdryer cord?' I snarled. I considered suggesting that he hang himself with it, but snapped the phone shut instead.

Then I rang Graeme. 'I'm so sorry,' I said miserably. 'I'm not sure how much longer. Twenty minutes, maybe? I'll be right with you.'

Graeme was not impressed. He was not the type of man you kept waiting.

Outside the hotel, I hailed a taxi that looked like it was stuck together with duct tape and a prayer.

The driver said something unintelligible.

'Sorry, I don't speak Glaswish.'

Even when repeated, it sounded like the Spanish dialect of Cantonese for all I could make out. Eventually, I took a chance that he might be asking where I wanted to go.

'Gordon Street?'

'Pah!' spat the driver – although I use the term generously. It soon became screechingly, honkingly, whiplashingly apparent that driving did not feature in his particular skill set.

However, his talents did include chain-smoking, and he puffed away with alacrity. Winding down the window I nearly gassed myself with exhaust fumes, so I glassed myself back in and choked on nicotine.

We were stuck in a traffic jam when I felt a rising damp around the area of my left buttock and realised to my horror that I was sitting on a wet patch.

I was thinking about screaming – or just shrieking vigorously to start with – when my chauffeur started ringing. In the palaver of extracting his mobile from somewhere under his seat and dropping it in the ashtray and pressing the answer button, he swerved violently and sent a cyclist into the kerb.

'Excuse me,' I quavered, 'sorry to disturb you and all, but would you mind not using the phone while you're driving?'

'Och effy geirn squicky the noo,' barked the driver (that was the phonetic version). He fixed me with a baleful glare in the rear-view mirror, reminding me uncomfortably of Begby in *Trainspotting* just before he uses some poor sap's face as a pool table.

'Stupid bitch,' he muttered into the phone.

I can recognise that phrase – or at least the sentiment – in many different languages. If I'd had the stomach for it, I would have happily chundered all over the back of his stupid taxi. But no, I was going to be the bigger person. I would retain the moral high ground.

Rummaging around in my handbag, I extracted a biro and wrote *Asshole* on the ID card hanging on the back of the headrest, with an arrow pointing to his head. When the taxi finally jerked to a halt in Gordon Street leaving four metres of rubber up the road, I sat there grimly while the 'driver' took his time counting out the change. I was determined to wrest every last sorry penny out of him.

'You still owe me fifteen pence,' I said, and sat with my hand cupped under his nose until he coughed it up.

As I walked into the Gragnoc head office, I was beyond cross. I was sweaty, hot, enraged, just a little bit panicky, and stinking with an overtone of reek to be exact. And sporting an unidentifiable damp patch on the seat of my pants.

Gragnoc's receptionists were deep in conversation. It was scintillating stuff. From what I could make out, the fat one – Eileen – had found her husband, Jambo, in bed with her mother, That Old Slapper.

In fairness, Eileen had been suspicious of Jambo ever since he started changing his scants every morning.

'Excuse me, sorry to interrupt,' I said. And really, if I hadn't been so late, I would have been delighted to hear all about That Old Slapper and Eileen's internecine showdown over Jambo the Studmuffin, who had taken to changing his underpants daily instead of – I dreaded to think about it – weekly? Monthly?

Annually?

'I'm here to see Graeme Dewar.'

'And?' yawned Eileen.

'And,' I said patiently, 'can you let him know I'm here?'

Eileen rolled heavily made-up eyes at her friend. The action dislodged one of her false eyelashes, which landed in her tea with a soft *plunk*. She picked up the phone and dialled the number with one hand, fishing the eyelash out of the cup with the other.

'Och aye,' she said, flicking cold tea at me. 'There's someone here tae see ye. Och aye, Ah'll ask.' She put her hand over the receiver. 'Who aire ye?'

'Olivia Anderson, from Puttock Leavitt,' I snapped.

The information was duly relayed and she hung up the phone.

'Whut?' said Eileen, surprised to find me still standing in front of her.

'I need to sign the visitor book,' I supplied.

If she rolled her eyes any more violently, she was in danger of dislodging an eyeball. She shoved the visitor book across the desk.

'Whut?' she said again, after I had signed in.

'Can I have a guest pass?'

Finally, standing outside Graeme's office, I knocked on the door.

'Coom in!' came Graeme's great roar. 'Well, it's aboot time,' he bawled. 'Ye're late!'

'I'm so sorry, Graeme. But in my defence, it took me a while to get past your receptionists.' I smiled at him. 'Good to see you.'

My hand was engulfed in his huge paw – Graeme's hands were like bunches of bananas. 'Guid tae see yeh too, lassie.'

'How are things?'

'Eh, ticking oaver, ye knaw. We brought oot a new admixture with an enhanced retarder last week, bu' Mantis beat us by a week. Cannae understand it. Ernest Thompson wouldnae knaw a ferrosilicon alloy if'n it jumped up an' bit 'im in th' napper.' He looked momentarily dejected.

'Who?'

'Ernest Thompson, CEO of Mantis. Buit enough aboot tha'. How aire you, girl? Ye haiven't visited us for a spell.'

'Well, you need to throw some more work my way, Graeme. Hasn't Nigel been up?'

'Tha' great fanny bawz!' shouted Graeme. I wasn't sure, but it didn't sound like a compliment. 'He's a nincompoop!' Graeme elaborated. 'Promised me the EnTire system months ago. Man couldnae find his erse in a bath wi' twa hands.'

'Mm-hmm,' I said noncommittally, although the assessment was fairly accurate.

Graeme flung open his door and pounded down the corridor. 'Lads are waiting in th' coanference ruim,' he shouted over his shoulder. 'Th' temporary soloution is handlin' traffic arigh', bu' we're all looking forward to gettin' th' full upgrade. By the way, lassie,' he said as he threw open the conference door. 'Ah've got a wee bone to pick wi' yeh.'

'Wh-what?' My heart sank. Graeme was not someone I fancied picking my bones.

'Later,' he said. 'We'll goa back the oaffice when yeh're done.' And he threw open a door and propelled me into the conference room, where thirty assorted Operations, Customer Care and Marketing staff waited less than enthusiastically for my presentation.

Even though I'd conducted hundreds – possibly thousands – of project kick-off meetings, they still break me out in a cold sweat. The introduction could have done with a bit more conviction, but I picked up speed in the project overview, ripped through the scope of work, and blistered past the division of responsibilities. Even though Drusilla froze twice and had to be restarted, by the time I got to the dramatic risk analysis denouement the only things missing were a trumpet fanfare and a Golden Globe nomination.

After thirty-seven emotionally draining minutes, I even got a standing ovation.

(Well, people had to get up to leave.)

'Tha' went arigh', ye think, lassie?' roared Graeme, stepping into his office.

'I thought so.'

'Have a seat.'

I sank into a chair. 'Graeme, before the meeting, you said there was something you wanted to discuss?'

I was referring to the bone. I really wanted it picked and buried before Luke showed up, but before Graeme could answer there was a knock on the door. It was Luke.

'Ah, yeh muist be Mr Wylie,' said Graeme.

'Delighted to meet you,' said Luke unctuously.

Smoothing his Dolce & Gabbana tie, he delivered an Extreme Smile and moved in for the power-handshake.

Given that Graeme was built like a steel-reinforced double-layer brick shithouse, it was not a wise move. I heard Luke whimper slightly as Graeme, rising to the challenge, ground his knuckles to a fine paste.

'I've heard so much about you,' said Luke rather tremulously, nursing his right hand. 'In fact—'

'Tell me now, where aire ye on the food chain?' Graeme interrupted. He wasn't a man for small talk.

'Er, ah, I eat Olivia. Ha ha ha,' said Luke in an ill-advised attempt at humour.

It was awful. A disaster. Complete trainwreck.

Then – horrifically – Luke went for a giggle-style effect. I think it was supposed to be charming, but it made everything much, much worse. Like a Greek tragedy with congenital herpes. Luke was accomplished at the pouty, sullen, underwear-model look studded with an occasional chopper-baring grin; he really wasn't accomplished at the wry chuckle.

Graeme looked relieved when his secretary rang.

'Nice of you to show up,' I said out of the corner of my mouth.

'Righ'! Where were we?' shouted Graeme, replacing the receiver. 'Now then. Ah've got a bone to pick wi' ye, lassie,' he said, and my heart nudged over the roller-coaster's edge.

I arranged my features in what I hoped was an interested yet unconcerned, competent but deferential assemblage.

'What seems to be the problem, Graeme?' I said in my best customer-care voice (with only a hint of tremor).

'Mah sairver. The v280R,' he said.

Oh, shite. How the heck did Graeme find out?

'Yer engineer misplaced it.'

'It was misplaced, but Keith found it, yes,' I said smoothly, hoping to head him off at the pass. No such luck: Graeme charged over it like a rogue elephant.

'Yeis, buit he loast it in the fairst place.' Graeme raised his voice to an eardrum-rattling volume. 'An' it wuis muived.'

'Muived,' repeated Luke, puzzled.

'Aye,' said Graeme. 'MUIVED!'

I gave Luke an I'll-handle-this-so-sit-back-and-try-not-to-get-in-the way-and-if-you-really-must-do-anything-at-all-please-limit-it-to-positive-karma look.

'That was regrettable,' I said. 'But it wasn't muived – er, moved – by my engineers. We're not sure—'

'Tha's beside the point!' bellowed Graeme. 'Why wasnae Ah told aboo tha incidaent? It maight've ben woaggled. D'ye knoa how mooch damage a fair woagglin' can du a sairver? Tha's three hundred grand's worth o' machine there!'

'Graeme,' I said slowly. 'We ran a full diagnostic check. In fact, I have the results of both tests here. Let me just . . .'

Thereupon, I spent what felt like half an hour fumbling around the pocket of my briefcase, although it was probably only ten seconds.

'The machine was fine, Graeme. Had there been any problem at all, I would have informed you immediately. But really, I didn't feel it was worth bothering you until we had identified a problem. Or not, as turned out to be the case.'

Belatedly, I produced several dog-eared sheets of A4. Kevin had couriered the report to me, complete with notations scribbled in the margins.

'Er,' I said. 'Er, yes. Sorry. These printouts were for

internal use. Only. If I'd known that you . . . I mean, if you'd been . . . I will print a fresh set and put them in a folder with – with maybe a label on the front and a nice clear cover . . . and without the, er, scribbles and the, ah, coffee stain on the title page.'

'Hand i' oaver,' said Graeme, with the barest hint of a grin. 'Ah jus' woanted to be sure yeh'd done yer hoamework, lassie.'

And then Luke pounced.

'Mr Dewar, I cannot apologise enough,' he declared theatrically. 'This incident was not brought to my attention either, or I would have—'

'It was a project issue, and I handled it,' I interrupted, trying to keep my voice neutral. What was he *doing*? It was case closed, until he went and blew it wide open again. 'We located the server, ran tests; everything is fine.'

'That's not the point. Mr Dewar, I am embarrassed you had to find out the way you did. I assure you it will never happen again. This will be dealt with severely.'

Graeme looked a bit startled at the grand declamation. He cast a quick look at me. I was working to get my jaw under control – it seemed to be having difficulty with the whole gravity concept.

'Och, thair's noa hairm done, laddie,' he said uncomfortably. 'I's no' a big deal—'

'With all due respect, it *is* a big deal,' said Luke. 'Puttock Leavitt holds itself to the highest standards. To produce this . . .' He snatched the papers out of Graeme's hand and brandished them at him.

'As loang as the information's there, I doan' reilly care—'

Luke addressed me. 'To present a document like this to a client is a disgrace.'

Now, I thought he got a bit carried away here, but it was certainly dramatic. He picked up the printout and tore it in half. Not content with that, he tore those pieces in two; then he tried to do so again, but there was too much pulp and he grunted a bit as he strained over the pages.

Then, in a final fanfare, he hurled the shreds into Graeme's wastepaper basket. Unfortunately, the paper sprinkled confetti-like in a two-metre radius around the bin.

There was a pregnant pause. I think I was gasping a bit.

'Olivia, I want a word with Mr Dewar,' said Luke.

'Okay,' I managed in a small, tremulous voice. I felt I might burst into tears without too much goading.

'Alone,' he snapped.

'Oh, of course, right.'

As I tottered out of Graeme's office on legs that barely worked, I heard Luke say in an undertone: 'I must apologise for Liv,' and Graeme say: 'It's really no' a problem. Liv's always done a great joab for us.'

And then the door closed behind me.

On the way back to the hotel, Luke acted as if nothing had happened. It was like a practical from *Manly Behaviour 101*.

'Nice guy, Graeme.'

'Mm.'

'Seemed to know his stuff.'

'Mm.'

'What would you like to do now?'

'Whatever.'

'Should we get some lunch?'

'Not hungry.'

If sulking were an officially recognised Olympic discipline, I would be a gold medallist: 'And it's Liv Anderson way out in front! She really is a class above the rest of the field! I don't think I've ever seen a pout so vicious! There's no catching her now! . . . And YES! She's smashed her own world record for the sixth time in a row!'

On occasion I've been known to maintain a hissy fit for several weeks, but I was so furious with Luke that this one only persisted until dinner.

We had been served our appetisers and Luke was waxing lyrical about his mushrooms stuffed with foie gras when I said conversationally: 'So, Luke, were you born an arsehole or did you wake up that way one day?'

Not a positive conversation-starter, as it turned out.

'Excuse me?' said Luke.

'You heard. Is there something about the question that requires clarification?'

We could have carried on indefinitely with the universal argument script, lurching around in circles with Luke acting dumb. He might not have been acting, but that was a concern for another day.

'Are you trying to pretend', I hissed, 'that you didn't absolutely *shaft* me in front of my client earlier?'

'Gragnoc is not your client, Olivia,' said Luke calmly, smoothing his tie. 'Gragnoc is Puttock Leavitt's client. And in order to ensure that they remain our client—'

'You fuck me over.'

'Look, Olivia, let's face facts, shall we? You screwed up. You screwed' – he chopped the air for emphasis – 'up!'

'That's crap, and you know it. A server was misplaced, and yes, I chose not to tell the client – for a number of reasons, not least of which was I wanted to know what I was dealing with before—'

'What if the server had been damaged? You're just lucky everything turned out all right. That's an expensive piece of equipment—'

'If there'd been something wrong with the server, I would have told you and Graeme! But we performed a thorough diagnostic and it was fine. So what, in your esteemed opinion, did I do wrong?'

'Much as you may dislike the fact, Olivia, I am your manager,' said Luke pompously. 'You should have informed me—'

'So that you could tell me to do what I did? You know, I am quite capable of making these decisions. I managed pretty well before you came along—'

'Well, that's a matter of opinion—'

'Whose opinion are you polling?'

'Look, Olivia, you seem to forget that there is a process for these things—' Luke persisted doggedly.

'If you wouldn't mind getting back to the question: what did I do wrong?'

'For Christ's sake,' said Luke. Throughout the exchange, he had remained unruffled, but now he rose to his feet.

'You're leaving?' I said in disbelief.

'I'm going to the bathroom.'

I could tell he was being sarcastic by the way his lip curled back – and the fact that he didn't return.

At least he had the consideration to prance off – and I'm delighted to be able to confirm that Luke did, indeed, prance; or to be quite specific it was a cross between prancing and *flouncing* – shortly after the main course was served, leaving me his lamb chops with chermoula paste and garlic mash. It would have been better had I retained my appetite, but never mind.

Unsurprisingly, there was no knock on my hotel room door later that night. So much for romantic notions of baths strewn with rose petals, rolling around naked in front of roaring log fires and licking chocolate sauce off each other. At that point, I would have happily smeared chocolate sauce on Luke's crotch – but only as a prerequisite to setting a Rottweiler on him.

I felt twitchy and sick to my stomach. Our previous argument had been resolved by Luke's lustily flinging me across his desk. In this instance, with no Luke to volunteer lusty flinging, I was not sure how we were supposed to sort this out if Luke refused to discuss it. Should I phone his room and ... do what? Apologise? Not likely. Call him names? Tempting.

Unable to sleep, I raided the mini-bar and cracked out the whiskey and a Toblerone. Then I watched the last twenty minutes of *A Dingo Ate My Baby*, followed by *Piranha Part II: The Spawning*, and an old episode of *CHiPs*. (Erik Estrada should have arrested himself for indecent exposure in those trousers.)

But my attention kept fretting back to the scene in Graeme's office and the argument with Luke over dinner. I couldn't explain it – any of it. I must have fallen asleep at some stage, because I awoke shortly after seven the next morning.

I felt calmer. Serene. Collected, even. I'd made peace with my Yin, although I still wouldn't trust my Yang with an armed weapon.

Perhaps we could salvage the rest of the weekend. I would be the mature party here. I would go and see Luke and calmly extend the olive branch. (As opposed to thrashing him to death with it, slowly and painfully, with a certain amount of regretful relish.)

I'd say, 'Sorry things got a bit out of control last night.' The subtle art of apologising without really apologising, you will note.

And then we would discuss things. I would composedly communicate how humiliated and betrayed I felt. Talk about the damage I feared it had done my relationship with Graeme. About where this left Luke and me.

However, when I knocked on Luke's door some time later, there was no answer. After breakfast and a newspaper, I returned to his room and found the door propped open with a laundry trolley.

'Luke Wylie?' said Reception. 'How do you spell that? Oh, right. Let me see . . . yes . . . he checked out this morning.'

34

There wasn't much point hanging around Glasgow dodging haggis, so I called the airline and booked a seat on the next available flight to London. It left in less than two hours. I felt I wasn't so much cutting it fine as slashing it to oblivion, but I just wanted to go home.

When I flung myself across the check-in desk wheezing something like 'Flight – London – bugger – gasp', there was barely three-quarters of an hour to takeoff. I was the last person to board the plane.

Being back in cattle class added seasoning to my humour or lack thereof. How come I never end up sitting beside some architect who moonlights as an underwear model who just happens to live just down the road from me ('Humber Road? No way! I live on Maze Hill! My ex-girlfriend didn't like it – said it was too close to Greenwich Park. She was a bitch. You're lovely. Mmmm.')

Traditionally, I'm wedged in between a fatty spilling over into my seat on the one side and Frankenstein's first prototype – the version with excess testosterone – on the other. If I'm really unlucky, I'll be surrounded on all sides: an underage kicker behind, and a recliner complete with big greasy potato-head in front.

On this occasion, as I clambered over Mr Ugly, I saw

there was a pair of teenagers diligently sucking each other's face on my right. It was a tangle of limbs and pimples. I could almost smell the sperm in the air. Inspired by the slurpy soundtrack, Mr Ugly gave me the glad eye.

'Hi,' he said.

Sigh!

At least there is one thing I can always count on, no matter what: the ugliest man in the plane will always chat me up. In a way, it's kind of comforting.

'Hi.' I smiled at him. 'Normally I'd love to chat, but I have a severe case of molluscum contagiosum and my doctor has advised me that talking will aggravate it.'

'I was only trying to be friendly,' said Mr Ugly with a huff.

His version of friendly probably came with a hot beef injection.

Tentatively, as one might prod a sleeping bear, I considered Luke. Although I suspected I had just been dumped, I wasn't entirely sure. Luke hadn't followed any recognisable break-up template. It's not like he had stopped calling and gone cold and distant, then turned up with lipstick stains on his collar and reeking of another woman's perfume and said: 'Look, I need some space. I'm not ready for a commitment right now. It's not you, it's me. I hope we can still be friends. You can have the dog.'

He hadn't said much of anything at all. Although abandoning me in Glasgow was pretty conclusive, I felt.

I was . . . cautiously I examined my emotions. Gutted? Devastated? Losing the will to live?

It took a while to realise that although I was angry and upset – yes, definitely upset – I wasn't ravaged with grief, sobbing helplessly into a sick bag and contemplating cutting my heart out and mailing it to Luke as a dramatic statement. In fact, I hadn't lost the will to *eat*, never mind the will to live.

It came as something of a surprise. Surely I should feel more distressed about losing the Perfect Man?

For the time being, let's overlook the momentary lapse of perfection when Luke marooned his lover in the middle of deepest Scotland. And his 'Heeeeere's Johnny!' turn the first day I met him; and the kinky office sex; and the honking, the runaway pubic hairs, the moisturising, and all the rest.

Because otherwise, Luke was a major contender. He got the small things right. He wasn't stingy with the flowers and was a reliable source of chocolate. He had impeccable taste and ironed his own shirts. As men's feet go, Luke's were relatively aromatic. He was considerate: he opened doors, he pulled out chairs, he helped me into and out of my coat. He let me commander the remote control and attended romantic comedies starring the likes of Renée Zellweger and Hugh Grant with minimal protest. And then there were the lashings of suave, the flashings of cash, the all-round handsome dashingness. He was almost charismatic.

But although Luke might have looked right on paper – not to mention other places – I had to admit there had always been something missing.

Actually liking the man, for a start.

Oh, it's not that I *disliked* him – nothing so passionate. That, I realised, was the problem: I didn't actually feel much of anything for him. And so, whereas I didn't dislike Luke, I didn't exactly like him either.

Never mind extremes such as adoration, devotion or love.

A particularly loud suction noise drew my attention back to the pair on my right. Romeo appeared to have a flip-top head, while his girlfriend was risking a serious rash. Suddenly, this physical manifestation of Young Love made me feel all misty. Ah, the innocence! The romance! The hickeys!

I couldn't remember the last time I had wanted to snog someone senseless like that. But I'll tell you, it had been a while – we're talking *decades*. And although I had been glad to escape the capricious, devastating hormones of puberty, I suddenly yearned for just a little of that turbulent emotion.

As I sorted through the jumble of thoughts in my head, it was as if my Id said: 'So, you want a spot of turbulent emotion, do you? Well, hold on to your hat, clench your cheeks and fasten your seat belt, my friend. Get a load of *this*.'

An image burst into my head, and the force of it knocked the wind out of me. There was a distinct Interruption of Service in the blood-pumping department too, because I'm pretty sure my heart stopped for several seconds.

I was kissing Jed, or Jed was kissing me – I'm not sure which. He had his hands in my hair, then they were cupping my face; now he was caressing my cheekbone, slipping a thumb into my mouth (that happened to me once and I nearly bit the guy's finger off, but in my fantasy Jed retained his digit). It was unbelievably, gut-wrenchingly thrilling.

Gosh, he really wanted me.

And here's the surprise: it looked suspiciously like the feeling was mutual, if not veering towards one-sidedness.

I know it was my own private thought process but

oh my God, I was acting like a shameless hussy. Look at me pressing into him, running my hands down his back, slipping them under the waistband of his jeans and . . .

Whoa! Back up! Reverse! Reverse!

What the *fuck* was that all about?

I felt like I'd just finished ten circuits on a violent rollercoaster.

Again, I thought about Jed and lust simply exploded in me like a Catherine wheel. My mind strayed back to his mouth closing on mine and, frankly, I thought I might be experiencing a heart attack.

Did I *fancy* Jed?

Surely not.

I had shared a cubicle with the man for over a year and never once considered bumping uglies with him. I mean, if the thought had ever crossed my mind, I might have spent some time deliberating it – but it hadn't.

And now that the thought was not so much crossing my mind as staging a porn movie in it, I felt it was time to assert reality. For a start, Jed was the biggest hound dog this side of the Thames. If the man charged on a per bonk basis, he could retire with millions. There wasn't a female with a pulse that Jed wouldn't screw, apart from maybe – let's be fair – Brenda Calburn; and even then, if she turned up on his doorstep with a bottle of massage oil, I wouldn't put it past him.

And for goodness' sake, Jed was my buddy, my mate – Cliff Richard would be hard pressed to get any more platonic. Jed was the person I called to unblock the lavatory, fix my toaster, or replace wonky hinges. If I had a dead stiff lying about the place, Jed would be my first choice to help dispose of the body. He might make a good partner in crime – but *boyfriend*?

Occasionally, I liked to give Jed an affectionate blue tit, but not once had he ever looked like he wanted to reciprocate.

Although . . . there had been that evening down in the Wine Cellar. Not that I had felt in danger of Jed's giving me a blue tit, but he had said . . . what was it? He had intimated that he liked me. He had said that I was special. And looked like he meant it, as I recalled.

And in contrast to the women he dated, Jed had always treated me with the utmost respect. Except when he rearranged the things in my drawer so that they were in the wrong place and – even worse – didn't line up.

But on the other hand, he brought me blocks of purple Post-its whenever he visited the stationery cupboard. He let me tidy his desk when I suffered a build-up of toxins and/or nervous tension. He cut out pictures of penguins to stick on my partition wall. He downloaded songs he thought I would like, and always remembered exactly how I took my coffee at any given moment in time.

I loved being with him and he made me laugh like nobody else.

Oh, shite.

Perhaps I did fancy him.

And with my usual impeccable timing, this revelation struck at a time when Jed and I were barely even talking to each other.

No doubt the situation would be better if, after Jed had bared his soul at the Wine Cellar, I hadn't picked it up, fecked it off the table, thrown it to the ground and stamped all over it in stilettos.

However, now that Luke had resigned his boyfriend-slash status, things with Jed would go back to normal.

Wouldn't they? Obviously, we'd take it slowly. I might casually bring it up in conversation. 'Hey, Jed, want to be my significant other? Could be for ever, but let's give it a couple of weeks for a start. What d'you think?'

But of course, it didn't happen quite that way.

35

L uke didn't call.

I hadn't expected him to. In fact, I was rather glad he didn't. Luke wasn't The One. He wasn't even runner-up.

All the same, I hoped it would be an amicable split. Luke returning my personal effects and CDs in a box, and throwing in *The Cream of Clapton* as a parting gift because he 'knew I liked it' and he 'never listened to it anyway'.

No call for throwing his clothes off a balcony (after cutting the arms off his suit jackets of course) or pouring nail varnish remover over his BMW or secreting fillets of haddock in his briefcase. Not at all; we would be mutually respectful in meetings, and civil – verging on positively friendly – when we chanced upon each other in the PL corridors. We could release a joint statement: 'This decision is the result of thoughtful consideration. We happily remain committed and caring friends with great love and admiration for one another.'

The skittering in my stomach as I wended through the Maze on Monday morning had less to do with Luke and more to do with Jed. It was an even conflict between anxiety and anticipation. Would he have arrived already?

Would my legs withstand the sight of him? What would I say to him? How would he respond?

Distinguishing my phone in the cacophony of background noise, I broke into a trot. My heart gave a great thump as I rounded the corner, but Jed was not there. However, the entrails of a computer across his desk indicated that he was in the vicinity.

Shrugging off my coat, I registered the caller display and snatched at the telephone.

'Graeme!'

'Livvie! How are yeh?' He sounded anxious.

'Fine! Fine! The grandest!' I injected a heartiness that was frankly unnatural for a Monday morning. 'And you?'

'Yes, yes,' he grunted.

'Is everything all right? There's no problem with the temporary system, is there?'

'No' at all,' he boomed. 'It's aboot yer boss man, tha' Wylie chap. He has i' in fer yeh a bi', Ah reickon.'

'Really?'

'Aye. He said some right unbeezer things aboot yeh after yeh left mah office.'

'Like . . . like what?'

'Och, they're no' worth repeatin',' he said. 'Now, yeh listen to me. That Wylie lad cares nowt fer yeh. Come on, lass,' he continued over my stuttering protests, 'Ah knaw ye're steppin' ou' wi' him. Tha' Wylie has a bad heart. All Ah'm sayin' is watch yer back.'

The hairs on my neck prickled.

'An' yer front too,' Graeme roared, just to ensure all angles were covered.

'What . . . what do you think . . . I mean, what might . . . ?'

'Hoo the scun should Ah ken, lass? Bu' be careful, arigh'?'

Hanging up the phone, I was in pensive mood. Graeme was not the type to spook easily. What on earth had Luke said to him?

My gut gave a big squeeze, alerting me to the fact that Jed had arrived. He looked tired – standard for Jed after the typical weekend excess – and intent and grim and knee-tremblingly sexy.

He nodded at me.

'Hello,' I said shyly.

'Hi,' said Jed shortly.

There was silence as I unpacked Drusilla, powered her up and fumbled around for something to say.

'Good weekend?' I tried.

'The usual.'

Another pause; then Jed, with an echo of his former self: 'How was the smutty holiday in exotic Glasgow?'

'Not much of a holiday, involving not a lot of smut.' I opened Microsoft Outlook. 'Er, Luke and I, we broke up.'

'Actually, I'd already guessed,' said Jed. 'You'd better take a look at your mail.'

'What?'

'Check your e-mail,' he said gently.

My laptop was taking a long time to boot up. Drusilla had been feistier than usual lately; I would have to ask Jed to take a look at her.

Glancing at my Inbox, I saw immediately what Jed was referring to.

! / Luke Wylie / Gragnoc project delays / Mon 14 May 07:42

My stomach yawed with fear. How did Jed know about this? It must mean . . . I double-clicked on the message. Yes, there he was on the CC list, along with most of the

BSS department and several Gragnoc employees, including Graeme.

> Olivia [Luke wrote],
>
> According to your original estimate for the Gragnoc EnTire system implementation, provisional acceptance was scheduled over two months ago. As you should be aware, PAC is a commercial milestone and I do not understand the reason for such delay. Please explain why this project is chronically late, and provide a definite date for PAC.

'That poxy git!' I gasped.

'Yep,' said Jed conversationally. 'That's a toasting if ever I saw one. And talk about airing dirty laundry – most of London has seen those skid marks. There were at least three members of Parliament copied on that, along with jesus.h.christ@heaven.com.'

'Oh, you don't know the half of it,' I said grimly. 'He worked me over with Graeme on Friday too. Don't ask – I'll tell you about it later.'

So, I thought bleakly, no *Cream of Eric Clapton*. It was slowly dawning on me that as boyfriend material, Luke was looking somewhat moth-eaten and frayed around the (faded) edges. Not only that, but evidence pointed to the possibility that he was something of a first-class prick.

And with spectacular timing, my annual appraisal with Luke was scheduled for Friday. Thank goodness he had submitted my appraisal form the previous week – there was a limit to how much rebound angst he could indulge himself in.

When time allows, I am an enthusiastic spectator of

flame wars between distant colleagues. They are invariably fascinating vignettes of corporate culture involving intrigue, politics, back-stabbing, gonad measurement, bitchiness and surprise twists.

Normally I do not engage in electronic handbag combat. Mud tends to slime both parties regardless of the facts, figures, rights or wrongs. However, I wasn't about to roll over and let Luke's missive go. I was beyond furious.

And maybe mud doesn't stick if you throw it hard enough.

Hitting 'Reply All', I paused only to remove my clients from Luke's original CC list.

If there was one thing an apprenticeship in PL had taught me, it was how to cover your arse. Layering, that was the key. Layers and layers upon layers of posterior defence. It was all in the minutiae.

Despite working with me for over six months – not to mention dating for most of that time – Luke obviously didn't know me at all. I rarely went to the bathroom without giving formal notice of my absence, the expected duration, and contact details in the event of an emergency. Being compulsively organised, I had e-mails backing up e-mails, all carefully filed and cross-referenced by project, product, subject matter, mood and hair status. All in all, it was a devastating munitions store.

I twiddled my fingers over the keyboard in the manner of a grand pianist.

Dear Luke [I responded], I hope you are simply splendid.

The original estimate was originally estimated by the Sales Team. With regard to the Gragnoc

PAC, please refer to correspondence dated 12/12, 21/12, 7/1, 9/1, 23/1, 24/1, 19/2, 20/2, 13/3, 27/3 and 28/3, all of which detail the estimated delays and associated risks. Alternatively, you might refer to my weekly reports, each of which exhaustively describes the project status and associated timeframes at that time.

You will appreciate there is nothing I can do about these hold-ups apart from keeping you and relevant parties, as always, fully informed.

Have a nice day and many kind regards,

Olivia

I may not be accomplished at reading between the lines, but boy I know how to write between them:

Dear Luke,

You asshole,

I hope you are simply splendid.

I hope you contract a double dose of Escherichia coli 0157:H7.

The original estimate was originally estimated by the Sales Team.

According to a date they made up optimistically yet largely randomly.

With regard to the Gragnoc PAC, please refer to correspondence dated 12/12, 21/12, 7/1, 9/1, 23/1, 24/1, 19/2, 20/2, 13/3, 27/3 and 28/3, all of which detail the estimated delays and associated risks. Alternatively, you might refer to my weekly reports, each of which exhaustively describes the project status and associated timeframes at that time.

Please let me know whether there is any way I can make the project reports easier for your perusal –

smaller words? Bullet points? Crayons? Please advise.

You will appreciate there is nothing I can do about these hold-ups apart from keeping you and relevant parties, as always, fully informed.

Asshole!

Have a nice day and many kind regards,

If I have anything to do with it, that's the last thing you'll have,

Olivia

I experienced a twinge of uncertainty as I hit the send button, but then, I hadn't started it.

Believe it or not, my life was about to get much, much worse.

'Hey, Anderson.' Jed had adopted a pop-eyed, faintly squinty aspect after poring over a hard disk drive with a pair of tweezers all morning. The disk was in so many component pieces that I doubted even Jed's ability to resurrect it to working order. 'How about a caffeine hit?'

'Sure,' I said casually.

Settle down there, I told the squirming ball of excitement in my stomach. It's only coffee, not a five-course dinner with rose petals and chocolate mints. It's not as if you haven't quaffed gallons of the stuff with him in the past.

But swirling through the doors into the drizzling May afternoon, I was flushed with nervous anticipation. Suddenly I noticed little things about Jed, like his solid warmth when we were crushed together in the revolving door; his breath in my hair; how he held his coat over my head as we dashed the ten yards into the station; the way he used his body to shield me from the swarming accountants.

'Take a seat,' he said at the Coffee Spot. 'My treat. Let me guess. Regular no-foam flat-top extra-caff low-fat soya latte with hazelnut flavour, easy on the soya?'

'Make it a grande.'

Jed returned with the drinks. An awkward silence permeated the ritual sugaring and stirring. Normally we would have squabbled amicably over something – anything – but things had changed.

'So what happened in Glasgow?' he said.

We eked a good quarter-hour out of the meeting with Graeme, Luke's actions and his subsequent misbehaviour. But words seemed to be going astray somewhere between my brain and my mouth.

'Listen—' said Jed.

'Hang on.' My heart sank as I saw Chanelle approach. She looked great; maybe she'd got lucky over the weekend. Or perhaps she and Uncle Bill had kissed and made up.

'Hey guys! Why didn't you say you were coming down?'

Then there was a jolt as the earth stopped turning. Because there was something different about the way Chanelle greeted Jed. Maybe it was the look that crackled between them. Or the way she sat on his lap and put a hand possessively on his chest and slipped a finger between two of the buttons and tickled him.

Or the way she snogged the face off him.

I was rooted in shock.

'Wha . . .'

I swallowed with difficulty; my throat appeared to have swollen. I'd better not be developing a coffee allergy – at that moment I was seriously considering whether life was worth living, and that would have pushed me into a definite negative.

'Wha . . .'

Perhaps, I resolved, it was better not to make further efforts to speak until my larynx had rebooted.

Chanelle drew a chair close to Jed's and sat down. She didn't even wipe it with paper napkins. She must be smitten, I thought. She put a hand on Jed's leg.

Jed's face was impassive.

'Wha . . .' I took a deep breath. 'You're seeing each other?'

'You didn't tell her?' Chanelle asked Jed. She gave his leg a horrid little playful slap. It was like a nightmare. A nightmare involving no clothes and flesh-eating zombies and Harrison Ford after the age of fifty.

'How long has this been going on?' I wheezed. For goodness' sake, I sounded like a cuckolded wife.

Jed shrugged, then stood abruptly. 'What can I get you?' he said to Chanelle.

'Grande latte,' said Chanelle.

I noted with dismay how Chanelle's eyes followed him to the counter, surfing the crest of a great big sloppy grin. She'd never looked at Uncle Bill like that.

'Sorry,' she giggled, snapping out of her lustful reverie. 'I am just in *shock*!'

Make that two of us.

'We've been shagging all weekend. I'm absolutely bandy-legged. Isn't it exciting?' She turned shining eyes on me. 'Can you *believe* it?'

Frankly, no.

'What happened?' someone asked.

Oh, right, it might have been me.

'Well, Friday afternoon someone suggested Spinker's after work. I didn't have much else on except going home to feed the cat and I haven't heard from Uncle Bill in a while – I think he's shagging his secretary at the moment. At least that's the word on the grapevine – not that I care. Anyway, where was I? Oh yes. So after downing a few at Spinker's, Jed and Nigel and I went on to the Wine Cellar, and somehow ended up at the Underworld. We lost Nigel on the way – he went to sleep in a shop doorway. I was pretty plastered, and we were on the dance floor and things were heating up. Jed is such an amazing dancer – I'd never noticed before. It was about three in the morning, and my shoes were *killing* me. I was wearing my Manolo Blahniks – you know the ones with the heels and the little strappy straps?'

That description fits most of Chanelle's footwear, but moving on.

'And Jed suggested we go back to his place. I was kind of lying across his sofa half asleep and Jed moved over and kissed me, and he was running his hands all over my back, and gazing deep into my eyes. Oh, Liv, he is an unbelievably good kisser. Masterful technique.'

I so did not want to hear about Jed's masterful technique.

'Then he picked me up and carried me into the bedroom. Threw me on the bed. It was so erotic! I had an orgasm right there on the spot. The first of many.' She gave a dirty giggle.

I scrambled to my feet abruptly and my chair crashed to the ground.

'Livvie? Are you all right?' Chanelle looked surprised.

'Yes. Yes. Sorry. I've just remembered . . . something. I forgot to do it . . . earlier. So I'd better go . . . now. I've got to go.'

'Are you all right with this?' Chanelle frowned. 'You know, Jed and me going out. Because you said—'

'Of course! It's fine, it's' – I made a monumental effort – 'great!' I touched her cheek and somehow dredged up a smile. 'I'm really happy for you.' Feeling tears jostling my retina, I said, 'Honey, I've got to go. I'll catch you later, okay?'

Tacking through London Bridge, I felt numb. Although, I thought with a flash of anger, Jed was obviously a flake if, less than a month after declaring his undying love and devotion to me, he was off knobbing Chanelle. It wouldn't last, I consoled myself. Jed's relationships never did. Fair play to her, Chanelle had done well to prevail past the weekend.

And she wasn't Jed's type. Although that said, she was female with a good complexion and no sign of a hump. On reflection, she was probably overqualified.

But another thing – Jed wasn't Chanelle's type. She went for professional footballers or upwardly mobile C-list celebrities; and if these were temporarily unavailable, perma-tanned men with enough spare cash for a penis extension *and* a Porsche. Jed just didn't have the finances or naked ambition to make the cut.

And the physical attraction wouldn't sustain them long. You can't run a relationship fuelled with carpet burns and lewd text messages.

But at the same time, Jed and Chanelle had always got on well. And surely Jed wouldn't risk going out with Chanelle unless he felt fairly strongly about her?

Then I felt dreadful. I had always hoped Chanelle would end up with someone special, and now she had. And what kind of scabrous monster was I who couldn't wish the best for my friends?

Opportunity had knocked, and I'd slammed the door in its face. This was my fault. The fact of the matter was: I'd blown it.

The only bleak ray of sunlight in the whole affair was that at least Jed and I reverted to a surreal normality. There were times when it was almost like it used to be – but not quite. Sometimes I caught Jed watching me with a curious aspect of stillness. Our eyes would catch and hold for slightly too long, before flickering away.

But I had other things on my mind, because the situation between Luke and me had disintegrated into open warfare. I might have been the undisputed champion of round one, but it was just the opening gambit in a battle that raged the rest of the week.

Outside the electronic arena, Luke proved to be a cunning and resourceful foe.

One of his favourite tactics included having Michelle ring: 'Liv, can you please hold for Mr Wylie?' Then, half an hour of 'Greensleeves' later: 'Sorry, Liv, Mr Wylie's not available right now.'

At our weekly progress meeting, Luke kept me waiting half an hour before cancelling. At the Project Support meeting, he interrupted and corrected me repeatedly in front of Jed, Max and the rest of the PM team.

He took to appearing in the Maze and loudly

demanding this or that brief, heavily hinting at incompetence – a brilliant manoeuvre, any response to which made me appear to be justifying myself.

He also liked to wait until the end of the day and then materialise in our cubicle with an 'urgent task' that had to be attended to right away.

Throughout the onslaught I pursued a position of aggressive cheerfulness, the objective being to cause maximum irritation. I dreaded meeting him in the corridors, where he would pointedly ignore me, staring stonily into the middle distance. However, I always flashed him a full set of teeth, and gushed: 'Luke, what a lovely surprise! How are you? How *are* you?'

Occasionally, I managed to score half a point by refusing to do something because it 'wasn't in my job description', but – and this came as rather a shock – I realised I just wasn't childish enough to keep it up. I had always assumed I was as childish as the next man – but evidently not if the next man happened to be Luke Wylie.

In between bouts of savagery unsanctioned by the Geneva Conventions, I wondered bewilderedly why Luke was being so unpleasant. I mean, it's not like *I* had left *him*, or belittled *him* in front of our client, or stolen his anti-ageing cream and hogged the hairdryer for hours at a stretch.

I had been a frigging goddess.

Most like in form to Venus.

So why was he being so vindictive?

It was all demoralising and energy-sapping, and obviously high time I reopened the job hunt.

38

On Friday morning I had a portent of doom – as if my appraisal that afternoon wasn't presage enough.

When I went to get dressed, my Friday underwear was missing.

There was no sign of my purple satin bra and knicker set with red trim in the Friday section of my underwear drawer. The only clean underwear available was a wispy pale green bra and black polka-dot hipsters. There was no getting around the fact that they just didn't match, and I felt completely discomposed.

It was a bad omen. Although on the bright side, at least a lone albatross didn't fly thrice around a scorched thorn tree ere the lowering sky.

All week, I had been getting progressively more nervous about the appraisal. Most of my colleagues had completed theirs. On Tuesday, Nigel had been devastated when he discovered that, in the 'Behavioural' section of his peer assessment form, Chanelle had ticked 'poor' next to 'Good sense of humour'.

'I've got a facking *great* sense of humour,' wailed Nigel. 'Haven't I?'

'Well, you always make me laugh.' I patted his arm soothingly.

'Really?'

'Oh, yes. You have an incisive wit.'

'Incisive,' confirmed Jed. 'And rare comic timing. You know that joke of yours – the one about the fly on the toilet seat? Always cracks me up.'

'And why did the booger cross the road? That's a facking classic,' said Nigel.

'Oh, yes.' Jed and I nodded vigorously. 'Hilarious.'

When I hadn't been fretting about Jed and Chanelle or revisiting situations-vacant websites, I'd spent the week compulsively preparing for the showdown. I'd summarised my projects over the previous twelve months with 3-D bar graphs and Technicolor pie charts illustrating comparisons between predicted and actual costs, resources and timeframes, all supported by sheaves of documentation.

In fact, I had exhibited stunning form over the year. The only project that had failed to come in on time was Gragnoc, but my original risk analysis had highlighted the Development delay and I had budgeted accordingly.

'Good luck,' said Jed as I gathered up my files and tucked Drusilla under my arm.

The hard knot of tension in my stomach was only distilled when I entered Luke's office and found Max ensconced in a chair.

'Olivia! Haven't seen you in a while, yang lidy. Keeping the nose to the squeaky wheel, are we? HAH!'

Instantly I wanted to scratch – even my *tongue* itched.

'Let's get right into it, shall we?' said Luke.

Clutching the files to my lap, I took the other seat across from him.

'I'm sure you are wondering why I have asked Max to join us. Frankly I have a number of concerns regarding your conduct.'

'Really?' I said coolly, although I was trembling. 'Strange that this is the first time in six months you've mentioned it. As I recall, you have been extremely positive about my work during our' – I paused for a quick mental calculation – 'twenty-six weekly meetings.'

'I don't think that is quite accurate,' said Luke crushingly. 'And there's no need to get defensive.'

He was right. Getting violent might be more appropriate.

I bit my tongue and tried to collect my scrambled thoughts. Luke had nothing. But if that was the case, why had he asked Max to attend the meeting?

I could not believe I'd been so mistaken about Luke. I mean, after a relationship breaks down, I expect a certain amount of twisted bitterness. But trying to ruin your ex's career?

That's just mean.

'I'm sorry you've been disappointed with my performance,' I said, realising the significant double entendre only after the words aired. It seemed a vast stretch of the imagination to consider that just over a week ago I had been looking forward to a saucy weekend with the man.

'Let's go through your appraisal form.' Luke slid a copy across the desk. I felt on firmer ground here – he had submitted the form the previous week, in that faraway time when we were still calling each other 'honey buns' and 'twinkle tits'.

But throwing an eye down it, I felt a rising tide of panic surge around my heels. Random phrases snagged my brain. 'Team worker – strongly disagree', 'Problem solving and decision making abilities – poor', 'Product/technical knowledge – poor'. And oh my God! I ranked with Nigel in the funny department: 'Sense of humour – poor'.

'Did you bother reading the questions?' I asked, trying to keep my voice under control. 'Or did you just tick "poor" and "strongly disagree" against everything?'

'No. Look here,' said Max, stabbing a furry finger at my form. 'Your time management skills are "adequate".'

'Oh, that's nice. Okay, well, let's take that one. Would you like to discuss my time management skills, Luke?'

'Olivia, I'm not about to take each point on the form and debate it with you,' said Luke.

'I thought that was the point of the appraisal process. To review performance and suggest areas for improvement?'

'You have a bad attitude,' said Luke.

'Well, you would too if you were ambushed like this—'

'I'm talking about generally, over the last six months—'

'Well, I'll try to work on that,' I said. 'But in the meantime, could you be more vague and simplistic?'

'Look, Olivia,' said Luke, slashing the air. 'There's no doubt that you're a capable project manager. If anyone asked me whether you were good at your job I would probably say yes. But if someone asked me, "Is Olivia a good *employee*", the answer would have to be no.'

'This is crap,' I said slowly. 'Max, you know my work. I've been with this company nearly six years, and my annual reviews have always been outstanding. I successfully managed more projects than any other project manager last year, including our two biggest clients. And they were all models of – of ...' I brandished my appraisal form in Max's face, mentally grasping for words. 'Models of top fabulousness.'

Not quite what I was going for.

'And – and – and you gave me a *rise* last year! What was that for? Poor performance?'

'Things change,' said Luke.

'I wasn't talking to you, mange head,' I snarled.

A look passed from Luke to Max, which clearly said: 'See?'

Not my finest moment, admittedly. Luke had come a long way from honey buns.

'You are only demonstrating my point,' he said smoothly. 'In addition to your attitude, there is also evidence that you have exhibited a certain – we'll call it "creativity" – with your expenses claims.'

My mouth fell open. '*Excuse* me?'

'Just a moment.' Luke riffled through some papers. 'Here we are. Yeah, on no less than two occasions you have submitted hotel receipts that include mini-bar expenses.'

'Can I see those, please?' I said in a remarkably calm voice. The pages swam in front of my eyes.

Gary Newbit's bottles of water.

'Is something funny?' asked Luke.

'You're having me on, aren't you? Fiddling expenses with three bottles of water?'

'Company fraud is no laughing matter, yang lidy,' barked Max. 'It might start with water and before you know it you're claiming all-expenses-paid holidays to the Bahamas with strawberry daiquiris and exotic lovelies with coconut oil . . .'

Max disappeared into a Bahamian-based reverie.

'I paid for them myself!'

'Not before attempting to pass them off as expenses,' said Luke. 'You know the policy. We have no option but to conclude that you were attempting to defraud the company. Then again, on the twelfth of January, you charged a taxi fare from Heathrow to Greenwich—'

'It was three o'clock in the morning—'

'Just last week, you claimed dinner for two in Glasgow. I have it on good authority that you dined alone.'

'You – you – I—'

'You can make all the excuses you want,' said Luke. 'However, you should consider this your first formal warning.'

Something about the way he worded it . . .

'*First* formal warning?' I said slowly. 'Should I be expecting my second any time soon?'

'Well,' said Luke after a pause. 'I suppose that's really down to you.'

39

After the meeting I fled back to the Maze. Jed had an answer for everything – well, ninety-seven per cent of most things. Maybe he could make sense of what had just happened. But he was nowhere in evidence.

I tracked him down to level minus two, but he was not alone. These days, Jed and Chanelle were like a pair of Siamese twins joined at the groin. I always felt uncomfortably like I was intruding.

'Hey!' said Jed when he saw me; then, looking at my face: 'Oh. What happened?'

I shook my head. Feeling perilously close to tears, I excused myself to order coffee and discipline the wobblies.

Chanelle appeared to be licking Jed's ear when I returned. I was surprised her tongue didn't reappear out the other one. I gave a discreet cough.

'So I gather the appraisal didn't go well,' said Jed, pushing Chanelle off.

I swallowed. 'Not really,' I said. 'It was an ambush. Luke and Max – he asked Max to sit in on it – they . . . my appraisal form . . . it was awful. According to Luke, I have no initiative, no . . . no people skills . . . basically, he said I can't manage my projects.'

'But that's ridiculous!' said Jed. 'You manage PL's

biggest clients! Didn't you close more projects last year than any other PM?'

'I know! I tried to argue – it didn't make any difference. Luke just lost it ... wild, staring eyes; throbbing forehead ...'

Although now that I thought about it, and putting the dramatic embellishment to one side for a moment, Luke had only ever given the impression that he was thoroughly enjoying himself.

'He terrorised me, called me names ...'

'He did?' Jed's mouth set in a hard line.

'Er, not exactly, no. Actually, I called him names. Well, just one.'

'What?'

'Mange head.'

'It's an accurate description.' Jed nodded. 'Although probably not recommended that you call your manager names in front of the Director.'

'I know, I know ... but he goaded me into it ... he was so smug, and all "Olivia, you hardly expect me to review each point, bitch". Okay, he didn't say bitch.'

Tears were flowing freely down my face by this point and I fumbled at the napkin dispenser. The napkins supplied by PL were only slightly more absorbent than laminated plastic, but they would have to do.

'Then he issued a formal warning—'

'*What?*' said Chanelle, looking up from debriefing Jed's erogenous zones.

'Luke said I tried to defraud the company because I cuh-claimed three bottles of water and a tuh-tuh-taxi fare to expenses.'

'And did you?' asked Chanelle.

'Did I what?' I blew my nose loudly.

'Claim the water and taxi fare?'

'Yes, but—'

'It hardly justifies a warning, Chanelle,' said Jed.

'There were extenuating circumstances in both cases,' I mumbled, rubbing a knot of tension in my forehead with the heel of my hand.

'Hey, don't do that,' said Jed gently. He reached over and removed my hand, then tucked it around my mug.

'What are you going to do?' asked Chanelle.

'Nothing I *can* do,' I said. 'If I resign now—'

'It looks like you *have* done something wrong,' said Jed.

'Exactly.' I shrugged helplessly.

40

That weekend, the conversation with Luke and Max churned round and round in my head. Both protagonists made guest appearances in my dreams, which quickly segued into nightmares. As soon as I'd banished one thought, three more popped out of a neuron or scurried up a synapse.

Sometimes I had difficulty breathing. I found myself gulping for air, fighting the tight band encircling my chest, trying desperately to fill my lungs.

The tide of panic was at my nostrils.

The confrontation with Luke and Max had distressed me on a deeply personal level. It may be sad, but I *was* my job. There was little else in my life; no hobbies apart from a mild obsessive-compulsive disorder; no extra-curricular courses; no significant others of any species.

So Luke's vicious, brutal and – I felt – unprovoked attack on my ability and integrity was about more than my professional prowess. It was about *me*. My character, my personality, my contribution to the human race.

I tried to reason away my feelings. It's not as if I were exactly happy at PL. It was only a job – and after all, I was actively looking for another. And let's face it; I would opt for lying on a sofa contemplating life, love, the universe and the cracks on my ceiling over work any day. It's not as if I had been fired.

But what became apparent as the weekend wore on was: it just didn't make sense. None of it. Very little of what Luke charged was relevant or strictly accurate.

Or was I in denial?

No, something smelled fishier than Molly Malone's bloomers.

The first thing that struck me on Saturday, as I energetically delinted my jumpers, was:

1) There was no valid reason for Luke's vindictiveness.

He hadn't caught me in bed with his best friend. I hadn't transmitted any manner of venereal disease. I hadn't slagged off his mother or earned more money than him or withheld sexual favours or committed any other traditional relationship-related crime.

Obviously, there can be any number of reasons for a break-up, but I just couldn't identify anything that might have led up to it. People have occasionally seen fit to mention that I have an annoying tendency to interrupt people mid-sentence with 'No, but—' or 'Yes, but—', and my obsessive need to polish can be a bit wearing, especially to those who aren't used to it. And apparently I chew really loudly; my molars perpetrate a *squelch!*-type sound effect.

But I'd always eaten carrots well away from Luke.

In summary, I really truly honestly felt that I hadn't done anything to inspire such passionate hatred.

Later that day, as I was cataloguing my DVD collection – cross-referencing movies by genre, running length, actors, year, languages (in case I ever learnt Spanish), and special features – it occurred to me that:

2) It was planned.

Luke had stitched me up even before the fateful trip to Glasgow. That awful appraisal form that had me on record as being a poor problem solver with humourless decision-making abilities had been submitted the week *before* we'd split up, while we were still enjoying a relatively happy albeit uninspired relationship complete with foot rubs and cute little in-jokes. In other words, before he went all psycho killer fafafafa fafafafafaafaa.

So there was more to this than Luke simply taking the break-up badly.

It was late on Sunday evening, while I plunged the sink (preventive maintenance), my memory perhaps jogged by the stench emanating therefrom and a particularly loud gurgle, that I remembered:

3) Max sitting by enjoying the show.

I'd kept expecting him to leap to my defence. After all, I'd worked for him for just under two years, and before Luke arrived on the scene Max himself had conducted my appraisals. Apart from the odd difference of opinion, they had generally featured glowing reviews with lush superlatives.

During Luke's rant, my subconscious had kept thinking: any minute now. Any moment, Max will bristle to his feet, and thunder: 'Your honour, I *object*! This employee is being unjustly accused. I personally can vouch for her unimpeachable character, her integrity, and her sense of humour.'

But he just sat there, nodding his head when Luke took the stage and shaking it when I managed to get a word in edgeways.

Yet while all this seethed about my head, a question remained unanswered.

Why would Luke want to bury me?

Why?

There was still a part of me that said, 'You're over-reacting. This is crazy.'

But wild and all as it was, the more I thought about it the more logical it seemed. (Although according to Luke's appraisal, my ability for logical/lateral thought was 'poor'.)

I was being set up, although for what I didn't know.

I had no idea what to do about it.

41

Despite my fresh resolve to part company with my company, I was anxious not to let my clients down. However, Drusilla had other plans. My laptop had contracted a severe case of multiple personality disorder.

On Monday morning she greeted me with threatening messages in Taiwanese, variations of which popped up at random over the next hour. Then, craftily waiting until I was just about to save a document, she had a spectacular meltdown and rebooted.

A trick she repeated at will.

Drusilla was but the start of my worries. Disregarding for the moment my decomposing career, my unrequited love for my colleague, my wholly requited loathing of my other colleague, my ailing laptop, and my stagnant life, I suspected that Chanelle and I had fallen out.

For the last week she had been a permanent fixture in our cubicle, perched on Jed's desk crossing her legs and adjusting her Wonderbra. Lipstick-encrusted polystyrene cups inflicted caffeine rings on my desk and I was frequently required to prise my Filofax out from under her bum. On Monday morning, I had to put Graeme on hold and ask her to stop giggling after he asked if I was in a brothel.

Chanelle and Jed exchanged a look that spoke of my unreasonable behaviour and their mutual desire to rip each other's clothes off.

Recently I had been experiencing a compelling urge to slap Chanelle extremely hard, preferably employing a blunt object. This inspiration was largely motivated by jealousy – although being self-aware didn't help much. I was ashamed to entertain such lemony thoughts about my two best friends.

Late that afternoon Jed excused himself to go to the bathroom. There was a protracted, tearful yet hopeful goodbye.

Sorry. That was unnecessarily catty – an involuntary meow.

But I mean really. It was as if he was going off to war instead of twenty paces down the corridor.

Sorry, sorry.

While I tried to coax Drusilla into recovering the file she'd just annihilated, Chanelle sat in Jed's chair throwing her hair around and doodling 'Chanelle Marshall' on a Post-it note.

'Livvie,' she said. 'Can I have a word?'

'Have a whole sentence,' I said, pushing away from Drusilla. 'I'm feeling generous.'

'I was wondering if you'd swap cubicles with me.'

'Oh! Oh. What, you mean . . . ?'

'I could move in here with Jed and you could have my desk. I mean, if that's okay with you. It's no problem if you don't want to, I'll completely understand. I just thought . . .'

'Have you talked to Jed about this?'

'No, not yet. I thought I'd talk to you about it first.'

'Well, that's very good of you,' I said. 'I'd like to think about it a while, if you don't mind.'

'What's there to think about?' asked Chanelle, applying lip liner without the aid of a mirror.

'Well . . . lots of things really. I . . . well, I like it here. And I'd be sharing a cubicle with Nigel.'

'Hey!' said Nigel from the other side of the partition.

'Hi, Nigel. It's not that I don't like Nigel . . . it's just that . . . well, I'm afraid I'd maim him.'

'I don't think anyone would mind that,' said Chanelle.

'I *say*! Fack off!'

'Although many aspects of it are appealing, I'd have an issue with the jail time and lesbian sex,' I said.

'Girlie action!' exclaimed Nigel, head popping up over the partition.

'You'd be closer to the window.'

'Chanelle, I work closely with Jed . . .'

'So you're saying no?'

'Well, not exactly . . . kind of.'

'Kind of?'

'Okay, yes. I mean, yes: no.'

'I see.'

'Okay then.'

'Good.'

'Grand.'

'Fine.'

Just then Jed reappeared in the cubicle and practically rebounded off the tension.

'What's up?' he asked.

'Liv and Chanelle are fighting over you!' chirped Nigel. 'It was just getting interesting, although there's never a mud-filled wrestling ring when you need one.'

'Usher, why don't you go and stick your tie in the shredder again?' I suggested. Nigel's head tossed and disappeared.

'What's going on?' asked Jed.

'Nothing,' said Chanelle and I simultaneously.

'Nothing,' repeated Chanelle.

On her way out of the cubicle, she crumpled up the Post-it note and hurled it in the bin.

'You going to tell me what that was all about?' asked Jed.

'No.' I turned back to my computer.

Drusilla gave a vapid *pop!* and the screen went blank.

'*Oh for fuck's sake!*' I bellowed. 'This piece of crap laptop! Bollocky bollocking bunches of bollocked bollocks!'

I picked up the machine and shook it until it rattled.

'Yeah, that'll sort it out. Still having computer problems?'

'Hail O Great Master of the Understatement! I salute you.'

'Give it here. I'll check it out this evening. Sounds like a virus – although I'd be surprised if it was. Your security software is up to date, isn't it? Have you been visiting dodgy websites? When was the last time you did a reinstall?'

'Yes, no, and what was the last question? Oh, just before Christmas. Six months ago. It's only been seriously banjaxed for the last few weeks.'

'Leave it with me.'

42

The noise that woke me wasn't the alarm. It was still dark. No, hang on – my eyes were shut.

I prised open an eyelid and squinted at the clock. 06:22:36. It *was* still dark.

My phone was inflicting the insistent ringing. I picked it up. 'Bleh.'

It is usually midday before I can construct a coherent sentence.

'Good morning,' said a familiar voice. 'This is your wake-up call.'

'Thanks,' I mumbled, and replaced the receiver. The phone rang again almost immediately.

'Oo is this?' I groaned.

'It's Jed,' said Jed patiently.

'*Oo?*'

'Jed. Jed Marshall?' he said when there was no response from my end. 'You obviously don't remember me but we've met once or twice. I work for Puttock Leavitt – you might have heard of it, big accountancy firm. We share a cubicle—'

'Jed. Wha' d'want?'

'I need to talk to you. Meet me at the Coffee Spot in half an hour.'

'Why, what—'

But he had hung up.

It normally takes me as long to apply eyeshadow, but forty-five minutes later I entered London Bridge station at a trot. Jed was already at the Spot. He looked like he'd been there a while, huddled deep in his leather jacket before the ravaged remains of a cappuccino.

'Jed,' I gasped. 'This had better be good.'

'Morning, Livvie. I'm fine, thanks. Although I have a slight rash on my left ear. Could be aural syphilis. And you?' He grinned wearily.

'Grand,' I muttered.

Jed looked exhausted; dark circles underscored his eyes and his face was darkened with stubble.

He'd never looked more gorgeous.

Although recently I'd thought that same thing every time I looked at him. I couldn't believe there had ever been a time when my heart hadn't skipped a beat in Jed's presence, my salivary glands sprung into overtime at the sight of him and a thrill skittered down my back.

'Sit,' he ordered, pushing a chair out with his foot. 'What are you drinking?'

'Is it too early for Jack Daniel's?'

Jed went to forage for drinks and returned with two lattes along with sugar packets, napkins and plastic spoons.

'You've got a problem,' he said.

'That's a gross underestimation,' I groused, stirring my coffee with little enthusiasm. 'I have no friends, my career is terminally ill, I hadn't time to even put on mascara this morning and I'm bloody ravenous—'

'Let's discuss one problem in particular,' interjected Jed before I could get on to my childhood and issues with my parents. 'Your computer.'

'What about my computer?'

'I found something.'

'Found something?' I repeated stupidly. 'What?'

'Keyword logging software.'

The cold clammy hand of doom tickled my innards.

'Keyword logging . . . but someone has to install—'

'Yeah. And we have to assume that whoever it was has been collecting all the data you type into your computer.'

'No. No. That's impossible.'

Maybe if I denied it, it wouldn't be true.

'Unfortunately not. You know what this means?'

'Yes.' My heart was hurling itself against my ribcage. 'Someone has all my usernames and passwords . . . oh, sweet Jesus!'

'You've got administrative access to your client's servers,' said Jed.

'So they could . . .'

'Access the system directories of all your active clients,' confirmed Jed.

My chest felt tight and a cold sweat prickled my hairline.

'Jed!' I gasped. 'I can't breathe . . . and there's no feeling in my toes. I think . . . Jed, I think . . . I'm having a stroke! Oh my God! I've lost the power of speech!'

'Livvie, I can still hear you,' snapped Jed, exasperated. 'Listen, sweetcheeks, you'll have to postpone your panic attack a while. This is serious.'

'How long? I mean, how long has it been on my computer?'

His voice came as if from a distance. 'It seems to have been installed at 03:40 hours on 24 April. Can you remember where you were at that time?'

What was he talking about? I could barely remember what I had for dinner last night.

'Let me see,' I said. In my head my voice sounded

high and squeaky. 'I can't recall *exactly*, but I was either face down in a flowerbed, or tucked up snugly in bed dreaming of penis-shaped vanilla ice cream coated with thick, creamy Belgian chocolate. Milk chocolate, not dark. What the fuck do you think? It was weeks ago! Of course I don't remember—'

And then something nibbled at the corner of my memory.

Luke hunched furtively over my laptop, his face fluorescing grey in the darkness.

'Oh, shite,' I whispered.

'What?'

'Luke,' I said bleakly. 'He sometimes checked his e-mail on my computer. One night . . . it must have been mid-April because it was after you . . . shortly after you . . . we . . . the Wine Cellar.'

I stopped to gather my thoughts, but they were not cooperating.

'It was really late . . . I woke up . . . Luke had my laptop. He was in the bathroom . . . I thought it was a bit strange . . . I didn't see what he was doing. I thought he was just downloading porn, but he must have been . . .'

'Yes, he must've been.'

'How screwed am I?'

'On a scale of one to ten? Pretty fucking screwed.'

I was about to be a hell of a lot more so because I sensed Jed's question coming like the stench preceding the Grim Reaper.

After an ominous pause: 'How did he access your computer?' he said softly.

Shite!

'He had my password,' I whispered.

'Well, you're in more trouble than I thought,' said Jed grimly. 'What the fuck were you thinking?'

'What—'

'You gave him your *password*?'

'He was my boyfriend! I never thought—'

'You certainly didn't. What a fucking stupid thing to do.'

'What are *you* getting so stroppy about?' I snarled, anger fuelled by panic and guilt.

'Well, just for a start, you've implicated *me*! In case you'd forgotten, I'm responsible for PL's system security—'

'Oh come on, it's not as if you care. You're always late for meetings, you sit around slagging off the company—'

'Don't pretend to understand me! You don't know anything. If you did you would know . . .' Jed trailed off.

'Know what?'

'Nothing,' he muttered.

'Know *what*?'

'Drop it,' he growled.

We fell silent, neither of us looking at the other. At least, when I stole a glance at Jed he certainly wasn't looking at me, but I can't vouch for the other ninety per cent of the time.

'Jed,' I whispered. 'What am I going to do?'

'Right, first things first,' said Jed, suddenly brisk. I could have cried with gratitude. My knight in shining armour! He had a plan.

'Yes,' I prompted.

'I need a fresh coffee.'

'Oh.'

Jed leaned across the table and took my face in his hands. 'Don't worry. We'll work something out, okay?'

I nodded dumbly.

'Hello,' said a voice. 'What's going on here?'

It was Chanelle, accusation written in every taut line.

'Nothing,' said Jed, dropping my face like it was red-hot – which admittedly it was. He got out of his seat and tried to kiss her, but she ducked her head and he got a mouthful of hair.

'Baby, Liv and I are working on something. Can I catch up with you later?'

'Working,' said Chanelle, in the sort of tone you'd use to say: "Horseshit."

'Yes. Working,' said Jed, in the sort of tone you'd use to say: 'How dare you question my integrity? Woman, witness at first hand the full force of my devastating masculine chill.'

'I'll see you in a while,' he said more gently.

Chanelle twirled so viciously she drilled a stiletto hole in the ground. Then she stalked off.

'Oh, God,' I moaned, dropping my head into my hands. 'Can my life get any worse?'

'I don't know. Are you scheduled for rectal surgery?'

'No.'

'Well then . . .'

'Will Chanelle be okay?'

'Yeah. I'll make it up to her later. By the way, she told me you refused to swap cubicles.'

'I didn't really refuse as such—'

'But you didn't agree. Why?'

I looked up into his face, which was studiedly blank.

'I didn't want to share a cubicle with Nigel,' I stuttered. 'So what about that coffee? I'll get it. By the way . . . I'm sorry about . . . about what I said earlier.'

'Forget it. I'm sorry too.'

'I'm *really* sorry.'

'It's an apology, Anderson, not a fucking contest.'

'You're right, you're right.' I stole a glance at him. 'Sorry.'

Jed looked as if he wanted to smack me, and then he laughed. I managed to return a wobbly grin before going to the counter.

'I was thinking,' I said when I returned. 'About my computer. The first thing to do is remove that software.'

'You don't think Wylie is going to notice?'

'I don't really give a damn whether he—'

'Well, you should.' Jed leaned forward, resting his elbows on his knees. 'Listen, Liv. Luke Wylie is a nasty piece of work—'

'You're telling me!'

I was well aware that Luke was not just a prick. He was a lying, cheating, immoral, fraudulent scumbag of the most slime-ridden lice-crawling proportions. (Actually, 'prick' just about covers that, but it just seems too ineffectual, if you know what I mean.)

'You don't know the half of it,' said Jed. 'Eleven years ago, three directors of Banco del Uruguay embezzled funds from their employer. The bank brought charges against them. Since no legal precedent had been established for that particular brand of scam, they walked.'

'What has this got to do with Luke?' I asked, although a nasty suspicion lurked in the pit of my gut.

'He was one of the directors.'

'That's impossible,' I said. Luke's apprenticeship with Banco del Uruguay hadn't featured in his résumé. Although, the more I thought about it, the more frankly inevitable it seemed. 'How do you know?'

'Er – I did a Google search on Wylie when you started dating him.'

'Why didn't you tell me about this earlier?'

'Would you have listened?'

'Well . . . are you sure it's the same person? There must be thousands of Luke Wylies out there—'

'It's him. Luke Damien Wylie.'

I swallowed.

'Livvie, you don't go secretly installing keyword logging software on someone's computer because you're bored or there's nothing on at the cinema. There's a reason Luke wants access to your client systems.'

'But *what*?'

'I have no idea. But I can't imagine it's good news for you.'

'So what – should I confront him?'

'No! We need to understand what his game is first. If you know the enemy and know yourself, you need not fear the result of a hundred battles.'

'Eh?'

'Sun Tzu, *The Art of War*. Great book, you should read it sometime.'

'I'll be sure to make that my number one priority—'

'We need to formulate a plan here.'

'Okay. How about I run away to Mexico? I could disguise myself as a sheep—'

'Look. The first thing to do is get rid of those bugs on your computer—'

'But you said—'

'I know what I said. We just have to do it in a way that means Wylie doesn't suspect anything.'

'How about I say my computer crashed and I had to reinstall it?'

'That would work. You'd have to act like everything's normal.'

' "Hot diggity dog, my laptop's crashed. I'm going to have to reinstall it. Hell and tarnation." Like that?'

'Yes, but it would be better if you didn't impersonate the Lone Ranger. Then we'll check all your client systems to see if anything is out of order.'

'Like what?'

'I'm not sure. My guess is Wylie's stealing data, in which case there might be some unusual activity in the log files. If that's what he's up to, then unfortunately the damage has probably been done. It's also going to be a bugger to prove. But I can't think of any other reason he'd want your log-on details.'

'But Jed, that doesn't make sense. I only have access to client executable directories – not the data centres.'

Jed blew out his cheeks. 'Well then, I don't know. But at least it's a starting point.' After a pause, he continued ominously: 'There's something else.'

'What?'

'I think Max knows about this.'

'Max? No. No, no, no.' But Jed had only put into words what I had been thinking all weekend.

'Yeah. Think about it, Livvie. He hired Luke – when you were the obvious choice for Projects Director. Then he gave you a raise when it looked like you might resign—'

'I'm a v-valued member of BSS—'

'Not on the strength of your recent appraisal.'

'But . . . if he knew, he would have stopped Luke—'

'Not if Wylie was following his orders.'

'I suppose it would – it would explain why he accepted what Luke said, even though he knows me better.'

'He may not know you better.'

I paused a moment to let that sink in. 'But there's nothing linking the pair of them . . . is there? I mean, Max is a corporate man, been with PL nearly thirty years, if you include his stint with BSS. But Luke—'

'I know. I can't figure it out.'

44

It was roughly three o'clock in the morning and I felt about as grizzled as Jed looked. The desk lamp bathed us in a conspiratorial glow, but the rest of the Maze was blacker and bleaker than a coalmine in hell.

Jed pushed away from his laptop and slouched so far down in his chair he was practically sitting on the floor.

'This is hopeless, isn't it?' I said.

'Hopeless?' he said. 'Oh, I don't know. Disheartening: yes; unpromising: undoubtedly; calamitous: quite possibly. But *hopeless*? You've obviously never attended one of Max's budget meetings. That's the true definition of despair.' Jed had obviously hit his seventh wind.

We had spent nine hours wading through my clients' system directories and turned up nothing. Unfortunately we had no idea what we were looking for, so it was like looking for straw in a haystack: a particular cereal plant of an exact length of a specific DNA profile – oh, and we'd only recognise it if we found it.

Depressingly, we'd reviewed exactly three client systems so far: comparing directory contents to the master list, running executables and combing through log files – an exercise only marginally less tedious than reading a telephone directory while paint dries.

I was haunted by the thought that we had missed something.

Even though it had seemed like all the pieces of the puzzle were falling into place, I now wondered whether we were trying to force a round piece into a square hole.

'You need a break,' Jed observed. 'How about some leftover pizza?'

'Tempting, but no thanks.'

He scrunched up a half-eaten slice of Pepperoni Supreme and bit into it.

'Mm, tasty,' he said around a mouthful of congealed cheese. 'Perfect room temperature. Sure you don't want some?'

'Would you eat *anything*?'

'No. I won't touch mushrooms, olives or Styrofoam.'

'Well, at least you have some standards.'

Jed unfurled himself from his seat and engaged in a prolonged stretch. His shirt tugged out of his trousers and for a breathtaking moment the lean plane of his stomach was on view: two sharp ridges flanking a rope of hair that increased in determination before disappearing behind his belt.

I imagined slipping my fingers down the gap between his big man-buckle and his stomach, then sliding lower . . .

My libido woke up with a great roar: '¡Ay caramba! That muchacho ees mucho bueno and hotter than a spicy tamale! ¡Arriba!'

(Don't ask me why my libido sounds like Speedy Gonzales channelling Errol Flynn at the height of his horny powers – I have no idea.)

Jed dropped his arms and the stunning vista disappeared.

'Hey, Space Cadet.' He waved a hand at me.

'What? Oh, right.'

I dragged my eyes away from his midriff and refocused on the screen, scrolling down the contents of Gragnoc's executable directory. I was so exhausted that the computer screen shimmered like a mirage. It took my brain a while to catch up with my eyes.

But something wasn't right.

I couldn't quite make out what it was at first.

Line by line, I scrolled back up the screen and consulted the master file list.

And there it was.

'Jed. Look. Here.' I pointed at the screen. 'This file is smaller than the same one in the master copy. See? Fifty-three megabytes. It has a different timestamp too.'

Jed leaned over my chair, one hand on the back and the other on my desk. He was so close I caught the echo of his aftershave and something else, possibly l'Eau de Hunk.

'Let me see.' He deftly wheeled me out of the way. 'It's a program file,' he said. 'Modified by user OANDERSON on the fifth of May. File name indicates it's an accounting application.' He keyed in a flurry of commands.

'What are you doing?'

'Copying the file to your hard drive,' said Jed distractedly. 'Then we tickle it and find out exactly what sort of beast it is.'

While Jed was occupied, I went to tickle the coffee machine. When I returned, Jed had advanced deep into command line territory. Not wanting to interrupt him, I scanned the remaining client systems for the rogue file and double-checked those we had already reviewed.

All other client files were in order.

Long after his coffee had gone cold, Jed swung round to face me and said: 'It's a Trojan.'

'What?'

'A Trojan.' I heard the rasp of stubble as he ran his hand over his jaw and around to knead the back of his neck. 'A file that appears to be a valid application, but—'

'I know what a Trojan is, Marshall. What type of virus is it? Security disabler? Denial of service?'

'No. This one's destructive. Think of it as a ticking time bomb. When it detonates, it'll wipe out all of Gragnoc's system files. It will also affect data files accessed by EnTire – I'm not sure to what extent yet.'

I paused to let the full horror percolate.

'Destructive,' I said stupidly. 'But . . . but . . . why hasn't Luke activated it? Oh.' I answered my own question. 'The system hasn't gone live yet.'

'That's right. I think you'll find this is timed for maximum impact. When's the system launch date?'

'Fourth of June. Monday week.'

'File is set to activate on the fifth.'

'But . . . but . . . I don't understand. *Why?* Why would Luke want to sabotage his own client?'

'I don't know. But you can bet your career and patootie fuzz with your eternal soul thrown in as guarantee that Wylie and Feshwari stand to gain from it. The only question is *what*. Have you any idea?'

'No, none.' When I shook my head my brain rattled. 'So when this file triggers, it's going to be—'

'Carnage,' said Jed with a small amount of morbid relish. 'The EnTire system handles all company processes, so everything will be buggered. Orders lost, shipments not sent, payments up Stool Creek.'

'In a company like Gragnoc, even a system outage of a few hours would cost millions—'

'In this case, you're talking about *days*.'

'What the hell are you looking so happy about?'

'Livvie, this is much better than I expected. You see? The situation is containable. We have plenty of time to address the problem—'

'Two weeks is hardly plenty of time—'

'But it's enough.'

'Oh!' I had just thought of something.

Jed had replaced my hard drive as planned, falsely advertising it as a reinstall. Although we had considered changing my log-in details at the same time, we decided that such action rather broadcasted the message: 'Hey, Wylie! You big white-collar crim! You're busted! Punk.'

'But Jed, my system access details are still the same. Luke can still log on as me. He could still—'

'Relax, babycakes.' Jed yawned. 'It's four forty in the morning. Luke's not likely to be doing anything apart from maybe Rosie Palm and her five sisters.'

'But—'

'No butts – or any other naughty bits for that matter. I don't know about you, but I'm going home.'

45

The following day – well, technically speaking, that same morning – I arrived at the office late.

'Hold the lift!'

A cadaverous man stared impassively at me from within the halo of scummy yellow light. He looked vaguely familiar.

'Hey! Excuse me! Can you hold—' I thrust an arm between the doors just before they clamped shut. 'Ow!'

The doors stuttered open again and I slipped inside, panting. The occupants of the lift glowered, as if the five-second delay had ruined their whole day – if not the rest of their lives. I felt their eyes scorch holes in the back of my neck.

'Thanks a million,' I said, rubbing my wrist.

The man remained immobile, but his eyes flicked over me. 'You expect everyone to wait for you?' he enquired.

'It was only five seconds!'

'It was nine seconds. There are four people in this lift, collectively resulting in thirty-six seconds of valuable company time, wasted.'

He was long and angular with teeth like an evolved vampire – sharp and pointy and lots of. Now I recognised him. It was James Henderson, last seen foraging around

Janine Clifford's corset at the BSS Christmas dinner.

Under normal atmospheric conditions – i.e. average humidity with light westerlies and the occasional sunny spell – I would have thought twice or even more about debating the matter with one of PL's senior partners. However, I was in the general vicinity of Not Giving a Shit. I had bigger things to worry about, what with potentially bankrupting my client and taking a long vacation at Her Majesty's expense. Anyway, the odds of his picking me out of a lineup were slim. But mainly, he was wrong.

'Well,' I said, 'I would have spent five minutes waiting for another lift, so you've actually *saved* four minutes and twenty-four seconds.'

'At a conservative estimate, my time is a hundred times more valuable than yours. Calculated accordingly, in actual matter of fact that results in fifteen minutes wasted in totality.'

'Actually ten minutes and twenty-seven seconds if you offset it against my five minutes and include the rest of the occupants. Oh, won't you excuse me? This is my floor. Great chatting to you.'

Luke caught me sidling out.

'What sort of time do you call this?' he demanded.

Rage surged up like flaming magma. I hated him, hated him with every fibre of my being, plus some of the fibres of Max's manky old nylon-mix sweater.

'I call it nine twenty-seven,' I snapped. 'Why, what time do you call it?'

'You look like shit.'

'That's probably because the sight of you makes me nauseous. Wreaks hell on my complexion.'

'Watch it, Anderson.'

'Can you specify what I am supposed to be watching?

Because if it's you, I might spew. Oh! That rhymes.'

Fun as it was standing around trading insults, I was experiencing a rising compulsion to give him a close-up of *my* Rosie Palm and her five sisters in fist formation. I was in absolutely no mood for Luke Wylie. I was still struggling to reconcile myself with the fact that he was trying to ruin not only my career but also my life.

Fucking exes.

With a flap of the bat-coat, I made good my escape with the final word.

When I reached the cubicle, Chanelle was sitting on Jed's desk. Her arms were folded across her front and her legs plaited around each other. She and Jed were engaged in lock-jawed conversation, which ceased abruptly when I entered.

'Hi, Chanelle,' I said cautiously.

'Hi, Liv.'

'How are you?'

'Good, and you?'

'Grand, thanks.'

'Glad to hear it.'

'Good.'

'Lovely.'

Still a bit of tension there then. Although now that Jed had joined me in the doghouse, at least I had some company.

While Drusilla powered up, I tried to catch Jed's eye. It was a tricky manoeuvre given that he didn't appear to be throwing it in the first place.

Michelle came into our cubicle brandishing an envelope. 'Hi guys,' she said. 'It's Michael's birthday next week—'

'Who?' asked Chanelle.

'Michael Carradene. He's a risk analyst with ISRM.'

I'd never heard of the man. 'I've started a collection for a present.'

Both Chanelle and I dutifully donated a fiver while Michelle produced a list and pencilled in the amount next to our names.

'Jed?' Michelle shook the envelope at him.

'No thanks.'

'Sorry?'

'Count me out.'

I risked a tentative smile at Chanelle and was cheered when she returned it. It was more of a gravity-defying lip-twitch than a full fang-baring grin, but the overall effect was undoubtedly positive.

'But . . .' stuttered Michelle.

'I'm not donating my hard-earned cash to buy someone I don't know a crappy present he'll never use.'

'If you don't give money, then you're not signing the card,' she said tightly.

'You think Mick'll be gutted if my signature's not there? Well, call me if he's threatening suicide and I'll help talk him down off the roof. Otherwise I'll pass.'

I felt a faint itching sensation; Max must be in the vicinity. Sure enough, next minute he catapulted himself into our cubicle.

I was starting to feel like a sardine, complete with fishy flavour.

'What's the problem, Mr Marshall?' enquired Max. 'Couple of quid's hardly going to break the bank, is it? Buy the man a birthday present. Good for morale.'

'Believe it or not, I have better things to spend my salary on than a birthday present for – what was his name again?' Jed asked Max.

'Er . . .'

'Michael Carradene,' supplied Michelle before Max

had fully availed himself of the opportunity for embarrassment.

'Yeh, yeh. Michael,' said Max. 'Nice bloke.'

'I'm sure he's a treasure,' said Jed.

Max bestowed an ineffectual glower on him. 'All right, all right. Now, everyone. Can I have ya attention please?' He rocked on his toes and clasped his hands portentously behind his back. 'Annual staff barbecue at my place. Sunday week. You lot up for it? Free beer: one can each. Know what they say: always grasp a gift horse by the horns. HAH!'

'I'd love to, but I spend Sundays fulfilling my potential,' said Jed.

Max's face darkened. 'Not much of a team player, are ya, Mr Marshall?' he snapped. 'How about the rest of ya?'

'I'm attending a funeral.' I adopted a mournful expression.

'Miss Fyffe?'

'Sorry, but I have an urgent appointment with the vet. My cat is having her teeth flossed.'

'How about you?' barked Max, rounding on Michelle. She did a fair impression of an electrocuted rabbit caught in headlights.

'Oh, er, ah,' said poor Michelle. 'Erm, I think . . . I . . . have . . . I, I . . . yes, I'll come.'

'Good! Good! Well, haven't you people got work to do? HAH!' he shouted by way of goodbye and charged off to sniff out reckless waste of toner or random stapling. Having pondered his last question, Chanelle and Michelle left soon after.

'Jed!' I whispered. 'I've had an idea! About – you know . . .'

He quirked an eyebrow at me and shook his head.

'Not here,' he mouthed and jerked his head rapidly. For a moment I thought he'd developed a nervous twitch until I realised he was indicating the fire exit.

Once on the stairwell, Jed said: 'Bit of an echo, don't you think? Someone might hear us—'

'You want to case the joint for bugs? There's nobody here, Marshall.'

Then I told him my plan. If I do say so myself, it was a model of understated elegance – although more so after Jed fine-tuned it with me. More important, there was a fair to middling chance that it might actually work. It addressed the immediate and biggest problem – protecting Gragnoc's system – although there was still nothing to link Max with Luke, or Luke to the sabotage.

There was only one problem.

Well, let's not be pessimistic here. It was more of a side effect of my plan.

A minor drawback.

A gentle hiccup.

I was going to have to tell Graeme.

46

'Listen, Graeme,' I whispered into the receiver. I extended an eyeball over the partition to check Luke or Max wasn't nearby. 'I need to speak to you about something.'

'Wha's on yer mind?'

'Not over the phone. I'll come up and see you. When are you free?'

'Hoo aboot Friday?'

'Friday's a bit late, actually.'

'It's day after tomorroa!'

'Now you mention it, how about tomorrow?'

'Must be impoartant.'

'It is.'

'Tomorroa then.'

To my surprise, Jed was vehemently opposed to my confessing the whole sordid story to my client.

'What the fuck are you thinking?' he hissed after dragging me outside. Since my computer overhaul he'd been jumpier than a flea-infested frog in a frying pan. I was strictly forbidden to discuss Gragnoc in the office. As a result, we were huddled under the pedestrian bridge on Great Maze Pond, glancing furtively over our shoulders as though we expected to be goosed by the long arm of the law any second.

'Jed, I *have* to tell Graeme. The stakes are too big. It's irrelevant that *we* think our plan is going to work. There are risks for Graeme; he needs to be fully informed of the implications. This isn't some TV show where we single-handedly hunt down the perp and drill him full of lead.'

'But Livvie – we don't even know what's going on yet! There's no compelling motive linking Max *or* Luke to the sabotage, or even to each other—'

'That doesn't reduce the risk to Graeme's company.'

'What if he doesn't believe you?'

'Well, there's a better chance he will if I tell him now. If he hears from another source he might draw his own conclusions.'

'Who's going to tell him? Livvie, *he doesn't need to know.*'

A stray newspaper wrapped itself round my leg and I kicked it absent-mindedly.

'Jed, believe me: I would *love* to avoid this particular conversation. Honest! I would prefer to discuss the man's favourite fetish with him than tell him about this mess. But this is Graeme's company we're talking about – not a Monopoly railway station! I've exposed Gragnoc to risk. Morally and ethically, it's the right thing to do.'

Jed remained stubbornly unconvinced in the face of my compelling arguments, but it didn't change anything. On Thursday I was on the early morning flight to Glasgow frantically rehearsing my speech.

Originally I thought maybe a casual, there's-no-need-to-panic sort of approach would be best:

'Yo, Graeme dude. Wassup? How've you been? Nice weather we're having. So there's a little bug in your system. Nothing to worry about. I wouldn't have bothered telling you except that I was stuck for conversation . . .'

Then I thought maybe that didn't fully convey the gravity of the situation, so I considered a more urgent declaration, along the lines of: 'ARGH! AAARGH! WAAAAAAAAAAAAAAAAAAAAAAAAARGH!'

But I didn't want to be mistaken for hysterical.

It looked like I was going to have to wing it.

I took a taxi directly to Gragnoc and managed to slip by Eileen on Reception without her noticing. She was busy picking a piece of chicken out of her teeth – or she might have been eating a buffalo wing; it was hard to tell.

My heart thumped painfully as I stood outside Graeme's office. I knocked before I could think about it further.

'Come in!'

'It's me,' I said, stepping into his office.

'Liv! Good tae see yeh.'

I was touched when he kissed me awkwardly on the cheek. A great lump formed in my throat, but I swallowed it down.

Crying was the last resort.

'Well! Whut's on yer mind? Mus' be important tae have enticed yeh oop here.'

I tried to return his smile, but my lips froze across my teeth and I realised the effect probably fell short of charming. Graeme studied my face carefully. 'All righ', lass?'

I probably wouldn't be after he'd finished with me. It occurred to me that I should have left a suicide note.

'Graeme.' My voice was husky. Clearing my throat, I tried again. 'We have a problem.'

Graeme's eyes narrowed. 'Whut sort o' proablem?' he said, suddenly sharp.

I sighed. 'Suppose I start at the beginning.'

'Aye, Ah think yeh'd better.'

Then I confessed everything.

I told him about dating Luke, about finding him hunched over my laptop in the bathroom, the appraisal, Jed checking my computer, the Trojan on Gragnoc's system. I left nothing out, although I played down the graphic sex scenes and skimmed over the gore and violence.

I finished to a charged silence. Graeme's arms were crossed, and the expression on his face chilled me right down to my spleen. As I eyed him warily, I thought that if he were Italian, Graeme would have been a hit man for the Mob.

'Yeh have proof o' this,' he said flatly.

'Only the Trojan on your system.'

'Weill then. Ah'd say yeh're in a lot o' trouble.'

I swallowed. 'Yes.'

'Ah could sue Puttock Leavitt, yeh knaw.'

I had already considered this. The way things currently stood, if Graeme pursued this course, I'd probably end up sharing a cell with a tattooed lady called Jack who restricted exfoliation to her cranium.

'You could,' I agreed. 'And I wouldn't blame you if you did. But if you do take it to court, PL will simply blame it on me. If you're lucky, Gragnoc will end up with enough damages to cover legal fees.'

'Yeh realise Gragnoc's a publicly listed company? The sort of outage yeh're talking about would be devastating. Investor confidence shattered, share price plummeting. We'll never recover. Mantis already has the edge in the market – they will kill us.'

'Well . . . hopefully it won't come to that.'

'Och aye?'

'We could deactivate the new release. Luke would still have access to it, so he wouldn't know that anyone had found out about ... well, whatever it is he's up to. If he checks, he will think nothing has changed.'

'Bu' Gragnoc needs the upgrade—'

'I know. We would install another version of EnTire on the second server, which would become the live system – essentially a replica of what is there already.'

Graeme massaged his great Mount Rushmore wedge of a jaw for several moments.

'Yeh think that will work?'

'There's no reason it shouldn't. It's technically sound. But you should be aware that with this setup you have no redundancy. In the unlikely event the primary server fails, there will be a system outage—'

'What's recovery time?'

'Seven minutes. I feel the risk is acceptable, under the circumstances. But it's your decision.'

'An' yeh'd take care o' all this?'

'Yes. My Support Manager is working on the mirrored system right now. We can have it set up by tomorrow.'

'An' yeh're teilling me Ah should jus' do nuthin'?'

'Essentially, yes.'

'All righ',' he said finally.

'In the meantime, I'll try to find out why Max Feshwari and Luke Wylie are sabotaging Gragnoc. Can you think of anything?'

'No. Ah've never met that Fishi fella an' Ah barely know Wylie.'

No clues there then.

'Weill a' least the immediate thrait has been

remuived. Doan' look so worried, lass. Eiveryone makes mistakes. An' thank yeh.'

'For *what*?' I said, astounded.

'Fer comin up here an' tellin' me. Cannae have been casy fer yeh. Yeh did weill.'

After leaving Graeme's office, I gingerly checked myself for bloodstains, broken bones or missing limbs. Apart from the occasional flesh wound, I appeared to be intact and relatively unscathed.

Previously, I had considered my continuing thriving and surviving to be a positive outcome, but now I felt almost euphoric. Even more so when, at the airport, I managed to score an upgrade.

Two hours later, ensconced in Business Class fending off caviar, I reconsidered the meeting with Graeme. The conversation hadn't gone half – or even a quarter – as badly as I'd expected. In my mind, I had built it into a great roiling mushroom cloud complete with nuclear fallout and hybrid badger-spiders with multiple flippers. Instead, it had been more like a hint of nimbus framed by a couple of pigeons. My brain rewound the conversation and played it out again: fast forwarding here, rewinding there.

Graeme clearly had no clue as to why Max and Luke were so keen to put him out of business, but something hovered portentously around the periphery of my subconscious. Every time I tried to coax it into the open, however, it skittered away.

The main difference between Business Class and

Economy is a better quality of weirdo. Undaunted by some of the most ferocious glares in my repertoire, the businessman beside me struck up a one-sided conversation.

After determining my availability for a shag (low), he produced pictures of his family holiday for my perusal. I was half-heartedly flipping through them when I came across a full glossy 4×6 photo of an aggressively unflaccid male member.

'Oh! Dear me, how did that get in there?' said the businessman with a ghastly giggle. 'That's my penis,' he continued conversationally, in the same way he might have said: 'And this is the Eiffel Tower.'

Why? Why? Why does this always happen to me? Not the willy photos, but more generally the sitting beside of freaks. Maybe I should resign myself to the fact that I attract them; that I simply have an irresistible sex appeal for losers, nutters, wasters, golfers, anyone yearning for codependency, and combinations of all the above.

'Isn't it lovely?' said my voyeur.

I wasn't really sure what to say. I mean, I didn't want to inflame – or even worse, engorge – the man.

'Very scenic,' I replied.

He didn't need any encouragement to state that a photo is just not the same as seeing it in the flesh.

I handed him back his photos.

'But you haven't seen them all!'

'I need a rest. I'm very tired.'

I pretended to fall asleep as a ruse to avoid him, but before long I really was touring the Land of Nod. It was a Daliesque landscape populated with penises, caviar and flashes of tropospheric sunlight. Just after Eileen's false eyelash made a cameo appearance as a chihuahua,

Graeme turned up in a suit of armour featuring a bright red PVC codpiece.

'The outage would be devastating,' he said. 'Investor confidence shattered, share price plummeting. Mantis will kill us – Mantis will – Mantis will—' He bent down to pat the chihuahua.

'Don't do it!' I tried to scream. 'It's not a dog! It's Eileen's false eyelash!'

The plane hit some turbulence and I was dimly aware of my head beating a brisk tattoo against the porthole window. And it was there in the half-state between waking and sleeping that the penny finally dropped with spontaneous terminal velocity. I came awake with a shock.

I marvelled at how I could possibly have missed it before.

If you've already figured it out, fair play to you. If I were wearing a hat I would take it off, but you'd really have to catch me at a wedding.

Max had shares in Mantis.

The letter I'd seen on his desk – it would explain – but no, was I getting ahead of myself? Yes but – no but – yes but – it accounted for – well, everything. The sabotage and – oh my God! – why Max had passed me over for promotion. He had hired Luke specifically. That explained why he hadn't leapt to defend me when Luke had savaged me in my appraisal – it was all part of his Master Plan.

How could I have missed it?

In my defence, can I point out that I have presented a heavily edited version of events to date, whereas I had to wade through the torrent of minutiae that adds up to what I generously call a life: the paper stapling, the conferences, the travelling, the reports, the endless meetings, the toenail clipping.

The plane had barely touched rubber to tarmac

when, under the bristling glare of a flight attendant, I switched on my mobile and called Jed.

'Livvie—'

'I've got it!'

'What's that? An exotic house pet?'

'I've figured it out. Why Luke and Max sabotaged Gragnoc.'

Jed's voice changed. 'Hang on.'

I heard the background thrum of the Maze, then a door swish open and closed.

'Where are you?' I asked.

'BSS conference room. So, tell me.'

'Max has shares in Mantis.'

'*What?*'

'Mantis and Gragnoc are the only two really big players in the concrete industry since Mantis took over Deco Concretes two years ago. Well, Max holds stock in Mantis. If Gragnoc's systems were to throw an Armageddon party—'

'Gragnoc's share price would fall—'

'And Mantis takes over the market.'

'How do you know this?'

'I saw a letter on Max's desk a while ago. It was a confirmation of shareholding or suchlike—'

'Why the fuck didn't you tell me?'

'I didn't remember until now. Something Graeme said reminded me.'

'Okay, think. Who was the letter addressed to?'

'I don't know. I was trying to read it upside down. Why?'

'It's pretty unlikely Mr Maximillian Feshwari will feature on the shareholder list. He's probably set up a skeleton company to buy shares. We need to find that letter.'

'No problem. I'll just pop round tonight, break into his house, disable his security system and crack the safe. Oh, that reminds me: I'd better stop off and buy a pair of gloves and a getaway helicopter.'

'Before you start getting all kinky, we need to think about this a bit. But Livvie, that letter would be all the evidence we need.'

'But it doesn't prove anything, surely? It only gives Max a motive, it still doesn't link the pair of them—'

'It's enough to clear you, which is the important thing. Let's concentrate on that rather than what a jury needs to convict Little and Large. We need to get our hands on that letter.'

For what was left of the week, the problem prowled around my head like a hungry predator. How the hell was I supposed to get my mitts on the shareholder letter? I had no idea where it was. Max's office at PL was unsecured, so it was most likely in a safe or filing cabinet somewhere in his home. But that was speculation.

I spent Saturday polishing the picture frames and refurbishing my CV. Despite months of rewriting, it was still duller than a six-part documentary on the life cycle of plankton, and hardly improved after three hours spent inventing achievements.

On Sunday morning, I was in no fit state to determine what godforsaken hour of the day it was when my door buzzer sounded. After a couple of exploratory blasts it reverberated jarringly around my living room, seeming to get louder and louder.

For a while I managed to successfully ignore it, but then I dimly became aware of my mobile ringing from the other side of the room.

Choosing the noise source closest to the bed, I stumbled to my feet and groped for the intercom. 'Wehbebe.'

'Good morning!' Jed's voice exploded out of the speaker, practically taking my eardrum out.

'Je. D. Whadya wan'?' I experienced a half-hearted squirm of excitement, but realistically it was too early to entertain it.

'I've come to collect you. I have planned a great escape.'

'Go 'way.'

'Open up.'

I buzzed him in and unlatched the apartment door before collapsing back into bed.

'Hey there!' Jed charged through the door. 'Come on, get up. We're going on an expedition.'

'I'm going back to sleep,' I corrected him.

'No you're not.' He strode over to the window and flung back the curtains with a flourish. It made no difference to the ambient light in the apartment.

'Jed.' I tried to muster up the Voice of Reason from the depths of a pillow. 'It's still fucking dark.'

'That's because it's early.' Jed switched on a light.

'What time is it?'

'Five o'clock. Get out of bed.'

I hadn't the energy to tell him that he'd need to apply a defibrillator at that hour of the morning.

'You have any hiking gear?' he asked, rummaging through my wardrobe.

'I live in London.'

'I'll take that as a no. Any boots? Oh, hang on – these'll do. Are they comfortable to walk in?'

He tossed a pair of ankle boots with pre-attached legwarmers on the bed.

'I can't remember.'

Jed pulled open random drawers and extracted jeans, a trendy fleece I had bought at the height of the rugged chic trend and a T-shirt that had last seen daylight in 1998 – although it was going to have to wait a couple of hours before seeing it again. Then he tugged open my lingerie drawer.

'What d'you think you're doing?' I didn't want Jed discovering my inadvertently crotchless Little Miss Naughty knickers from circa 1991.

'Picking out some underwear. Unless you'd prefer to go without, you minx. Do you have knickers for each day of the week?' he asked incredulously.

'Only some of them!'

'Jesus. Okay, these'll do.'

He deposited matching bra and knickers in turquoise and brown on my bed. The man knew his lingerie, I acknowledged grudgingly.

'Jed, why . . . what . . . I don't—'

'I thought it would be a good idea to get out of the city for a while. Clear your head.'

'My head is clear enough.'

'Stop stalling.'

While Jed retired to the kitchen to brew coffee, I resentfully showered and dressed and threw some tinted moisturiser in the general direction of my face.

'Where are we going?' I asked as we made our way downstairs.

'We're going to pay homage to the Great Outdoors.'

'Why can't we do that from here?'

Having spent most of my life in cities, I am not naturally predisposed to the countryside. The only type of wildlife I have ever associated with is of the drink, drugs and rock 'n' roll variety.

That's not to say I don't appreciate nature. Hey, there's nothing I appreciate more than a brilliant sunset in thrilling shades of orange, red and purple – provided I'm observing it from a hammock on the balcony sipping frozen margaritas. I appreciate the miracle that is life and growth, as long as it is not my waistline showing symptoms of either.

At five twenty in the morning I was in absolutely no humour to appreciate anthing at all, whether natural or synthetic. I was even failing to appreciate Jed's posterior, which will tell you how bad I was.

To my complete irritation Jed was in great form. He'd probably just got in from the Underworld and hadn't bothered going to bed at all.

'Why the frig are you so cheerful?' I said sourly.

'Lots of reasons. It's going to be a beautiful day. I'm spending it with you. We're having a picnic. We get to wear wellies. Does life get any better?'

'Yeah, at around midday,' I muttered. 'Is that thing roadworthy?' I pointed at his ancient Aston Martin.

Jed was outraged. 'Of course she's roadworthy! Have some respect, woman. This car is a classic.' He carefully polished the cracked wing mirror with his jacket sleeve.

I am ashamed to admit that, for the first couple of hours, I was not monosyllabic so much as semi-syllabic. There was also something of a grunty quality about my conversation. However, I perked up considerably after Jed pulled over at a refreshment stop and hunted down a newspaper, a herd of low-fat muffins, and a parliament of apples and bananas. And, of course, two buckets of cappuccino.

'Jed, have I ever told you what a special place in my heart you hold?' I said, falling upon a muffin and demolishing it in a very unladylike fashion.

'No. Why don't you tell me now?'

'D'you have a couple of hours to spare?' I said, spraying crumbs all over him.

'Yeah, I've got a few.'

We carried on up the M40 in companionable silence, only broken by the odd munch. The world had been waking around us for some time when Jed drove into a parking area on top of a hill and pulled me out of the car.

I was just about to ask Jed what the bloody hell I was doing standing on top of a hill when I could have been huddled in front of the car heater stuffing muffins into my face when, in a single magical moment, the sun sprang into the sky with a great beam of joy and every bird in the world burst into song at once and flowers seemed to bloom spontaneously.

All of a sudden, I understood why Judy Garland believed her dreams really would come true somewhere over the rainbow, while Julie Andrews felt compelled to enervate the hills with the sound of music and climb ev'ry mountain. If I had not been tone deaf and without the ability to make up words as I went along, I would have burst into song right then and there. And had I ever experienced any formal dance training other than half a class of Irish jigging when I was eight (the teacher was very frightening), I would have followed the Blues Brothers' advice to go loop di loo watootsie and bent over to shake my, shake my, shake my, shake my tailfeather.

But because I was feeling marginally better disposed towards him, I decided to spare Jed the trauma.

He smiled at me brilliantly. 'Wasn't it worth getting up early for this?' he asked.

'Maybe,' I conceded.

I might have been moved, but not that much.

Jed got a tarpaulin out of the boot and draped it round our shoulders. Then we spread what was left of breakfast out on the bonnet of the car and watched the sun rise.

There had been something on my mind from the moment Jed charged into my apartment.

'Jed, does Chanelle know about this?'

'What?'

'You bursting into my apartment like the Milk Tray man and whisking me off to some exotic location—'

'It's Oxfordshire, not the Bahamas.'

'You know what I mean.'

'No,' said Jed. 'I haven't told her.'

'Are you going to?'

Jed didn't answer.

I resolved not to think about it. Bit late now, anyway.

'So where are we going?' I asked when we were back in the car.

'It's a surprise.'

For a while I flicked through the paper and read out pieces of interest. Then we turned up the radio and sang along.

'I wish I could sing,' I confided.

'Right now, so do I.'

'Although I wish I had psychic abilities more.'

'How about being indestructible? I'd like to be able to regenerate.'

Two hours later, Jed turned on to a small forest road and I rolled down the window and sucked in the glorious pine fragrance.

I felt as if I hadn't breathed properly in months.

'Jed. This is . . . this is . . .'

'Isn't it?'

We wound through the forest, climbing for a while and then dropping gradually. Then Jed turned off the main track. He had to stop twice to pick branches from the road, but the Aston laboured gamely.

Finally we broke into a dappled glade where the track petered out.

When Jed turned off the engine the sudden silence was shocking.

Jed threw me a bottle of insect repellent.

'Mm, that's not bad.' I sniffed. 'Citrus. An advertising agency would describe it as having a top note of lemon, with base notes of DEET and picaridin.'

'It's better if you spray it on your hands and rub it on to your face and neck.'

'If Giorgio Armani packaged this in a minimalist bottle – preferably phallic shaped – it would leap off the shelves. Sixty pounds a pop.'

'Most likely. Right, let's go,' said Jed, clapping a floppy hat three sizes too big on my head.

'Where are we going?'

'Fishing.' He hefted a huge rucksack.

'No, really.'

'Wait and see.'

Shafts of sunlight slanted through the pine trees and I could hear hints of a distant river overlaid with piercing birdsong.

Now, unless it's to get to a bar, I've never seen the point of walking. Certainly, if there are seats free *at* the bar I have serious difficulty condoning it. So generally speaking, I would never set out to tramp aimlessly through the countryside. But as I meandered after Jed with bluebottles lazily humming in the undergrowth and butterflies dive-bombing my face, I found myself reconsidering.

It was only when the tension released its grip on my shoulders that I realised it was the first time I had relaxed for *months*.

It was a galaxy away from London.

After a long hike, we emerged from the forest on to a stretch of marshland. Fifty yards away a river chuckled busily.

'This is it,' said Jed. He offloaded the rucksack, dived in the top and emerged with the tarpaulin, which he flapped open on the ground.

'What the hell are those?' I asked as he extracted some complex-looking pulleys and sticks.

'Fishing rods,' said Jed.

'I thought you were *joking*!'

'Why would you think that? This is a great spot for trout. Rainbow mainly, but occasionally brown.'

'Er. Right.'

Jed carefully fingered through a small plastic box full of barbs and brilliant feathers.

'What are you doing?' I asked, interested despite myself.

'Selecting a lure.'

His long fingers deftly affixed a tasty-looking fly to the line.

'Here you go.' He handed one of the rods to me.

'What the hell am I supposed to do with this?'

'Catch us lunch. Come on, I'll show you. Now,' he said at the water's edge. 'You need to think like a fish.'

'Like: do my gills look fat in this? Are my scales dull?'

'Not quite. Okay, fish are very intelligent—'

'Marshall, they're *fish*. They're not building underwater nuclear reactors and plotting to take over the world.'

'That's what you think. Now, if you were a fish, where would you hang out?'

Privately I rather thought I'd be staying far away from noisy people in wellingtons brandishing fishing rods. However, I pointed to a deep spot beneath an overhanging tree on the far side of the river.

'Good choice. Well, give it a go.'

I unclipped the line and attempted to cast. I was probably a bit overenthusiastic; the lure whipped through the air and embedded itself in Jed's trousers.

'I caught one!'

Jed extracted the lure from the general region of his right buttock while I rewound the reel.

'Here, I'll show you,' he said.

He put his arms round me from behind and gripped my right wrist. His stubble brushed against my temple and my breath caught in my throat. It took full reserves of willpower not to lean back and press into him before ripping his clothes off and doing all manner of al fresco things to him.

'Reach the rod back gently . . .'

There was nothing gentle about what I wanted to do with Jed's rod. Sorry, but seriously though: you didn't think I could talk about fishing without some unsubtle smutty entendre?

'Slowly, like this . . . now, flick your wrist.'

I nearly had an orgasm. Who would have thought fishing could be so erotic? The lure dropped under the tree with a faint *plop*.

'You need to start reeling right away or the lure will get caught in the rocks,' said Jed, stepping away and leaving my legs all wobbly. 'Here, give it a go. Steady . . . that's right. Reel it in. Good.'

'Now what?'

'Do it again. Repeat until lunch.'

Jed left me and wandered off downriver. Watching him, I realised I'd been supplied with the training-wheels beginner's rod along with the *Fishing For Dummies* tutorial. Jed was in a different league altogether. He had a different type of rod which he twirled like a magician his wand, the delicate line looping and swirling, tracing complex patterns. Dreamily I fancied he was writing me secret messages in the air.

On my fourth cast I got the lure stuck under a rock. Discarding shoes and socks, I made a futile attempt to retrieve it but gave up when the water lapped playfully at my groin.

Jed manfully waded in and freed the lure. Bafflingly, he appeared to seize upon any opportunity to leap into the sub-zero waters. His theory appeared to be that the greater the suffering, the better the experience – a bit like Catholicism, only wetter and minus the angst.

It was half an hour before I could feel my toes again – and at that, only a painful tingle now and then.

Despite all this, I'm about to make a confession that might make you reconsider your opinion of me. I'm a bit nervous because it's very uncool – like admitting that your hobbies include picking fluff out of belly buttons or filling in tax returns, or you like a nip of Ovaltine before bedtime. But in the interests of full disclosure, I'll 'fess up.

I *loved* fishing.

I was at one with the universe, getting down with Mother Nature, finding my inner Earth Child. I would have hugged a tree if I hadn't worried that the rest would feel left out.

I had no idea how long I'd been there when I felt a tug on the line. For a second I thought the lure was caught again, but then there was an unmistakable wiggle.

'Jed! JED!' I roared. 'I think . . . I think I've caught something. No . . . yes . . . no . . . yes, yes it might be . . . it might be . . . it's a FISH! JE-E-ED!'

Jed threw his rod on the ground and splashed over at a gallop.

'What do I do?'

'Keep the tip down!' he instructed. 'You don't want him to break the surface because he'll flop around and spit out the hook. Keep the tension in the line.'

'Aren't I supposed to play with him?'

'What were you thinking of – a game of Monopoly?'

'Like, tire him out.'

'Not in a stream like this – he'll wrap the line round a rock.'

The rod was jerking all over the show and I was having some trouble keeping the reel taut.

Next thing, a *whale* broke the surface of the water.

'Look!' I shrieked, trying to point, but the reel whirred madly so I figured I'd better keep a grip on it.

A great chortle of pure unadulterated joy bubbled up from somewhere deep inside Jed. I stared at him in wonder – he was a different person, with the lines gone from his face and his eyes sparkling in the sunshine.

'What are you looking at me for? Over there! Make eye contact with your prey. Show him who's boss.'

'Oi! Trevor,' I addressed my unfortunate quarry, heaving on the reel. 'I'm in charge around here and don't you forget it.'

'That told him. Tip down.'

The hook must have been embedded fairly solidly in poor Trevor's mouth because I gave him every opportunity to swim away to snap at minnows another day. But after several minutes' cursing and hauling, Trevor was within wriggle distance. Jed reached into the water, plucked him out and juggled the thrashing fish up the bank.

'What a beauty! Around two – two and a half pounds, I'd guess. It's a rainbow trout – see his markings? And that pink colour? Isn't he a pretty fellow?'

Then he knocked him on the head with a large rock.

'Jesus, Jed! Wasn't that a bit vicious?'

'Did you want to eat him alive?'

'Well no, but . . .'

'Stop being such a woman.'

'I *am* a woman, in case you hadn't noticed.'

'Oh, I'd noticed.' Jed gave me a look that liquefied my insides.

He extracted a hunting knife and used the blade to pry out the hook.

'Hungry?' he said.

I wasn't sure after that display of aggression, and even less so after Jed had deftly gutted poor Trevor. Freddy Krueger could have taken lessons in horror from the man. Then Jed rubbed the skin with rock salt and packed the cavity with foliage.

'Is that grass?'

'Wild mint. Found some growing upstream.'

While Trevor grilled over a small campfire, Jed produced a bottle of white wine from his bottomless rucksack. He garnished two plates with crusty bread rolls, cream cheese, tomatoes, cucumber and lettuce.

It was quite possibly the best meal I'd ever had.

For dessert, we threaded marshmallows on twigs and melted them over the fire.

'Hey! Who ate all the marshmallows?' I said, upending the bag.

'Who what?'

'Ate all the marshmallows?'

'I have no idea.'

'*You* ate all the marshmallows.'

'That is a lie, Anderson, and completely unfounded. There is a total lack of evidence—'

'There is a total lack of marshmallows! There's the evidence!'

Later, we lay back on the mossy grass and drowsily digested. Jed's head rested on my midriff. It was a full-time job resisting the impulse to touch him: smooth his hair, run my fingertips over his eyebrows or trace the curve of his lips.

My belly gave a great gurgle, which echoed around the forest.

'Your stomach is making a meal of it,' murmured Jed. 'Can you tell it to shut up?'

'Sorry. I don't have much authority in that area.'

Jed picked up my hand and wove his fingers through mine.

I was starting to feel uncomfortable about the direction things were taking. So far I'd been able to justify Jed's using my belly as a pillow by persuading myself it was a practical arrangement. Why not rest his head on my stomach? It was soft, warm and squashy and featured an intestinal soundtrack. But this was too intimate.

'Jed. Stop.' I pushed his head off, rolled over and sat back on my heels. 'This isn't right.'

'What?' asked Jed, propping himself up on one elbow.

'This. All of it. You're going out with Chanelle.'

'Not any more.'

'What?'

'We broke up,' said Jed.

A great surge of excitement welled up, which was quickly replaced by dread.

'But . . . but . . . why?'

'We weren't right for each other,' said Jed carefully. 'And I've realised . . . well, life's pretty short. Chanelle and I . . . well, we had fun together. But there's not much point in mucking around, you know?'

'Is that what you were doing with Chanelle? Mucking around?'

'No! No, I like her too much for that. We had fun together, but we were never going anywhere. Oh, I'm sure we could have happily dated for a few months, a year – who knows? But marriage, babies – it was never going to happen. Chanelle was not for ever.'

'Oh.'

'You are.'

'Jed . . .' I said despairingly.

'Livvie, I shouldn't have gone out with Chanelle. It seemed like a good idea at the time. You were with Wylie, and I . . . well, Chanelle and I kind of fell—'

'Into bed.'

'Into a relationship. She ended up at my place after a night at the Underworld—'

'Jed, I already have full details of your technique and the size of your penis.'

'Well, after that I couldn't just not see her. It kind of went from there. And I thought . . . I thought it would show you that I could be serious—'

'You think a three-week affair with Chanelle demonstrates your monogamous aptitude?' I rubbed my forehead with the heel of my hand, but there was no blotting out the desolation. 'Jed, I'm sorry.' And I was. I was sorry for everything – for going out with Luke, for rejecting Jed that night in the Wine Cellar, and most especially for what I was about to say. I took a deep breath. 'I can't go out with you.'

The cheerful sounds of summer intruded on the grim silence that stretched between us. The gap between us widened until it was as if we stood on either side of the Grand Canyon.

Eventually, jaw clenched tight, Jed said: 'Why not?'

'Because Chanelle is my friend, Jed. And I've seen the way she looks at you—'

'I don't love her.'

'But I do. And I can't do this to her.'

I spent that night trying to convince myself I had done the right thing, but I kept interrupting by kicking myself. I woke exhausted and empty.

Monday was chill and overcast, although a lone ray of sunlight occasionally stumbled through the dinge of the Maze and collapsed across my desk. It was as if that magical Sunday had never happened, but sometimes, when I wondered whether I had dreamed the whole thing, I would look up and catch Jed regarding me with a watchful stillness. Otherwise, he was grim and brooding.

In the meantime, I was in an agony of indecision about Chanelle. Should I call her? Bring her bunches of flowers and grapes? Jump into filing cabinets to avoid her?

Around midday we bumped into each other at the printer. (Technically speaking I bumped into her, since she was relatively stationary.) Chanelle was swearing and beating the machine – a not uncommon response to the BSS network printer.

'Let me help,' I said.

I opened the drawer and eased out the paper stuck in the rollers. This exercise usually resulted in crumpled confetti littering the floor, but I took my time manoeuvring the sheet while I considered what to say.

'I heard about you and Jed,' I said.

'Yeah.'

'I'm sorry.'

'Are you?' said Chanelle.

'Yes.' I handed her the paper.

'Thanks.'

I hesitated. 'Would you like to go for lunch sometime?'

Chanelle looked almost more perfect than usual, not one rogue follicle out of place, the pleats of her miniskirt pressed into razor sharp creases. But underneath her flawless mask of make-up, dark circles underscored her eyes and her mouth was set in a bitter twist.

'That would be nice,' she said with an effort. 'Maybe next week. I'll call you.'

'Okay.'

As she turned away I put my hand on her arm but when she looked at me I didn't know what to say, or even how to say it.

There was so much on my mind that I was finding it impossible to concentrate on anything. Gragnoc's user acceptance testing started that morning, after which the system was scheduled to go live. At the end of last week, Jed and I had set up the second EnTire system on Gragnoc's servers. This measure effectively protected the company, but after the launch Luke would know his plan had failed. We had to locate the shareholder letter before then.

Later that week, I had a eureka moment, illuminated by a giant imaginary light bulb above my head. At the time, Jed and I were down on level minus two with Nigel.

'How's Amber?' I asked for the distraction.

'Superb, fabulous, excrement,' enthused Nigel. 'Our relationship is like nothing I've ever known. It transcends the physical.'

'Is she into Buddhism?' asked Jed.

'Amber's a very special girl,' said Nigel, ignoring him. 'She makes me want to be a better person. I'm thinking of taking up charity work.'

'Really?' said Jed. 'Like what?'

'Well, I thought I'd start small. Maybe people without a property portfolio.'

'You're all heart,' I said.

'I'm thinking of asking Amber to marry me.'

'You're *what*?' said Jed and I in unison.

'Well, we've been together nearly six months. And when you know, you know.'

'You know fuck all, Usher,' said Jed wearily.

'She's coming to the barbecue on Sunday.'

'You're actually *going* to Max's barbecue?' I asked.

'We have to,' said Nigel, stuffing half a cream dough-nut into his face. 'Max made attendance compulsory after everyone refused.'

'Well, you won't find me there,' said Jed. 'My job description does not include mandatory barbecuing.'

'You're rilly nat mach ava time plya, ah ya, Mashall?' I said in what I considered a fair impersonation of Max. Jed grinned.

Jed and I left Nigel bonding with his cream bun in the canteen. We were waiting for the lift when it occurred to me.

'Jed, maybe we *should* go to Max's barbecue,' I said.

'I'd prefer to grind stale nachos into my eyeballs.'

'Well, I'd prefer to grind stale nachos into your eyeballs too. But I'm thinking that the shareholder letter

– or documents of some kind, anyway – must be in Max's home office. Maybe I could sneak in and find it—'

'No way. You don't even know it's there.'

'True. But I don't think it's here, do you?'

'No, it's not.'

'Really? How do you know?'

'I looked.'

I was on a roll, so didn't pause long enough to think about that.

'Well, there you go,' I said. 'It must be at his house. If I go to the barbecue I can break into his office while he's distracted and riffle through his filing cabinet—'

Jed laughed.

'I'm serious!'

'No. It's too dangerous.'

'Rubbish. It's not as if I'll end up buried at the bottom of Max's garden in a shallow grave. Probably. I mean, what's the worst that can happen? Max finds me in his office, he calls the police, I end up in prison. My life is simply fast-tracked.'

'Livvie, I really *really* don't like this—'

'You can keep me updated on Max's whereabouts by phone—'

'You think his home office will be open?'

'I have no idea.'

'I don't think you've thought this through.'

'Look, Jed, we've got to do something. And it's not as if you've come up with anything better. My life is on the line—'

'Don't you think that's a bit dramatic?'

'No! Jed, my career as I know it is over, I'm looking at a spell in prison smuggling contraband up my anus—'

'It won't come to that.'

'Oh no? How do you know? Look, Jed, I need you.

You might have to set fire to his moustache or something if it looks like Max is about to rustle me—'

'Livvie.'

'Jed.'

'Let's think about this a bit more.'

'Sure. The barbecue is on Sunday, so that gives us two and a half days. You'd better get thinking.'

However, another opportunity was to present itself in the meantime.

At first, I didn't recognise it as an opportunity. It was the internal Gragnoc Wrap Party, traditionally held after the client signs Provisional Acceptance. Normally I love wrap parties, but as the Projects Director, Luke was attending this one. I couldn't completely avoid him since Spinker's was too small, but I was successfully ignoring him.

In twenty-one months with PL, Chanelle had never missed an opportunity for free booze and I admired her for not stopping now. She and Luke had just spent half an hour nose to nose discussing tips on ex-partner-avoidance techniques.

Thankfully Luke finally left to go backslapping and guffawing and wafting bonhomie and minty breath freshener. Amber disengaged herself from Nigel with a slurping sound effect.

'Where's the bathroom?' she asked Chanelle.

'Far side of the bar, down the corridor. You'll see a sign that says Ladies, but just ignore it and go right in.'

'My round,' I said, getting to my feet. 'Another pint of Murphy's, Jed? Chanelle, can I get you a drink?'

'No thanks, I'm going to head off,' said Chanelle, applying lipgloss with a practised fingertip.

Two men chatted me up, which would almost have

been flattering had they been of the same species. The first accosted me en route to the bar and propped himself up against my bosom.

'Y'know,' he breathed, gazing soulfully up at me from his vantage point around my clavicle, 'you are the most beautiful womang I have ewer shet eyesh on in m'life?'

'Have you considered seeing an optician?' I suggested chillingly. I prised him off my front and tunnelled through the floor to make my escape.

My second amour ambushed me on my way back.

'Hi!' he roared above the surge of background noise.

'Bye!' I responded, attempting to push by him, but I couldn't achieve optimum leverage with an armful of drinks.

'I'm a banker.'

For some reason, financiers seem to think that their job description ensures guaranteed and spontaneous access to a woman's knickers. On me, it normally has exactly the opposite effect.

'Did you say *wanker*?'

'No! I'm a banker!' He leaned in uncomfortably close and nibbled my outer ear. 'You look like a nice girl. Would you like to suck my cock?'

I was surprised that being a nice girl was a necessary prerequisite. I would have thought that being a naughty girl would be a better qualification.

'I'd prefer to suck on a buzzard's claw,' I responded. 'Excuse me.'

The standard of men in London was definitely eroding, I mused, as I edged back to the table. Or was it me? Could it be that I was getting old? The other day, I'd found two liver spots on the back of my hand. On closer inspection they turned out to be overweight freckles, but still. And since the age of twenty-seven I'd noticed that my face had gone all furry, like the surface of a peach: a somewhat dingy, three-week-old one. I supposed men would opt for the odd blackhead on taut, luminous two-decades-young skin instead of a grey-haired, liver-spotted old prune.

So perhaps it wasn't the quality of men; it was the quality of *me*.

Manoeuvring through a knot of shiny revellers, I came eye to canine with Luke.

'Olivia.'

'Good grief, is this place *full* of assholes?'

Luke's eyes narrowed and his nostrils flared.

Now, I swear it was an accident, although I'm not saying I wouldn't have been voluntarily prompted along this course of action of my own volition. Someone jostled me from behind and I poured half Jed's pint of Murphy's down Luke's shirtfront.

'Aargh!' screamed Luke, leaping backwards. He crashed into a chair, overbalanced and cannoned into a table. As he scrambled to his feet, the look on his face made me take a step back. I hadn't seen Luke look like that since Lynott's. He obviously didn't take well to having his Calvin Klein shirts defiled.

'You shouldn't have done that,' he said, ever so gently. He ran a finger lightly down my face, a gesture which may have seemed affectionate to an outside observer, but was in fact more menacing than a strike. I flinched.

'Get the f-f-fuck away from me,' I quavered.

'Excuse me, madam,' said a deep voice behind me.

It was seven foot nine of bouncer. He had the consistency and demeanour of a brick shithouse, and wore an ill-fitting black T-shirt with *Security* stretched tight across the chest.

'Madam,' he repeated, 'is this man bothering you?'

'Oh! No. No . . .' But then I thought about it, and I realised Luke *was* bothering me. He had been bothering me for at least three weeks.

'Actually, yes. Yes, he is,' I said tragically.

'Madam, did he threaten you?'

'Yes.'

Well, technically Luke *had* threatened me during my appraisal.

'What!' broke in Luke furiously.

'Quiet, sir. Madam, are you hurt?'

'Yes.'

'I'm the one who's fucking hurt!' snarled Luke, picking a shard of Heineken bottle out of his finger.

I was in danger of losing the bouncer's attention and wondered whether I could coax a tear to the surface. Then I thought about how much Luke really, really bothered me and how very hurt I was and – yes! There it was – I managed to launch a lone teardrop down my face.

'Don't cry, madam. Sir, will you come with me?'

'I will not.'

'Sir,' said the bouncer, taking a firm grip of Luke's upper arm. Although Luke was a big man, the bouncer had a good thirty pounds on him.

'Get your fucking hands off me.'

The bouncer nodded towards the corner and a colleague materialised beside him.

'Come along now, sir,' the newcomer said affably.

Protesting loudly, Luke was frogmarched to the door so quickly his feet barely touched the ground.

I returned to the table.

'Did you see that?' I laughed at Jed.

'See it? I had a ringside seat! You're a genius, Anderson.'

'Here you go.' I pushed the Murphy's at him.

'Where's the other half?'

'Down Luke's shirt. Sorry. Here, you can have some of my JD and Coke. And this packet of peanuts.'

'Thanks.'

'Jed. Jed!' I shook his arm. 'Do you see what I see?'

'You mean Nigel passed out in the corner?'

'No, look. Wylie's briefcase.' I pointed at the leather briefcase tucked under a barstool at the far side of the table.

I looked at Jed and our eyes locked.

'Throw it up here,' I said.

'What?'

'Hurry!'

'Livvie, are you sure about this?' said Jed, laying the briefcase out on the seat between us. 'What if Luke comes back?'

'Fuck him. There's nobody watching, is there?'

'No. Usher's comatose and Amber's chatting up that bald bloke over there. I haven't seen Chanelle for a while.'

'Keep a lookout.'

'There's no combination lock or anything. Livvie, I seriously doubt there's anything in there.'

'You never know. Here: Wylie's Filofax. Check out the day the Trojan was loaded on to Gragnoc's computer system.'

'When was it again?'

'Fifth of May.'

'Nothing.'

'Check out any meetings with Feshwari and see if there are any strange references.'

'When did you turn into a Charlie's Angel?'

'Well, I've always had the looks. From there it was a short step.'

'E-mail printouts,' said Jed, riffling through a bundle of A4 sheets. 'Copies of the Gragnoc proposal and contract—'

'Here's a bank letter . . . interesting. There was fifty thousand pounds deposited into Wylie's account on the twentieth of May.'

'Really? From where?'

'Doesn't say. But it has Max Feshwari written all over it. Figuratively speaking. Hang on. Hang on.' Something had caught my eye in Luke's briefcase. Something I'd seen many times before but failed to notice the significance of.

'I think I know how Luke and Max know each other,' I said. I held up Luke's key ring, with its unusual logo: a gruesomely ugly phoenix, enwreathed in flames. 'There's a photo in Max's office, beside the shredder, of Max with three other businessmen—'

'Shit! Is that the logo—'

'On the wall behind them! Max said it was one of his clients, in South America. You said Luke embezzled funds—'

'From Banco del Uruguay! How the hell did we miss it – Livvie, you—'

'Jed!' I hissed. Luke was coming straight towards us, ripping a path through the crowd like a tornado. 'It's Luke! How the fuck did he get back in? He's coming! Jed!'

'Take it easy. I'll stall him,' said Jed calmly. 'Here, take these.' He bundled the papers and Filofax into my lap. 'Put everything back as it was. Hurry.'

Luke was not yet close enough to see his briefcase flattened out on the barstool, but any minute—

I watched as Jed intercepted Luke barely ten paces away. It all seemed to be happening in slow motion. Then, with a jolt, I started frantically arranging the papers, packing them level on a barstool before stuffing them back in the briefcase. There was no time to consider what went where and in what order, but hopefully Luke wouldn't notice. I jammed the bank letter back in its envelope and threw it in, the Filofax following hot on its heels. I was closing the briefcase when I remembered Luke's keys. I tossed them in, then latched the briefcase and replaced it.

Sidling back to my seat, I turned my attention to Jed and Luke, who were doing what appeared to be the diametric opposite of male bonding. Over Jed's shoulder I could see Luke's forehead, bright red and shiny, with a throbbing vein standing out in stark relief. He was giving Jed a close-up of his tonsils at high volume.

It all happened so fast that afterwards I wasn't sure exactly what or how it happened. Luke hauled back and swung a long arm at Jed.

As perfectly balanced as a Bolshoi ballet dancer – only not as gay – Jed weaved gracefully to the left. Bracing his feet against the floor he crouched low and, in a movement that was a blur, lashed up and punched Luke soundly on the snout with the heel of his palm.

Blood sprayed out of Luke's nose like a geyser.

'By dose!' wailed Luke, clutching at his face. 'You boke by boody dose!'

'Right on all counts,' said Jed flatly, in a voice that gave me a shiver. 'Just be grateful I didn't break your fucking neck.'

This time when Security and his buddy escorted Luke out, Jed was not far behind.

'Wow!' I exclaimed, skipping along beside Jed. 'You were *awesome*! Wow! Jed Marshall, cooler than a liquid nitrogen enema. Wow, he didn't stand a chance! How did you *do* that? I didn't even see your arm move! It was a blur!'

'I know how to take care of myself,' said Jed shortly.

'It was pretty sexy.'

'Turned on, were you?'

'Hell, yes. But that could have been the sight of Luke Wylie's bloody nose. What'll we do now? Find some muggers and beat the crap out of them? Do a few one-arm pull-ups off a barbed wire fence?'

'Thought I'd act as your personal detail to the station.'

'Gee, thanks. Would you take a bullet for me?'

'Yes,' said Jed simply.

'That's . . . that's very nice of you,' I said after a moment, the words having to force their way through my strangled throat. I steered us back on to lighter territory. 'Just so you know, I'd take a bullet for you too. In fact, I'd steal a whole packet.'

Jed smiled.

'What time is it?' I asked.

'Half eleven.'

'If we hurry I might catch the eleven thirty-nine.'

Clattering through London Bridge, we clipped up the ramp and came out on to platform two. At that hour, only a few stragglers were scattered about. One was propped up against a vending machine, no doubt wishing it would stop spinning. Another was slumped on the ground, performing a poignant cover version of the Bangles' 'Eternal Flame'.

Jed walked me to the far end of the platform where we emerged from under the domed roof. Under the light cast by an overhead lamp, his eyes sparked like chips of mica.

'Three minutes,' I said quietly.

From somewhere far off a sad, slow song floated across on the summer breeze.

'Dance?' said Jed, his tone mocking.

Our eyes snagged for a long moment before I took the hand he proffered and he pulled me into him.

Although we fitted together perfectly, at first we moved like a pair of mismatched marionettes: upright and stiff and jerky. I was embarrassed by the way Jed gazed at me, his look unfathomable. He dared me to look away, but I could not.

At first he held me the old-fashioned way, one arm encircling me, his hand supporting mine. Behind my back, I felt his fingers moving gently up and down my spine.

Although the song was diluted by distant sirens, horns and screeching brakes, it still throbbed with a bruised melancholy.

Jed's jaw brushed my hair and I ducked my head nervously.

So far we had maintained a decorous space between us. But then Jed's long fingers curled round mine and held my hand against him, and, applying some insistent pressure at the small of my back, he pressed me close. I could feel the heat of him through his cotton shirt and caught a lungful of pure pheromone that made me feel light-headed.

His head rested against mine and I closed my eyes, suddenly painfully aware of his closeness. His hair tickled my cheek and I smelled shampoo and a lemony aftershave which had a devastating effect on the supportive ability of my knees.

Running his hand down my flank, Jed pressed really rather firmly. The song was coming to an end. I clutched at Jed's shirt and held on desperately. His shoulder muscles were bunched and tense, but his breath against my ear was soft as a butterfly's wing.

'Attention please,' whined the speaker over the fading melody. 'Last train from London Bridge to Gillingham, stopping at Deptford. Greenwich. Maze Hill. Westcombe Park. Woolwich Arsenal. Last call for London Bridge to Gillingham.'

I ripped myself off Jed and faced him shakily. My train was leaving in thirty seconds. Jed leaned towards me and for a thrilling moment I thought . . .

Putting a hand to my face, he kissed me lingeringly on the forehead.

Then, without a backward glance, he turned and walked away.

'Listen, Livvie,' said Jed. 'Why don't I do this?'

We were in Jed's Aston Martin en route to Max's barbecue and my nerves were stretched tighter than a stripper's G-string. Jed gripped the steering wheel as if he were about to rip it from the dashboard.

'What?'

'Search Max's office.'

'No, Jed.'

It wasn't the first time he had brought it up. In fact, over the last two days Jed had proffered his break and entry skills on average every half-hour on the half-hour.

I have to admit, the offer was hugely tempting. Courage has never been one of my particular talents. I'd like to think that if I came across a mugging in the street, I'd do the noble thing. March up to the mugger and demand that he cease and desist with immediate effect. Then wrestle the knife and/or gun off him. Realistically, it is more likely that I would be sprinting in the opposite direction, throwing my handbag and jewellery over my shoulder as I went.

I took a deep breath. 'This is my problem,' I said. 'It's up to me to sort it out.'

'Liv, I know a bit about this sort of thing.'

'Me too. I read a John le Carré novel once.'

'That's great, but I've had some experience in this area.'

'It's okay. Thank you, but no,' I said. 'We'll stick to the game plan. You'll be on the phone updating me on Max and Luke's whereabouts. I'll have plenty of time to get out if Max comes into the house. I'll be fine,' I added, with more conviction than I felt.

A muscle flickered in Jed's cheek and I wished the two of us were anywhere but here.

'All right,' he said. Then, after a moment's pause: 'Have you charged your phone?' he asked for perhaps the fifth time.

'Yes.'

'Is it on silent?'

'Jed!'

'Just checking,' he muttered.

I rolled my eyes. We had spent the last two days obsessively planning. Nothing had been overlooked. My phone was charged and on silent. My mad hair had been tamed into sanity with the aid of a squeegee and several packets of clips (the type with a fastener, so I would not leave any incriminating hair accessories in Max's study). I was wearing trousers for manoeuvrability, and rubber-soled shoes for maximum silence and/or creepage. I had considered every angle (although if Max's floor was unusually hot, I might stick to the floor. But that would be unlikely and dreadfully unlucky).

'This is it,' said Jed, cruising past a mansion.

'Big,' I commented.

'Cost him three point two two million quid four years ago. Worth four point two one mill now,' said Jed.

'How do you know that?'

Jed paused. 'Educated guess,' he said shortly.

'Educated to within two decimal places,' I observed.

'Mm,' he said noncommittally. 'Look at that.' He pointed to Max's six-foot-high fence with skewers on the top.

'The man's definitely guilty of something,' I muttered.

There were cars everywhere: up on the pavement, on the lawn, stacked on top of each other. Jed found a space that was more a vacuum, and somehow managed to wedge the car in.

'Let's go,' he said.

Most of BSS was already at the party. Brenda Calburn was levitating on a chair while everyone ignored her. Nigel and Amber were at the bottom of the garden, Nigel earnestly addressing Amber's cleavage.

Chanelle looked less than riveted to be conversing with Max, who was presiding over a smoke-belching barbecue. The tableau was missing only a pair of horns and a forked tail.

'Excellent,' said Jed quietly. 'Max will be occupied for a while.' He turned back in time to confiscate the glass of wine I'd snatched from a passing tray. 'No you don't! You've got to stay focused.' He hauled me into a bush and peered out of the foliage. 'Where's Wylie?'

'Over there,' I murmured, flicking a finger in Luke's direction. 'By the . . . er . . . incontinent cherub.'

Luke had a big white bandage across the middle of his face. Every so often he raised a hand to touch his nose and winced.

'Right,' said Jed. 'Let's do this. Are you all set?' His face softened and he reached up and brushed his thumb across my cheek. 'Everything will be okay. I won't let anything happen to you. You know that, right?'

'Yes,' I said, and I did.

'Okay. Anyone catches you inside the house, you say—'

'I'm looking for the bathroom. Got it.'

Jed had his hand in my hair, and his face was very close to mine, and he was so clean-shaven and his aftershave smelt so very spicy. 'You can't have him,' said a bleak little voice in my head, before Jed leaned in and administered a ferocious kiss. And I sincerely apologise if I sound like a bad romance novel – the kind with a picture on the front of a brooding hero propping up a semi-conscious heroine with her skimpy dress ripped to her navel – but there's no getting around the fact that Jed did, in fact, crush me to his manly chest; and what I felt of his manhood – which was quite a lot – appeared to be throbbing.

Sorry.

(Just be thankful he didn't rip off my bodice with his tongue.)

Just as abruptly, he pushed me away. 'You'd better go,' he said. I'm ashamed to have to report that his voice was husky. Perhaps he had a head cold coming on.

My legs felt like spaghetti as I turned and tottered towards the house. Although I was absolutely terrified, I was also exhilarated. But there was no time to think about my furtive pash.

I was on a mission.

Unfortunately, my mission got off to an unpromising start, because right outside the bush I ran straight into Luke Wylie.

'Olivia.'

'Wylie. Let's skip the pleasantries, shall we? I can't think of any.'

'I'd like a word—'

'Talk away. You don't mind if I leave, do you?'

'You think you're awfully smart, don't you?' he said calmly, but the vein in his forehead gave a seismic throb.

'I do. And if you were half as smart as you think you are, you'd know it too,' said my adrenaline, which was on top form.

My phone vibrated. 'My phone,' I said. 'Excuse me.'

Turning away from him, I pressed 'Answer'.

'Thought you needed rescuing,' said Jed's voice. 'Move away from the arsehole. Good. Right. Max and Wylie are now stationary. You're all clear. Be careful. Let's see what we can find.'

54

As I made my way towards the house, I had to keep reminding myself to walk naturally.

I caught myself creeping on tiptoe, and there was a huge temptation to dive over bushes and commando-roll across the lawn.

At the front door, I affected nonchalance and slipped inside. The interior of Max's house seemed gloomy after the hard sunlight outside, and I paused to let my eyes adjust.

'I'm in,' I whispered.

'Livvie, I watched you walk through the door,' came Jed's exasperated voice out of my handset.

'Okay,' I muttered. 'There's a long hallway with doors leading off it. Stairs on the right. Kitchen at the far end.'

'Talk naturally so that if anyone hears you they won't suspect anything. Have a look around. Hang on, Wylie's on the move. Wait . . . wait . . . you're okay, he's just getting a kebab. And now he's talking to Chanelle.'

I tried the first door on the left. Shit! It was the guest bathroom. I closed it firmly, and tried the next couple of doors. One was a formal dining room with a grand piano bedecked with family photos, the other a living room, both of them the size of football fields. I was checking out the cupboard under the stairs when—

'Hellair!' came a loud, Sloaney voice from behind me, and I nearly blasted off through the roof.

'Arrgh!' I shrieked. I whirled round, hands flying to my face. I recognised her from the photo in Max's office. It was his wife with a tray of canapés.

She looked at me curiously. 'Can I help you?' She pronounced it 'hyelp'.

'B-b-bah . . . bah . . .' I tried to get a grip on myself. 'I'm trying to find the bathroom,' I said in a voice that sounded like I'd been snorting helium.

'Certainly. The guest room is here.' She indicated the door.

'Oh, thank you. Thank you. That's great, thanks so much.' Then something struck me. 'Er, I was wondering whether I could possibly, if it's not too much trouble, if I could possibly use a bathroom upstairs? It's just that I have this thing about using loos on the ground floor. Sometimes, ah, er, rats swim up the, er, the pipes, the sewerage pipes, and swim around. If the, ah, the loo is on the ground floor.'

Max's wife was looking increasingly horrified.

'Rayllay?' she said.

'Oh, yes. It's, ah, a big problem in London. And they sometimes, you know. Nibble. Your bits. Happened to my uncle. Terrible tragedy. He lost a testicle. But you see,' I went on hurriedly, fearing I was overdoing it a bit, 'at – at higher levels, the rats can't, er, can't swim up. So if there is a bathroom upstairs, I'd really prefer to use that.'

'My God, of course,' said Max's wife. 'It's the third door on the left at the top of the landing.'

As I went upstairs, I saw her peer round the door of the guest bathroom, reach out cautiously and close the toilet lid.

'Fuck, Jed!' I hissed. 'Did you hear that?'

'It's okay. Although . . . rats? All right, I don't need to know.'

'Where is she now?'

'Abusing a waiter outside. I'll keep an eye on her. What are you doing?'

'I'm on the first-floor landing, shitting myself.'

There was a significant pause. 'Livvie, you know I could—'

'No! Stay where you are. I'm fine. I'll try these rooms now, Where's Max and his Manky Me?'

'Don't worry about them, they're still out here. Be careful.'

I wished he'd stop saying that. I was hardly throwing caution to the wind and acting in a reckless, irresponsible manner.

I decided to start with the furthest door, and hit the jackpot.

'This is it,' I murmured to Jed. The room was large and masculine and – my heart sank – there were three large filing cabinets against the side wall. How much crap could one man possibly file? I went to the largest one, and pulled at a drawer.

It was locked.

'Fuck!' I informed Jed. 'It's locked.'

'Have you got a nail file?'

'Jed, I hardly think I have time for a manicure!' I snapped.

'To pick the lock,' said Jed patiently.

'Oh. Er . . . well, I don't have one, and even if I did I doubt I'd be able to pick the lock.' I tried the next filing cabinet and the drawer slid out. 'Hang on, this one's open.'

But as soon as I looked inside, I realised that this was

a complete waste of time. There were thousands of files, and they were arranged – if you could apply the term – according to a system – and I'm also reluctant to press that word into service – of disorganised chaos. It was like picking up a phone book and finding the entries arranged according to colour code. It seemed ridiculous that I had expected to fling open Max's filing cabinet, spend three seconds riffling through the files, and pick out the folder clearly labelled 'Mantis Corporation Stocks and Shares – incriminating documents'.

'Max's wife has just come over to him and . . . he's turning off the barbecue.'

'Jed, there're hundreds of these things,' I said despondently. 'And they're all over the place. "Wood treatment preparations", "Invoices", "Bognor 1977", "Cat flaps", oh my God!'

'What?'

It was a few seconds before I could speak.

'There's a file here on me. "Olivia Anderson". In between "Paint Samples" and "Electrical Wiring".'

Crouching, I laid it out on the floor.

'Livvie.' A charged note had crept into Jed's voice. 'You need to get out. Feshwari is moving towards the house.'

'It has my CV in it, medical reports from my last PL physical, my appraisals . . . it has, it has e-mails here that I sent to . . . to Graeme—'

'Livvie – get the fuck out of there! Wylie and Feshwari are going in!'

55

When people talk about 'fight or flight' mode, they forget the third option: 'freeze to the spot and suffer complete brain failure'.

It seemed like days, *eons* that I stood rooted, all thoughts having departed on extended vacation. I wouldn't have been able to tell you the year, my name or how many fingers I had at the end of how many arms.

'Livvie. *Livvie!'* Jed's voice grabbed me by the metaphorical scruff and hauled me back into the moment. 'Are you there?'

'Yes,' I croaked.

'Okay.' His voice was urgent but controlled. 'You have about fifteen seconds. Listen carefully. Conceal yourself. I will be outside the door. I'll be in at the first sign of trouble. Remember: worst that can happen is you are discovered and get fired. Okay? *Go!'*

Actually, I figured the worst that could happen was I could be discovered, tortured, chopped into pieces small enough to fit into a sack and thrown into the Thames at the dead of night. But it was a small quibble and hardly an appropriate time to debate the finer details. Anyway, I seemed to have cut us off, so I couldn't have argued even had I wanted to.

Conceal myself. I looked around wildly. Where was

my brain? And why was it operating so slowly? The options were sadly limited – in fact, there were only two places that offered full cover: behind the curtains and under Max's desk.

I briefly considered the curtains. If I were discovered, I could plunge through the window and evade capture, although I didn't fancy landing on my face on the gravel drive below. Also, it was possible that a guest might look up and see me through the glass.

Max's desk then.

I was halfway across the room when I remembered my file splayed open on the floor behind me.

Shit!

I whirled round, scooped up the folder, and jammed the pages back into it. The cabinet was still open and I stuffed the file hastily into the drawer and slid it shut. I could hear nothing through the heavy office door. I galloped back across the room and squeezed myself into Max's desk.

I had barely whisked my arse under when the door opened. There came the sound of footsteps accompanied by a whiff of charred buffalo wings, then the click of the closing door.

The desk was a solid affair. There was a set of drawers built into one side with a cavity behind them, into which I squeezed my upper torso.

'What's all this about?' Max's voice got louder as he came closer.

I clutched my phone to my chest and tried to make myself as small as possible. I badly wanted to giggle – it must have been nerves.

'I bubbed indo Olibbia Addeson in de garden—'

'How's the nose?' asked Max with what sounded suspiciously like a snigger, hastily turned into a cough.

'I'b wowwied aboud her,' Luke continued, ignoring the question.

'I didn't know you had a caring side.' To my horror, I saw Max's legs heave into view under the desk before he threw himself into his chair.

'No, nod dat way,' said Luke impatiently. 'I'b wowwied dat she dows—'

'Knows?' said Max, suddenly sharp. 'What makes ya say that?'

'She arribed wib dat viowent fucker Barshall. In de garden, she said someding aboud how I'b nod as smart as I dink I ab. Den she disappeared – your wipe said she caught her sdooping around dowdstairs – I haben't seed her for at least halb ad hour—'

'Relax,' said Max. 'She's probably off in a corner getting drunk.'

'I hab a bad feeding.'

'A feeling? That's not good enough. Have you—'

'Yes, yes,' said Luke impatiently. 'The bug is still dere. I checked de system dis borning.'

'Nothing ta worry about then.'

'I hobe dot. Is dere anyding here—'

'In this office? Nothing that she'll find.'

Aha! So there was something!

'Hab you got by condract?' asked Luke.

'What?' came Max's voice. He hitched up his trouser leg and his furry ankles poking out the top of his socks made me want to scratch.

'De condract,' said Luke impatiently. 'Transferring twenty per cent ob Mandis common shares to me. You said you had it weady.'

'Don't ya trust me?' said Max.

'Dust you?' said Luke, and gave a nasty laugh. 'Hell no, Feshwawi, wid all due respect, I *don't* dust you.'

'Flattery will get you amongst thieves, eh?'

'I believe de expession is dere's no hodour abongst thieves. And in your case, Feshwawi, dere cerdainly isn't.'

'That's a bit rugged, isn't it? I'm no thief—'

'So whad do you call sabodaging your owd client for fidancial gaid?'

'Smart trading.'

'And Olibbia Addeson?'

'A business casualty.'

Damn it! Where was a tape recorder when you needed one? Hang on – as I recalled, my phone had an electronic recording feature, didn't it? I remembered reading about it in the user manual. Where was it again? I cautiously clicked the menu key.

'De condract, Feshwawi.'

'All right, keep ya hair on. I've got it here.'

The click of a lock turning sounded awfully loud, and I realised it was one of the drawers I was crouched behind. There was the sound of the drawer sliding out on casters, and then a rustle, which I presumed was the document falling into the wrong hands.

I tabbed through the menu options on my phone. Messages, Call Register, Contacts, Settings – where the hell was it? It must be either Applications or Media – think!

'Stock option for de purchase of a hundred thousand shares of Mantis Corp . . . exercise pwice two hundred and eight pence per share,' read Luke. 'Looks in order.'

I selected 'Media' and scrolled through the list of features. There it was – Voice Recorder! I selected 'Record', and surreptitiously inched my arm round the side of the drawers. I hoped it wasn't too late.

'One binute – date of grant – de end ob dis bonth! What's dis about, Feshwawi?' barked Luke.

'A little insurance policy,' said Max smoothly. 'If anything goes wrong . . .' I thought I heard him shrug, but it might have been my traumatised imagination.

'Just rebeber I hab dirt on you too, Feshwawi,' said Luke sourly.

'Yeah, yeah,' said Max impatiently. 'Everything is set?'

'Yes. De Trojan will acdibate in two days' time and de Gragnoc systems will be down for ad least a beek.'

'Mantis shares will skyrocket. And that fucker Henderson won't know what's hit him.'

'I'b nebber udderstood whad you've got against Hedderson. I thoughd you were buddies.'

Max laughed without mirth. 'No. About ten years ago, he screwed me over on a deal in Chile. When it went rotten, Henderson claimed he knew nothing about it. He got promoted to partner – and I ended up Director of Bullshit Services.'

'Ad this is payback.'

'I like to think of the damage to his reputation as a partial down payment. I intend to destroy him.'

I had never before thought of Max as dangerous – apart from hazardously hairy – and his words made me swallow. It sounded awfully loud in my ears.

'There is no way this can be traced to us?' Max's query was more a statement.

'Impossibbe. I wogged on wib Olivia's username to upwoad de bug.'

'So now we wait.'

'Exaddy.'

T hey had barely left when my phone vibrated.

'Jed!' I whispered. 'Did you hear all that?'

'You hung up on me, remember?'

'Oh, Jed – Luke said he suspected – and then Max said not to worry – and then Luke asked for the – and Max handed it over – and Luke said what about – and Max said it was smart trading – and Luke asked about me – and Max said I was a business casualty – and I recorded it all! Or most of it. Well, some of it—'

'Stop talking, Anderson. I'm in the room next door. Come out – Feshwari and Wylie have gone.'

With a bit of applied wriggling I managed to squirm out from under the desk. 'Anyone outside?' I asked Jed at the door.

'No.'

When I put my hand on the doorknob and turned it, I thought the door was stuck. Then I realised—

'Jed! Max must've locked the door! The door's locked!'

'One second.'

There was a scraping noise and then something rattled in the keyhole. Twenty seconds later the door swung open.

'Jed!' I fell on him.

'Get off me, woman.'

'Wow!' I said, peeling myself off him. 'How did you do that?'

'What, repel you? Seems I've been successfully doing that for weeks.'

'No, I meant unlock the door.'

Jed quirked an eyebrow and twiddled what looked like a nail file, although I'd never seen one like it before.

'Keep a lookout,' he said.

While I peered over the banisters, Jed worked the lock until the bolts slid back into place. Then he slipped the file into his pocket.

'Let's blow this joint,' he muttered.

Double-checking there was nobody downstairs, we charged down the steps two at a time and burst out into the garden giggling wildly.

I felt absolutely giddy with relief. There's something to be said for living on the edge. Now and then everyone should flirt with danger: taunt bears, walk under ladders, drink full-fat milk past its expiry date. I felt like ripping my clothes off and somersaulting across the garden, or giving Max a great big wedgie or shoving Luke into the swimming pool and then pushing a piano in after him. I felt invincible.

I hadn't been chopped up and stuffed in a bin liner! That in itself was a positive outcome, never mind—

'Jed – the recording.'

'Let's find a quiet spot and see what you've got. Hold it!' Jed hijacked a waiter and relieved him of his drinks tray.

He handed me a glass of champagne. 'Here. You deserve it.'

'God, this stuff tastes like it was distilled from a cement truck,' I said. 'Aren't you having any?'

'After that recommendation? No. Anyway, I'm driving.'

We were on our way to the bush next to the fountain when we were accosted by Max. He was carrying his son, whom I recognised from the family portraits.

'Oh, crap,' I muttered. 'Give me another drink.'

'Enjoying the party?' roared Max solicitously.

'It blows,' said Jed.

'Hellooooo,' I cooed at the baby. He was between one and eight years of age. I'm not that good with children – I don't get exposed to them much. Although newborn babies are fine, I generally have problems when they start to talk, laugh and point.

'Who's this cute little fella?' I enquired of Max.

'This is my *daughter*,' snapped Max, moustache bristling with paternal outrage. 'Maxine.'

Shite!

'Oh, isn't she lovely?'

I went to stroke the child's head and she whipped round and sank her choppers into my wrist.

'Ow!' I shrieked, jumping back. I was lucky to retrieve my arm. Max stamped off carrying his daughter like a rugby ball.

'Come on,' muttered Jed.

'Can't I stick around and call the little monster names?'

'She's *three*! Come on, you can be the bigger person.'

'You're right,' I conceded grudgingly. 'But she's uglier.'

'She's going to be a real growler all right.'

'Poor child takes after her father.'

We navigated the depths of the bush and I located the recording on my phone and pressed 'Play'. It was hard to hear with the splash of the fountain nearby.

'I can't make out *anything*!' I wailed.

'Don't worry. We should be able to isolate the voices. We'll copy the file to the computer later. Let's get out of here.'

I wasn't sure where he was planning on going, but when we crept out from under the foliage we nearly ran into Luke and Chanelle, who were sitting together at the edge of the plastic fountain. They had their backs to us, but it looked like – it looked like—

'Jed,' I whispered, picking at his sleeve. 'Jed! Is . . . is Chanelle getting off with Luke?' I wasn't sure whether my eyes were faulty.

'Well I don't know about you, but I would describe that as serious foreplay.'

As we watched, Chanelle picked the maraschino cherry out of her drink and, maintaining eye contact with Luke, spent an unreasonable amount of time sucking on it. I mean really, it doesn't take that long to detach the fruit from the stalk – it takes me on average three milliseconds, although admittedly I've never tried the manoeuvre with only my tongue. Somehow Chanelle managed to make it look wildly erotic as opposed to totally unnecessary and bordering on silly.

'Maybe they're just flirting.'

'Livvie, she's fellating a maraschino cherry. How long do you think it'll be before she moves on to bigger and better things?'

'Mmm, tasty,' I heard Chanelle say in a breathy, throaty voice with a slight hiccup at the end.

'I have something else that's tasty,' responded Luke.

He leaned over and whispered something in Chanelle's ear. She laughed and threw her hair around – her patented flirting technique. Luke was administering the Wylie slow-burn smoulder while massaging one of her feet.

'Well?' said Jed in a low voice.

'They haven't actually rented a room yet.'

'You want to tail them? Or do you want to get out of here?'

I looked at him for a long moment.

'Let's go.'

57

The roads were clear and Jed drove fast, deftly whipping around cyclists and the occasional bollard. We didn't talk much; there was too much sexual static crackling through the air.

'Jed, do you think I should warn Chanelle about Luke—'

'She's not eloping with him.'

'But she doesn't—'

'Chanelle's a big girl. She can look after herself.'

Anyway, she shouldn't have been getting off with my ex-boyfriend, I thought. Although it did mean Jed and I could be together. I was too overjoyed to feel aggrieved.

'Where to?' said Jed.

'I don't mind.'

For just a second, the practical side of my nature got the better of my raging libido. If I turned up at work tomorrow in the same clothes, the gossip could reach dangerous levels. The coffee machine would be thronged; people might die of thirst. Of course, I was assuming Jed wanted me to stay over, as opposed to drop-kicking me into a taxi at three in the morning with assurances that he would call.

Jed pulled up with a jerk at a red light.

'We'll go to mine then: it's closer. You sure about

this?' he said, raising a hand to my face.

'When was the last time you hoovered?'

Jed grinned. 'No, I mean about this. Us.'

'Are you wussing out?'

'Not at all.'

'I'm sure.'

'You know how I feel about you?'

I nodded, feeling his thumb caress my cheek. He dropped the hand to my leg, and I thought he might roast a hole through my trousers.

'Listen. There's something I have to tell you—' he said.

'Later.'

'But I—'

Before I could consider how wanton it was, I put my hand over his and moved it further up my thigh. What had got into me? Next thing I'd be straddling him right there at the lights and wrapping my legs round his neck.

When I released his hand, Jed pressed his fingers into the soft flesh of my upper thigh. Although verging on painful, it was also unbearably erotic. I looked down at his long, long fingers and the sharp curve of his thumb and thought I might die of lust – seriously.

I wondered what Jed's apartment was like. Probably a typical bachelor pad: bottle tops strewn across the table, empty pizza boxes sporting half-eaten garlic bread and long-lost lacy knickers abandoned down the back of the sofa.

As we drove through Wandsworth I grew increasingly nervous. What if Jed was disappointed? I had dressed with breaking and entering rather than seduction in mind, right down to my underwear: a viciously practical pair of granny knickers featuring maximal VPL and minimal flirty charm. And I was hardly at my aromatic best; I could do with a quick shower – or a very long one would be even better.

Jed manoeuvred the car into a parking spot on York Road.

'This is it.'

'You live *here*?' I indicated the swanky block of flats opposite.

'Yes. I keep trying to tell you: I'm a classy guy.'

We walked to the door in a state of super-charged silence. When we got into the lift, we stood diametrically opposite, looking everywhere but at each other: the floor, the ceiling, the buttons.

Jed led me to number 601. He unlocked the door and held it open for me. Then he closed it carefully and turned to face me.

And then we were grafted together in a bruising kiss. Jed had his hands at my throat, the pads of his fingers caressing. He swung me round and his rock-hard thighs pressed me against the wall. (Please accept my apologies for that metaphor and assurances that I considered all possible variations. Unfortunately, hard as nails does not quite fit the occasion and mallow hard doesn't cover it either. Viagra hard is plain inaccurate.)

Through my eyelashes, I got a marvellous close-up of his finely arched eyebrows and the lines of his jaw and the way his cheek furrowed as he kissed me.

His hands were wreaking all sorts of havoc. They were in my hair and he tucked stray tendrils behind my ears. He ran his fingers lightly over my face and then moved south, where he paused to brush his thumb over my nipple (I swear the thing retracted before springing violently back to attention). Then he made his way to the small of my back, where he pressed firmly.

Now, you might be wondering what I was doing, and

believe me I wasn't standing passively by wilting and gasping – although admittedly there was a fair amount of both going on. I had undone the buttons of his shirt and was feeling my way around the taut planes of his body.

The clash of teeth was mainly my fault. Well, I got a bit overexcited when I came across a particularly bristly tricep and gave a jump.

'Sorry,' I murmured.

'No problem.'

Jed was breathing heavily. He moved away slightly, but I grabbed him by the belt and pulled him back.

'Livvie. We need to talk—'

'Chat away.'

I stitched a line of kisses down his jawline and was gratified when he tensed in all the right places.

'There's something I need to tell you—'

'Isn't it a bit late to be playing hard to get?' I said cheerfully.

I slipped my hand behind his belt and ran a finger around the top of the most stonking great erection.

'Goddamn! Livvie—'

'Shut up.'

'I—'

'Me too. Now, shag me senseless.'

So he did.

And then he did again, and again.

It was 5 June. EnTire had successfully gone live the day before, and the Trojan was due to harmlessly infect the redundant Gragnoc system any moment now. By the end of today, Luke and Max were expecting to be rich men getting considerably richer.

Were they in for a surprise – I hoped. Not coincidentally, Max had scheduled the annual strategy meeting for 10 a.m. the following morning. Instead of being ignominiously fired in front of my peers, I planned to present evidence of Max and Luke's treachery and extract my bloody retribution. Gracme had also agreed to attend – he would take care of the 'bloody' aspect.

However, I was getting a bit anxious. Jed had taken my recording of Luke and Max to some undisclosed location and unleashed the full force of his inner nerdiness on it. So far, he had failed to isolate anything amidst the static and crackles. Since he seemed unconcerned, I tried to ease up on the teeth-grinding.

At least I was sure of one thing. I was in love with Jed Marshall.

You know how, in any good song, there's a perfect moment where everything comes together? Usually at the end of the arty instrumental when the music soars, the electric guitar writhes and on the video the star clutches the air and yearns at the camera. It's the bit that gives your heart a good goosing and makes you want to wave your head around Stevie Wonder-style and grimace with the sheer emotion of it all.

Well, that's how I felt *all the time*.

Although you'll no doubt be grateful to hear I kept the facial contortions to a minimum.

I couldn't get enough of Jed. There weren't enough hours in the day to talk to him and touch him and think lusty thoughts featuring Jed wearing a negligible amount of clothing. I was only sorry there was no way to demonstrate the extent of my feelings without Jed thinking I was some sort of stalker-nutter; the type of woman who would ritually stick herself to a window by the vagina.

Sometimes I was overcome with such a flood of emotion that I wanted to squeeze him until he popped, but I knew Jed probably wouldn't be so keen on that. As an alternative, I considered snuggling up in his arms for ever, but there were certain logistical problems associated with that – namely eating and going to the bathroom. I could give up food, but I loved Jed too much to ask the same sacrifice of him. And of course a relationship was likely to go a bit stale without external influences – it might get boring after a decade or so.

Sometimes I got swept away in a lustful reverie and snapped out of it minutes or possibly hours later having scribbled a Picasso reproduction on my cheek, or with a neatly shredded contract strewn across my desk.

Oh yes, I had it bad.

The wonderful thing was that it seemed my feelings were reciprocated (although I wasn't sure whether Jed wanted to squeeze me until I popped). I had been worried that once The Chase was successfully concluded, Jed might go off me. After all, it had happened with every other woman he'd ever dated.

But he had been right: with us it was somehow different.

Sometimes, when roaming dizzily around a Vaseline-smeared romantic fantasy, I wondered whether maybe I had found The One.

We were in our cubicle instant-messaging sweet nothings to each other when, in a low voice, Jed said, 'Hey, baby.'

sigh! He called me baby!

Jed nodded at Luke winding through the Maze. 'It's show time.'

All day, Luke had looked harried. Behind the big vein throbbing in his forehead, you could just about make out his hair all churned up. He and Max had already held one power meeting, no doubt postulating theories as to why nobody was running around shrieking about Gragnoc's system crash. Walking by the closed door, I had heard staccato bursts of syllables. Max had not sounded happy.

'Good morning,' said Luke, pulling up outside our cubicle. The effort to be polite was making his eyes bulge slightly. 'How's everything?'

'Fine, thanks, Luke,' I responded. 'Nice of you to care.'

'I just thought . . .'

'What?'

'I wondered . . .'

'Look, Luke, if you want to get back together again, just say so. The answer might involve physical violence, but you'll never know if you don't try. Although I'll probably refuse because I can't stand the sight of you.'

'Anderson, if you don't watch that attitude I will not

hesitate to issue you with a final warning,' said Luke, his fists clenching in time with a muscle in his jaw. 'You know what that means.'

'That I'll be fired and never have to see you ever again? You realise it's got one hell of an appeal?'

'I have more important things to worry about,' said Luke. 'Are there any problems on the client systems this morning?'

'Problems? Like what?'

'Anything.'

'Not that I'm aware of.'

'I heard there was a problem with the Gragnoc system,' persisted Luke.

'Really?' I said.

There was a long pause.

'Have you heard anything?' said Luke doggedly.

'Not a thing. Jed – has Gragnoc called the support desk?'

Jed leaned back in his chair and put his hands behind his head, making me want to throw myself on him and snog the face off him. But then I wanted to do that all the time. Just a little bit more at that moment.

'Nope.'

'Nothing?' said Luke.

'No. Although – hang on—' Jed pulled his jaw. 'There was that thing . . .'

'What thing?' said Luke sharply.

'Oh yes. No. Nothing.'

My phone rang.

'Graeme,' I said, picking up the receiver while Luke hovered behind me like a Nazgûl. 'Great to hear from you. How are you? Oh, sorry to hear that. What? *Really?* No, of course. Not a problem. Absolutely. Yes, sir. Bye-bye.'

I replaced the receiver and yawned.

'Jed, d'you fancy a coffee?'

'What?' roared Luke. 'A client has just reported an outage and you're going for *coffee*?'

'Goodness no. Whatever gave you that idea?' I said coldly. 'Graeme called about the weekly report. Now, if you'll excuse us.'

Luke's stride was jerky as he stormed back to his office.

'I don't need my jacket, do I?' I said.

'Watch! Any minute now . . . Wylie's going to scratch his head in hopeless confusion . . . wait . . . wait . . . there!'

Sure enough, Luke dropped his head and rummaged around in his hair.

'Well, he is just outside Max's office,' I pointed out. 'Get a wiggle on, Marshall. And don't fondle my bottom until we're out of the office.'

'I bet Wylie's logging on to Gragnoc's system to check the Trojan activated,' said Jed as we approached the Coffee Spot. 'Oh, bugger! You know what we should have done?'

'What?'

'Shame we didn't think of routing the live traffic to the secondary system. Hopefully he won't notice there's no activity—'

'I'm way ahead of you, lover.'

'You directed—'

'Yes.'

'God, you're sexy.'

'And nasty. Mwah hah hah hah!'

'Mwah hah hah hah haaaaah. My evil laugh is better than yours.'

'I don't think so. Mine is modelled on Ming the Merciless.'

'Grande low-foam double-shot soya latte with—'

'You know what? I fancy an iced coffee, hold the crap.'

'Jesus, that's a bit daring. No hazelnut flavour?'

'Nope. Shall we get a takeaway?'

'Good plan.'

Jed threaded his fingers through mine and I gave his hand a squeeze, marvelling at the charge it gave me. We strolled down the road and crossed Borough High Street. It was a perfect day, the sky an impossible shade of blue, interrupted only by the occasional jet trail. Everyone looked happy – even the accountants.

Although it was late afternoon, there were hordes of people scattered about the grounds of Southwark Cathedral with their shoes off, trousers and skirts hiked up to reveal fluorescent skin. Jed settled against the trunk of a sprawling oak tree and I leaned back against him.

'Let's play hookie for the rest of the day,' murmured Jed, draping his arm round me.

I sighed. 'I'd love to, but I need to prepare for the big meeting tomorrow. After that, I can mitch off indefinitely. Speaking of which, shouldn't you be working on the recording?'

'Stop worrying. It'll be ready. Listen, Livvie,' said Jed. He nuzzled my hair. 'There's something quite important I need to tell you.'

I felt a twinge of alarm. I knew it was too good to be true. This was where Jed confessed that he was actually married with eight children; or that his name was really Juan; or that he included cross-dressing in his list of hobbies.

'What?' I said cautiously.

'I'm not who you think I am.'

Oh, God, I was right: he was a transvestite mother of eight called Juanita.

But then I realised: I didn't care. This was Jed/Juanita and I loved him/her. There was nothing he could tell me that I couldn't handle.

'I'm not a support manager.'

I swivelled round to face him and tucked my legs under me. 'What are you talking about?'

'I work for the Met.'

'You *what*?'

'I'm an undercover police officer.'

I gawped at him. To be honest, I felt a bit short-changed having geared up for a confession involving all sorts of personality kinks or bizarre fetishes or worse.

Then again, the revelation was still in the process of registering.

'Wait. Let me get this straight. You're . . . a bobby?'

'Er, a DI. Detective Inspector,' said Jed. He looked deeply uncomfortable. 'With CID.'

'CID?'

'Criminal Investigation Department. With the Metropolitan Police.'

'You have a nipple hat?'

'Yes.'

'A gun?'

There was a pause.

'Yes.'

'Whoa! Whoa! Fuck.'

Jed sighed and rubbed the bridge of his nose. 'Okay, look. For a number of years, we've kept an eye on Max Feshwari. We've never been able to pin anything on him, but we're fairly certain he's guilty of major accounting fraud on at least three occasions.'

'When you say we—'

'CID. I asked for the assignment in BSS – you'll recall

I joined slightly after he came across from Tax Management. At the time, we thought he was involved in a money-laundering scam for the Russian mafia—'

'You *what*? And was he?'

Jed sighed. 'We think so, but again . . . I found nothing. Certainly not enough to press charges – even when an accomplice of his disappeared in Tajikistan—'

'Hang on: "disappeared"? You mean, wearing concrete shoes?'

'Your lingo is seventies Sicilian, but yes, you have the right idea. We wondered whether he had an inside contact in PL – for a long time we thought it was James Henderson, but after what Max said to Luke in his office, we don't think it is. If he has another contact, we haven't identified him.'

'Maybe you're just crap at your job.'

'Maybe.' Jed grinned briefly. 'Then Luke Wylie entered the equation. We knew it was hardly coin-cidence. You were the best qualified person for the job, and Feshwari made sure Wylie didn't go through the usual PL screen. Later, we found out Wylie has a prison record. Unlike most white collar crims, Wylie started out with petty crime. While he was in pokey—'

'Pokey?'

'Prison. Two years for assault and battery.'

'Oh.' All of a sudden, I was producing industrial quantities of saliva. I felt a bit sick.

'While he was inside, he did an MA to pass the time. Probably realised he could make more money as a career criminal. But fundamentally, Wylie's a street thug.'

'And that business with the Uruguayan bank—'

'It's on our database. The case went to court in Uruguay, although Wylie wasn't convicted. Feshwari's involvement wasn't even suspected, but in retrospect it was probably his idea.'

I thought for a moment. 'So that's how you . . . the recording—'

'Yes. We have an AV guy – Audio Visual Forensics – working on it.'

'But how . . . Jed, you're a computer geek. I've seen you – installing patches, testing laptops, taking calls—'

'I know my way around a computer. I have a master's in Computer Forensics and Enterprise Security, courtesy of the Met.'

'How come you've stayed with PL for so long?'

'In fact, I was about to take another assignment when Wylie turned up. It was my job to get enough evidence to convict Feshwari. And now we have, if we can isolate your recording.'

'Well, that's great. You're welcome. My consultancy fee is in the post. How come *you* weren't crouched under Feshwari's desk doing your own dirty work?'

'I did offer, as you may recall, but you were having none of it. I have to tell you, my Super wasn't too happy about it either. But we took every measure to ensure your safety. Remember the caterers?'

I recalled the – now that I thought about it – rather burly waiters dispensing food and lukewarm champagne.

'The canapés were foul.'

'Not surprising. Those were our boys. They didn't know a lot about food. First sign of trouble and a whole team would have kicked down Feshwari's office door and blown him and Wylie away.'

'Really?'

'No, not really. But you were as safe as I – we – could possibly ensure.'

We fell silent and I shredded the petals off an

unfortunate daisy that happened to be in the wrong place at the wrong time.

'But I thought you were supposed to keep a low profile undercover – what about all those women?'

'Would you believe I was gathering intelligence?'

'Not with the type you normally go for.'

'Fair enough. I was going through a James Bond phase.'

'Is it over now?'

'I think so. Although I still have the suavity and sophistication.'

'How did you end up in the police?' I asked.

'Well, I was in the army—'

'Okay, you'd better start at the beginning. How the *hell* did you end up in the army?'

'I got into a bit of trouble. In my teens. Stealing cars, that sort of stuff. Ended up in prison—'

'Am I the only one around here that hasn't done time?'

'Realised I was on a short cut to Nowhereville, so I joined the army. Didn't fancy my life expectancy there, too many people shooting at me. But the army got me qualified, paid for my degree. Which was nice. Then I joined the police—'

'Stop. Stop talking.' I dropped my head into my hands.

'Livvie.'

'Shush.'

'Livvie.' He stroked my hair gently. 'I'm still the same person, you know.'

'I don't know who you are,' I said, my voice muffled in my hands.

There was something else. The big question that I was afraid to ask. Raising my head, I gave him the benefit of full frontal eyeball.

'Jed, why . . .' I cleared my throat. 'Why didn't you tell me all this before?'

From the look on his face Jed had anticipated the question – or maybe he had detected its imminence with his previously unsuspected sleuthing powers.

'I couldn't.'

'Why not?'

'Livvie. Please. Don't do this—'

'You were just using me. All this time, and I thought – I thought you loved me.'

'I did! I *do*! Livvie, I don't – I didn't—'

'Jed. I don't believe you.' My heart twisted as I said, 'You must have had such a laugh.'

'No! Livvie, no.'

'You let me go out with Wylie when – you – you knew he had a history of – of – oh my God – assault and battery—'

'I didn't know that until recently—'

'How recently?'

'After you left him. I felt sick when I found out.'

Him and me both. We stared mutely at each other for a long while. Then I got carefully to my feet, brushed the grass from my trousers and replaced my sunglasses.

'We have to talk about this,' said Jed.

'We just have.'

Jed looked anguished, but then I knew what a good actor he was now. 'Livvie, I—'

'Jed. I have a strategy meeting tomorrow, where my managers are going to frame me for corporate espionage. I still have no evidence, apart from a demo recording of static, and a fishy smell. So I can't deal with this right now. I'm sorry.'

Then I walked away.

Back in the Maze, I powered down Drusilla and slipped her into my case. It wasn't five o'clock yet, but I couldn't handle any more of the place. On the way to the train platform, my phone beeped: message received. It was from Jed.

Call me. Whatever you think please do not doubt that I love you.

It was the longest text I'd ever got from Jed, who usually limited his telecommunications to 'yes', 'no' or 'maybe'. My heart had a seizure, trying to expand and contract at the same time.

It rather hurt.

I switched off my phone.

On the train I pressed my throbbing head against the window. I was experiencing significant issues processing Jed's information.

I tried to focus on the imminent strategy meeting rather than Jed. Yet every time I tried to put thoughts of him to one side, they crept back in, making a little more headway every time until they occupied full space again.

Jed had said he was the same person, but that wasn't quite true, was it? I mean, I had no issue with Jed's sudden career change (and blue was a very flattering colour on him; really set off his eyes). The problem was this: I had thought I *knew* Jed.

But now he was throwing around initials like DI and CID and AVF and saying 'pokey' instead of prison and referring to crims and using words like 'money-laundering' and 'fraud' as if that were in any way *normal*. All of a sudden Jed spoke a language I did not recognise, accessorised with a secret life that I knew nothing about and from which I was excluded.

Our whole relationship was built on a lie.

I didn't want to believe it, but it was possible – maybe even probable – that Jed had been using me to manipulate Wylie and obtain information.

Yet we had been friends before the Gragnoc affair.

But then, why hadn't he told me about his real profession before now?

And what about sending me into Max's office like a lamb to the horse's mouth (as Max might put it)?

In fairness, he had offered to infiltrate – goodness, Jed had me talking like him now – Max's office himself. In fact, several times.

If Jed didn't care for me after all, he had no incentive to return the recording. Anxiety electrocuted me. No, no, I was being paranoid. Disregarding his true feelings, Jed had never let me down; and anyway it was in his interests to compile evidence against Luke and Max.

Wasn't it?

The following morning, I came instantaneously awake at 04:30:27. The roiling mass of dread in my stomach was almost indistinguishable from nausea. I tried counting bottles of valium for a while, but sleep was the furthest thing from my mind. I eased out of bed, and pulled on a shirt Jed had discarded two nights previously. It gave me some measure of comfort as I fixed myself a cup of coffee.

The strategy meeting was in – I checked my watch – five hours and nineteen minutes, and I still didn't have Exhibit A. Oh, God, why hadn't Jed been in touch?

When I reached the office, for some reason I expected things to look different. Yet everything was the same as I emerged from the lift on level six: the grey commercial carpet tiles, the flickering fluorescent light at the far corner of the Maze, Nigel picking his nose with the staple remover.

From Max's office came the soothing strains of him bawling at Luke, although unless Luke had the eardrums of a bat there was no way he could have made out half of what Max was shrieking. When Michelle opened the door to deliver Max's PornFax, I heard Luke say: '. . . definitely! There is no mistake . . .' and on her way out Max was roaring: '. . . raining cats and headless chickens . . .'

Jed was at his seat in our cubicle. He was grey and drawn, and looked anxious. Since I had never seen him look more than mildly concerned – and that in the face of a real disaster (Spinker's ran out of Murphy's) – it took a few seconds to identify the emotion.

'Why didn't you call me?' I said, without preamble.

'Well, your mobile is off; and if you check your voicemail, you'll find roughly eleven messages from me.' He sounded harried.

'What's wrong?'

'I've been on to the boys.'

Jed was referring to his colleagues in the Met. Not having met any of the boys, I found it difficult to imagine them as individuals, as opposed to a large collective operating as a single entity.

'Yes? What did the Borg have to say?'

'They haven't been able to clean up the recording.'

'So we've got nothing—'

'They're still working on it—'

'But Jed! The meeting is at *ten*!' I hissed.

'Okay, look, I've seen these guys at work. They can do amazing things—'

'Obviously not within amazing timeframes!'

'We'll get something.' He lifted a hand to my face, but took a detour halfway there. 'Breathe, my love – Livvie. Everything's going to be fine.'

'It's less than two hours away—'

'I know, I know. Just hold it together and try not to worry.'

But I *was* worried, and getting more so with every second that whipped by.

Minutes before the strategy meeting, I collected myself, and some files. Jed had been muttering expletives into the phone to his colleagues all morning.

'Wait a moment,' he said into the receiver. He took my hand.

'What's the story?' I asked.

'We're almost there—'

'Well bring it—'

'It's not quite ready. We can't make anything out—'

'Then what do you mean, you're almost there?' My stomach squirmed around issuing nauseous storm warnings. 'If you can't bloody *hear* anything—'

'We can make out some words. There's a you, a be and a we—'

'I'm going down now,' I said tremulously, as if facing the green mile.

'Shit, is it that time already?' asked Jed, dispersing any lingering shreds of confidence. 'Listen, sweetheart,

I'll get you the file as soon as it's ready, okay? Don't worry. Everything will be fine. Just . . . trust me. And trust yourself. Okay?'

I nodded automatically. He kissed my palm. I wanted to lean into him, but instead I pulled away.

I was as nervous as an accountant cooking the Mafia's books when I reached the conference room. I paused outside and took a deep breath. Had I got everything? Too late now. I pushed open the door. Ironically, it was the same conference room – 614 – where all this had begun.

The only person there was—

'Mr Henderson.'

For the first time, I noticed his forehead was disproportionately wide.

'I'll have Earl Grey, black, three sugars,' he said.

For a moment I considered pointing out that he was standing right beside the refreshments, but I didn't want to antagonise him.

There'd be plenty of time for that.

After I prepared his tea, I took a seat near the head of the table and watched my colleagues filter in. Nigel sat opposite me, braying happily into his mobile and unaware that his tie was in his cup – again. Next to him, Chanelle avoided my eye. Brenda performed some voodoo with a fountain pen.

The tension built until it was almost a relief when the conference room door was wrenched open and Max leapt in, followed by Luke.

'Right, folks,' said Max briskly. 'Let's get this show across the bridge.'

Despite the bawling, both Max and Luke looked calm and collected. In fact . . . were they looking smug? They were! The expression on Max's face brought the words 'cat', 'cream' and 'total bastard' to mind. My anxiety levels increased exponentially. Did they know that I knew that they knew that I knew?

'James,' said Luke smoothly, shaking James Henderson's hand. He turned to me. 'Olivia, Graeme Dewar left a message for you.'

What? Why hadn't Graeme called me on my mobile? Maybe he had – where was my phone? Oh God, I must have left it upstairs! How would Jed get in touch with me—

'He has been delayed,' said Luke. 'Car accident on the way from the airport.'

And then he gave such a diabolical smirk I actually caught a whiff of brimstone. Suddenly I felt real fear. Could he and Max have tampered with Graeme's car? Cut the brake lines, or concealed an explosive in the ignition?

Although Jed had presented Max and Luke's criminal résumés, it had all seemed slightly surreal – as if I were watching a television show. I had never seriously considered that they might be capable of murder. What did they have planned for me? Maybe a trench-coated henchman, pushing me down a dark alleyway: 'I have a message from Mr Feshwari. He says, "Never tango with the hairy parrot."' Then taking out a gun and putting a bullet between my eyes and sliding my still-warm body off London Bridge.

Okay. My first priority at this moment was breathing. PL's receptionists were more than a match for trench-coated henchmen, so they were unlikely to charge the conference room any time soon. I was safe for the time being.

It usually took half a day for everyone to settle round the table, which would have suited me just fine, but on this occasion my colleagues arranged themselves uncharacteristically efficiently. Thankfully, Max was distracted by the HobNobs. Since this was to be my last meeting in the building, I had taken the initiative of ordering chocolate HobNobs and Jaffa cakes. A little gift for Gary Newbit – with any luck he'd have a heart attack deciding what expense code to charge it to.

With no recording, Jed MIA, and Graeme possibly dead in a hospital morgue, I hoped Max would take his time getting round to my business.

'Right,' he said, settling into the seat at the head of the table. 'I'm glad you're here, Jimmy,' Max addressed James Henderson, and I was heartened to see Henderson shudder delicately, 'because a grievous situation has come to my attention.'

Fabulous. It appeared I'd made the top of the agenda. All right. The situation called for confidence, coolness, calm under pressure – and totally blagging it.

'Recently, a client system was recklessly sabotaged by one of my employees,' said Max. He paused for a dramatic beat, and to pick a HobNob crumb out of his back molars with a stubby finger.

A babble arose from the rest of BSS, accompanied by the optical equivalent of Chinese whispers.

'This reckless act was planned with premeditation and cunning, over a period of weeks,' continued Max over the noise.

'May I ask what you are referring to?' said James Henderson.

'Olivia Anderson installed a virus on her client's system, which wiped out half of Gragnoc's database yesterday afternoon. Regrettably I was not aware of the disaster until it happened.'

'You're telling me a virus wiped out a client system

yesterday?' said James Henderson. He was finally paying attention; he was grafted to his chair, face set in shock.

'That's correct,' said Max. 'Miss Anderson—'

'Who the bloody hell is Miss Anderson?'

Oh, sweet Jesus.

'That would be me,' I said desperately. 'How – how are you?' I half stood, then sat down again. Shit, this was going from bad to cataclysmically dreadful.

'And who are you?' said Henderson.

'Er – sorry – I'm Olivia Anderson, Project Manager with BSS.

'Is this true?'

For a second I panicked, wondering what he was referring to. 'Er, yes. Sorry? Which bit?'

'I am referring,' said Henderson tightly, 'to the accusation levelled at you.'

'Not at all. F-five years ago, one of PL's clients, Gragnoc Concretes, contracted PL to supply its proprietary enterprise resource system, EnTire. I was the project manager in charge of implementation.'

My throat was drier than a diva's tonsil and I paused for a sip of water. Max had subsided so willingly that I wondered whether I was making a horrible mistake, but there was no turning back now.

During the course of many rehearsals over the previous week, I had decided that short, sharp and vicious was the best approach to presenting the next sentence.

'Two weeks ago I discovered that Luke Wylie and Max Feshwari had sabotaged Gragnoc's EnTire system.'

BSS gave a collective gasp, but when I cast a glance at Max a vortex of dread opened up in my gut. He appeared entirely unruffled. But then I saw that Luke had gone a whitish green. His skin was stretched across his face, as if someone had him by the hair.

'Luke used my password to log on and upload a Trojan virus to Gragnoc's EnTire system,' I ploughed on. 'It was designed to bring down Gragnoc's system yesterday morning.'

'This is ridiculous!' said Luke, his voice shimmering.

'It's a serious accusation,' agreed Max pleasantly.

'Olivia Anderson reports to me,' Luke told Mr Henderson. 'Frankly these are the ravings of a desperate woman. Her work is substandard. I have had to issue repeated warnings—'

'Is this true?' asked Mr Henderson.

'Well, I am a bit desperate, but working for Luke Wylie should come with a health warning.'

'No! The sabotage.'

'Of course it's true. Spending quality time with a plate of HobNobs in a conference room isn't my idea of fun, you know.'

Luke leaned forward earnestly. 'Mr Henderson, this doesn't surprise me. That Olivia would do something like this, I mean.' Luke broke for a Dramatic Pause. 'I had problems with Olivia as soon as she started working for me – I had to issue a formal warning. But I thought she had changed. I sometimes think it is one of my flaws, that I trust too much.'

'Miss er – Erderson—'

'Anderson,' I said. 'Similar to Henderson in many ways.'

'Quite. Er, what evidence do you have to support this accusation?'

'Yes, yang lidy,' said Max. 'Ya can't go around pointing the greasy finger of shame at whoever yah fancy.'

'When I found out what Max and Luke had done, I

replicated the system,' I said. 'The primary system is fully operational and in extremely good health, as my client will verify when he arrives.'

Watching realisation filter into Luke's face was like watching the dawning of a brand-new day. The revelation had also pierced Max's hairy hide. He looked uncertainly at Luke, before deciding that offence was the best defence – although personally I didn't notice any difference.

'Yang lidy, you're in enough trouble without throwing groundless accusations around now that the golden goose has hit the fan. Assuming this is malfeasance rather than malicious sabotage – and before this, I was prepared to give ya the benefit of the doubt – it is the sort of incompetence I've cam to expect of ya.'

'Bollocks,' I said, which caused a bigger shockwave than the revelations minutes before. 'I reported directly to you for two years, during which time you purported to be entirely satisfied with my productivity. Anyway, why would I wittingly sabotage a client I've worked with for five years?'

'Who knows? I'm not expected to know the workings of a criminal mind—'

'Oh, I don't know about that. Unlike me, you had motive.'

'What the—'

'You are a major shareholder in Mantis Corporation. Gragnoc's major competitor,' I explained to the assembly, who emitted a collective 'Ooh!' 'So it is in your interests that Gragnoc fails.'

Max pointed a hairy appendage at me. I think it was a finger.

'Yang lidy, I was going to support ya through this mess, but ya have crossed the camel's back! You're fired!

Jimmy, I would recommend extracting restitution for any damages Miss Anderson has incurred.'

I waited until he had filtered a slug of tea through his moustache before proceeding.

'I have a recording,' I said. 'Of you and Luke discussing how you decided to sabotage Gragnoc to adversely affect its share price.'

Max sprayed tea over the conference table in a cloud of droplets that glinted in the sunlight. It was a pretty effect.

'*Wha-at?*' yelped Luke.

'That's crap!' said Max. 'I don't know about Wylie here, but you have nothing on me. Nothing!'

'Slightly more than nothing,' I said, 'to the extent that it almost qualifies as something.' I stole a glance at my watch – nearly eleven o'clock.

'You have it here? The alleged recording?'

Where, where, where was Jed with the file?

'No. But I can tell you—'

'So where exactly is this "recording"?' sneered Luke, recovering some of his aplomb.

'It's . . . it's in a safe place.'

'Waste of my time,' said Max, rising from the table (although it was difficult to tell). 'When you have this recording, then talk to me. But until then—'

'Sit down, Max,' I said, surprised at myself. 'I have not involved the police yet – but I will not hesitate to do so.'

Suddenly there was a noise like someone trying to batter the door in with a sledgehammer and then Graeme's granite noggin appeared round the frame. The sight of a friendly face made me want to burst into tears of gratitude.

'Livvie!' The sonic boom rattled the windows of the conference room. 'Yeh all righ', lassie?'

'The grandest!' I cried. 'How about yourself?'

'Och aye. Haing oan a moment—'

He swung wide the door and a swarm of pinstripes flooded in.

'Woan' bother wi' the introductions,' said Graeme. 'Reinforcements. Lawyers and suchlike. Piranhas,' he said without much enthusiasm or, for that matter, bothering to lower his voice.

There was an unseemly scrum over the biscuits in the middle of the table.

'Mr Henderson, may I introduce Graeme Dewar?' I said. 'Graeme is CEO of Gragnoc Concretes.'

Graeme evicted a group of developers and seated himself strategically at the other end of the conference table, flanked by his lawyers.

'Mr Dewar,' said James Henderson faintly.

'And this is the Director of BSS, Max Feshwari,' I said.

'Feshwari,' said Graeme in the same tone he might have used to discipline a naughty dog. 'Wylie.'

'Max wants to leave,' I said, 'but he'd be missing all the best bits.'

'Si' down,' said Graeme amicably enough, yet leaving little room for debate.

Max sat.

'Oh, by the by, a friend asked me to give this to you, lassie. Special delivery.'

And he handed me a package.

'Help yourself to tea and coffee,' I said to Graeme and his posse.

'Can we just get on with it?' snapped Mr Henderson.

'Ah think Ah'll have a wee cup o' tae,' said Graeme easily.

I've never experienced anyone take so much time to fill a cup – Graeme managed to eke out the process for a good five minutes. While he measured out sugar to the last grain, I surreptitiously opened the package. There was a note in Jed's scrawl: *Sorry about the delay*. And a tiny, slimline electronic device, slightly bigger than a credit card, along with a small pair of speakers.

Graeme finally finished pounding the bone china with the teaspoon and eased into the chair facing Henderson at the other end of the table.

'Let me get this straight,' said James Henderson, running a hand through what was left of his hair. 'Mr Dewar, did someone sabotage your company system?'

'Aye, tried to,' said Graeme. He fished a pipe out of his breast pocket along with a pouch of tobacco. Given that his fingers were three times the diameter of the bowl, he was surprisingly efficient at packing it.

'Pardon me,' said Mr Henderson. 'Smoking is not

permitted in the building, Mr Dewar. It is unlawful and PL is ultimately liable—'

'Ah think yeh've got a bit more tae be worryin' aboot than a wee pipey,' said Graeme companionably.

'But—'

'Ge' oaver i'. Noo, if we can get back to business. Miss Anderson foun' oot aboot th' virus and informed me. A week ago, was it, Livvie?'

I looked up from where I was connecting the speakers to the MP3 player.

'How awful for you, Mr Dewar.' Luke took the grandstand. 'But if you recall, I warned you – I offered to replace Olivia with a competent—'

'Laddie,' said Graeme, 'Olivia has looked after mah interests for over five years. As fair as Ah'm concairned, *her* intaigrity is no' in question.'

Luke swallowed hard and looked to Max for guidance, but Max was vandalising company property: studiously chiselling a splinter of wood off the edge of the conference table.

'Mr Dewar, I understand this must be hard for you. But I think you will find that Olivia planted that file—'

'An' then tol' me aboot i'? An' then replicated the whole system with an exact copy so that business could continue uninterrupted? Och aye, son.'

'Excuse me,' I said. 'I have something here which may help clarify things.'

Max looked up and sniffed at the air.

'Hold on a sec—'

I pressed the large button on the MP3 player. For a moment, there was only static, but then amidst the crackles—

' "Just rebeber I hab dirt on you too, Feshwawi," ' came Luke's snuffled tones out of the device.

'What the— How the— That doesn't mean anything,' said Luke with a ghastly laugh that sounded more like a quack.

'The sound on this thing is amazing,' I said conversationally to Graeme.

' "De Trojan will acdibate in two days' time." ' Luke's voice reverberated around the faux suede conference room walls. ' "De Gragnoc systems will be down for ad least a beek." '

'That could be anyone,' said Luke. He was so white he was almost luminescent.

'Yes, I suppose it could,' I said. 'But this is definitely Max. Wait . . .'

' "Mantis shares will skyrocket. And that fucker Henderson won't know what's hit him." ' James Henderson's eyebrows shot into his comb-over. ' "There is no way this can be traced to us?" '

'That your voice, Max?' I queried, pausing the recording. 'Can you identify whom you were addressing?'

'I have bitter things to do than sit here and listen to this – this—'

'Singing canary?' I suggested.

'Sounds moare like a fat lady,' said Graeme.

'How did you—' spluttered Max.

'I was under your desk. Needs dusting, by the way.'

'*What?*'

'That is – that is hardly conclusive,' stuttered Luke into the silence.

'What d'you want – photographic evidence?' I asked happily. 'Maybe a couple of snaps of you uploading the bug, or a picture of Max scheming in his office?'

'I'm going,' said Max, standing up again.

'Ah doan' think yeh'll get that far,' said Graeme

comfortably. 'There's a couple o' detectives waitin' on yeh outside.'

'You said you hadn't gone to the police!' hissed Max at me.

'I lied,' I said. 'You once said I should be more imaginative with truth. I took the advice literally.'

Luke had gone even whiter and his bloodshot eyes stood out like neon blobs. Then he made a bolt for it, shunting his chair back, pounding across the floor and flinging open the door.

'About time,' said Jed, appearing in the doorframe. He gave me a ghost of a wink.

'Get out of my way!'

'You're going nowhere,' said Jed softly, and his voice made me shiver. If there is a fine line between love and hate, I might want to reconsider crossing it. 'We'd like a little chat with you and Feshwari.'

'Who d'ya think ya are, Marshall?' snarled Max.

Jed flipped out a badge. 'CID,' he said with what I recognised as Job Satisfaction. 'What is it we do again?'

Another figure appeared in the doorway. Although wearing a suit, he looked like he would be more comfortable giving his horse a piggyback up one of the rockier gorges of Marlboro Country.

' "Work together for a safer London"?' he asked. I was amazed he could speak with a jaw that craggy.

'That's our slogan, is it?' said Jed. 'Actually, I like it.'

'It's very inspiring,' I said.

Marlboro man prowled stealthily into the room. 'Can you come with me, please?' he said to Max, although I suspected it was not a question. He wrenched Max's arms behind his back and slapped on a pair of handcuffs that appeared magically in his fingers.

'What the fuck!' squeaked Max.

'You might want to restrain Luke Wylie as well,' I said, thoroughly overexcited by seeing the handcuffs in action. 'He's a dangerous criminal too.'

'No problem. Got your bangles, Marsh?'

'This is outrageous!' squealed Luke.

'This is *justice*,' said Jed.

This is such a turn-on, I thought.

'Let's take a little trip down to the station, boys. Lots of people looking forward to a chat with you.'

Although Luke went quietly, Max was manhandled out the door bawling: 'Don't think you'll get away with this! Get your fucking hands off me! I'm an innocent man! You'll pay for this!'

'Righ',' said Graeme once the excitement had died down. 'Would the raist of yeh mind please buggerin' oaff?'

Even had they managed to form a makeshift scrum, BSS weren't about to take on Graeme and his lawyers. They surfed out on a wave of vicarious adrenaline.

'Excuse me,' said Mr Henderson, looking like he was sucking on a rancid pickle. 'Naturally, I am frightfully sorry for any damage inflicted on Mr Dewar and his company by this unfortunate and truly regrettable incident—'

'Very sorry?' I repeated. 'That's nice. What do you think, Graeme?'

'Och aye, i' was beezer. Quality apology. I haiven't been that muived since braikfast.'

'However, I don't see what this has to do with Puttock Leavitt or myself—'

'Don't you?' I said. 'You should have your eyes checked; I suspect you're nearsighted. If this were to go any further, it could be very bad for business.'

'The PR would be draidful,' said Graeme. 'Altho' bu' they say no publicity is bad publicity.'

'Not in the accounting industry,' I said. 'People take their money very seriously. And this is your classic what I like to call "pants down" publicity. That's never good, unless you're in the prostitution business.'

'Which Puttock Leavitt kind of is when you think about it,' agreed Graeme.

'Yes. I like to think of it as sort of like . . . an actuarial brothel.'

'Hey!' barked Mr Henderson.

'What? You screw people for money. Doesn't sound a million miles away from your traditional trick-turning variety of tart,' I said.

'We all have to make a living,' snapped Mr Henderson. 'Is there a point to this?'

'A point?' I repeated. 'Gosh, I'm sure I had one here somewhere. Let me see – ah yes. Okay, it might not be the sharpest of points, but in essence, I'm not that keen on working for a company that has treated me so shabbily—'

'I don't know what you expect us to do,' interjected Mr Henderson. 'This incident has nothing to do with Puttock Leavitt.'

'So you keep saying,' I said frostily. 'However, you are a partner with PL, are you not? Making you liable for any case brought against PL.'

'I didn't know—'

'Ah yes, the old "I didn't know" argument. A rock solid defence which I'm sure will play a terrific tune in court.'

'Come now,' said Mr Henderson. 'This doesn't have to go to court, surely?'

'I can't see any alternative if you keep insisting this has nothing to do with you,' I said.

'Perhaps you misunderstood me. I'm sure we can come to some amicable arrangement—'

'Oh, I'm sure we can too, Mr Henderson. I've always liked you. Whenever anyone said you were an avaricious prick who would sell your grandmother for a pound, I always stood up for you. I know you wouldn't sell your granny for less than market value. As I was saying: I am not about to waste one millisecond more of my life working for PL. At the same time, I am only slightly more interested than you in a court case which might drag on for years—'

'We could look at an out of court settlement,' said Mr Henderson eagerly. 'Under the circumstances, I'm prepared to be generous. I could offer monetary compensation of the order of . . . let's say fifty thousand pounds. Which I'm sure you'll agree is a more than fair recompense for—'

'I'm pretty sure I *don't* agree,' I cut in. 'Under the circumstances that sounds frankly scabby, Mr Henderson.'

'Did you have an alternative figure in mind?' said Mr Henderson through clenched teeth.

'I was thinking more in the order of a million.'

Mr Henderson choked on his tie.

'A million!' he shouted. 'For what?'

'Emotional trauma? I still feel very upset about the whole affair. When I think about it, I get all tense and my hair goes frizzy. Tell you what, if you prefer we could just call it a thank-you for my loyal years of service.'

'Outrageo—'

'Lassie, yeh're selling yerself short,' said Graeme, thoughtfully puffing on his pipe.

'You think so?'

'Daifinitely.'

'Okay. How about, maybe, I don't know.' I took a deep breath. 'One point three million.'

'One point three million!' Mr Henderson again.

'Henderson, that's oanly a fraction of what yeh give the defence industry in annual kickbacks and yeh know it,' said Graeme, his head wreathed in smoke. 'And one seventh what yeh buried in the profit and loass statement last year. In faict Ah'd be startin' wi' at least one point five.'

'Thanks, Graeme,' I said happily. 'One point five million then.'

There was a stony silence.

'I hardly—'

'Non-negotiable.'

That was me, much to my own surprise. Graeme nodded approvingly.

'It will be necessary to consult the other partners,' said Mr Henderson.

'No deal,' said one of Graeme's lawyers. 'You walk out of this door and it goes up to two million. Excuse me, is that all right with you?' he asked me.

'Of course. Hey, thanks very much.'

'This is extortion!' said Mr Henderson.

'Not at all,' I said. 'You have three valid options. One: you settle with me for the stated sum. Two: consult your partners and settle out of court for two million. Or three: let the law decide.'

'She's not kidnapping your daughters,' pointed out Lawyer #1.

'Please don't think I'm rude, but I'd rather you kept the quips to yourself if you're charging by the hour,' I said.

'Oh, er, sorry.'

'What d'ye think yeh'll do with the money, lassie?' boomed Graeme into the silence.

'Well, I certainly won't be buying Mantis shares.'

'All right,' said Mr Henderson eventually. 'On behalf of PL, I will settle for the amount agreed.'

'Lovely,' said Graeme, taking a sheaf of papers from his lawyer. 'Hope yeh doan' min', Livvie. Ah took th' libairty of havin' lawyer boy here draw oop a coantract on yer behalf.'

'Oh, Graeme, you shouldn't have,' I said, feeling genuinely misty. 'Thank you. Mr Henderson: can you please initial each page, and sign and date those areas marked with an X. And make it snappy.'

'In case you were wondering, the contract is watertight,' said Lawyer #2. 'Very favourable terms.'

Mr Henderson finished signing.

'I'll sign as witness,' said Lawyer #3. 'Mr Dewar, perhaps you'd also do the honours—'

'No' a proablem.' Graeme looked thoroughly happy.

'If that's all,' said Mr Henderson icily, pushing back his chair.

'Actually, tha's noa all,' said Graeme easily. 'Let's discuss Gragnoc's compensation.'

'*What?*'

'Ah think Olivia wen' rather easy on yeh,' said Graeme, giving me a broad wink. 'Yeh migh' find me a tougher prospect. Lassie, if yeh wouldn't mind excusin' us, Ah have business with Mr Henderson.'

Ever the gentleman, he rose and kissed me on the cheek.

As I left the room, I almost felt sorry for Mr Henderson.

As I left the conference room, it was as if I hit a wall of exhaustion. I returned to the Maze to clear out my desk. Jed wasn't there, presumably still processing Luke and Max at the station. It felt all wrong without him. I couldn't wait to be out of there. I sent him a text message from my mobile: *Thank you.*

And received one back: *Welcome.*

Oh. Okay.

That was that then.

I walked out of the Puttock Leavitt building and resolved never to return.

Later that same day I contemplated another evening alone prolonging my Emmy-award-winning hissy fit, and realised I'd much prefer to spend it with my Dirty Harry ex-colleague instead.

I knew why Jed hadn't told me about his profession.

I decided to be honoured he had chosen to confide in me now.

It took me over an hour to get to Jed's. Some-one came out the front door as I arrived, enabling me to slip in. I had flutters in my stomach as I knocked on his door.

Jed swung the door open, unshaven and clad only in a pair of jeans.

'Livvie!'

His brilliant smile was chased away almost immediately by uncertainty. Then his face went blank. My whole body ached for him.

'Hi,' I said.

'Hi.' He leaned against the doorjamb and hooked his thumbs in the loops of his jeans. I smiled in what I hoped was a saucy manner, although I'm only truly skilled in the ketchup variety.

'I wondered whether you'd be interested in strip-searching me.'

The beginnings of a grin stirred his mouth. 'You know, I've wanted to do that since the first time I met you, but I never mix business and pleasure.'

'Why ever not? What if I told you that underneath these clothes I'm wearing spangled knickers and a conical bra?'

'In that case, it would be irresponsible of me not to check it out,' said my lover and, gripping me by the front of my trousers, he pulled me to him and kissed me very thoroughly indeed.

'About before,' I murmured against his mouth. 'You realise the correct time for your full confession would have been *before* we slept together the other night?'

'Yes,' said Jed, nibbling on my upper lip. 'Sorry. I did try, you know.'

'But?'

'Your tongue was in my mouth at the time. And my mother always told me' – he moved down and gently nipped the side of my neck – 'you should never talk with your mouth full.'

'Is that right?'

'Yes. Apparently it's very rude.' Jed's thumb brushed across my nipple and I gave a bit of a porn star gasp. 'Not only that, but it's very difficult to talk with your mouth full. Here, let me show you.'

The kiss he delivered made my legs buckle. At the same time, he deftly undid my bra.

'One-handed. Impressive. Did you learn that at police school?'

'No, the local comprehensive.'

'Thorough education.'

Jed was doing astonishing things to various erogenous zones and my breath was jumping around all over the place.

'Yes. Learned everything I know behind the bike shed.' Pushing apart my top, Jed affixed his mouth to my left breast.

'Would you like me to demonstrate the policeman's lift?' he enquired when he paused for breath. I gave a yelp as he swung me over his shoulder.

'Much the same as the fireman's lift, I see.'

'There are similarities,' said Jed, depositing me on his bed.

'Could you arrest me for swearing?'

'If you were breaching the peace or creating a public nuisance.'

I got tingles at the way he said 'public nuisance'.

'What about if we had a fight? Like if I refused to have sex or something?'

'You think that's likely?' Jed placed a hand on either side of me and gently rotated his groin against mine.

'Hypothetically.'

'Well, presently, refusing to shag your boyfriend is not a criminal offence. I'd probably have to make something up and plant some evidence. A smoking blood-stained gun with your fingerprint on it. You know, stuff like that.'

'Have you a pair of handcuffs?'

'Of course,'

'Standard issue?'

'Oh yes.'

'With pink fur?'

'No, I had to glue the fur on. Maybe I'll show you later.'

And then we didn't talk any more.

Epilogue

I felt a bit bad about not saying goodbye to my colleagues at PL.

'Never explain,' said Jed. 'It generates an aura of mystique.'

'Isn't that what perfume is for?'

The following week, Jed told me to leave Friday evening free. 'A surprise,' he said.

He had arranged a leaving party for me. Chanelle, Nigel and Amber were there, but regrettably Brenda Calburn couldn't make it due to a personality crisis.

''M gong fackin' mish you, Livvie,' said Nigel, zooming in for an embrace and lurching into the jukebox. However, he was like a determined pinball and I didn't duck fast enough to miss an open-mouth slobber.

'I'll miss you too, Nigel,' I said, realising that I probably would.

Much later, I bumped into Chanelle in the bathroom reapplying lipstick.

'Hi!' I said delightedly.

'Hello.' She smiled at me in the mirror.

'Chanelle—'

'Don't. It's not important.'

'I just wanted to say I'm so glad you came.'

'Wouldn't have missed it,' said Chanelle.

Moving towards me, she gave me a brief, regretful hug.

'Whatever happened between you and Luke?' I asked. Chanelle coloured delicately.

'Oh. Well, we went out. But ... he was so unbelievably crap in bed. And what *was* the licking thing all about?'

'I never figured it out. Come here, there's someone I want you to meet,' I said and, taking her hand, I led her back into the brawl of Spinker's. He was leaning awkwardly against a pillar at the other side of the bar.

'John,' I said, thrusting Chanelle at Marlboro Man. 'Have you met Chanelle yet? Chanelle, this is John. Detective Inspector John – isn't that right?'

'Yes, ma'am,' said John. Chanelle stared at him with her mouth open. John seemed to be equally mesmerised, or else he was *really* into leopard print. It looked remarkably like love at first sight. Even *I* could hear the orchestra playing.

'Hi,' said Chanelle and there was a loaded pause.

'Well, I'll leave you to it,' I said.

Spinning away from them, I bumped into—

'Aw fuck!' I said.

'Olivia,' said Gary Newbit. 'Heard it was your leaving do, thought I'd come down and pay my respects.'

'Well, I suppose that'll be a nice change,' I said, desperately trying to catch Jed's eye.

'You and me,' he continued philosophically. 'What d'you say we get out of here? Have a glass or two of champagne, see what pops up—'

'Are you making a *pass* at me?' I said incredulously.

'I suppose I am,' said Gary Newbit, looking down my top.

'You have got to be joking. *No!*'

'Oh, come on.' He pouted. 'Is it because I'm married?'

'Well, yes, there is that. But more because I despise you.'

'Really?' He looked genuinely distressed. 'I always thought we had something.'

'That would be mutual loathing, Gary.'

'Hey! There you are,' said Jed, dropping a kiss on my shoulder. 'I've been looking all over for you.' He nodded at Gary.

'That was fun,' I said on our way home.

The following week, my bank called to ask whether I was expecting any incoming payments.

'Yes, I am.'

'How much are you expecting to receive, Miss Anderson?'

'Is it any of your business?'

'It's just that we are concerned you're dealing in drugs,' they responded – although I'm paraphrasing.

The balance on my next bank statement came to £1,502,023.67.

'Jed, look!' I shouted, waving the statement at him. He was chopping an onion. It was yet another thing I loved about Jed: the man could cook. The smell of lightly sautéing spices almost distracted me, but not quite. 'Have you ever seen that many numbers?'

'Only once, on a dodgy munitions deal in Uganda.'

Seriously, Jed and I needed to talk.

'Let's go wild! Let's buy a new telly! And organic food! And . . . and . . . a bicycle!'

'Are you going to chop those peppers?' said Jed, punishing the onion. 'You're a millionaire now—'

'A multi-millionaire!'

'Not quite. But screw organic food. You should be

thinking big. How about organic truffles? You can treat me to a motorbike. And we could get a yacht—'

'You know what I'd really like to do?'

'What?'

'I'd like to travel round the world.'

'Really?' said Jed slowly. 'Is this some sort of midlife crisis?'

'Probably.'

'How long were you thinking?'

'Maybe six months? I don't know. Six months, a year.'

Jed attacked the pepper and then stopped, looked at me.

'Sweetheart, if that's what you want to do, you should go for it. Absolutely. But I'll really miss you. I've kind of got used to having you around.'

'Yeah? How much?'

'An amount barely falling inside the bounds of common decency.'

'Well, that's nice. Because I meant both of us. You and me.'

Jed started to grin. 'Yeah?'

'Yeah.'

Jed came round the bench and kissed me soundly. 'Suppose we might as well explore our midlife crises together. You're on! Let's go.'

'Okay, but let's have a shag first.'

Jed took a year's sabbatical, I gave notice on my apartment, and within a month we were gone. First stop Africa. We started off easy, working on a nature reserve in Namibia for a couple of weeks. Jed nearly got bitten by a shark off Capetown, but claimed that working for Puttock Leavitt was worse. We rode camels across the Sahara until our backsides wore out. In Borneo, we picked nits out of orangutans. I puked on top of Kilimanjaro while Jed, robustly oblivious of the altitude sickness, held my hair back. Jed was cavity-searched in Dubai airport and then we left the UAE in a hurry when I accidentally set fire to our hotel room. We rode elephants in India, upgrading to the Orient Express in the Far East. For one magical month we lived in a shack on a beach in Thailand.

You don't truly know someone until you've had amoebic dysentery with them. Jed and I looked out for each other; we talked and argued and made love. By Cambodia, I knew Jed was the man I wanted to share the rest of my life with.

Coming back to London was surreal. Of course, the city was the same as it had always been, but everything seemed slightly skewed. It was a little dingier, more shrill, not as vibrant as I remembered. It was time for some major decisions – but not just yet.

Hidden in the hillock of bills, brochures and bank statements on Jed's hall floor was an invitation. We had returned just in time for Nigel and Amber's wedding. It was the society event of the year; hordes of beautiful people attended. Amber was delivered in a glass carriage, a vision in a froth of hot pink.

'Could only have been less tasteful if she'd worn white,' murmured a voice I recognised. It was Chanelle, accompanied by John and looking rudely radiant in – a maternity dress.

'Oh my God!' I shrieked. 'You're pregnant! How – what – when?'

'Five months,' said Chanelle, with a dazzling smile. John put a protective arm round her.

'Congratulations! D'you know if it's a boy or girl?'

'Not yet.'

'We're going to call her Lily if it's a girl,' said John shyly.

'Tiffany,' said Chanelle. 'We haven't quite agreed—'

'And Jack if he's a boy,' said John.

'Rock,' corrected Chanelle.

'As in Hudson?' asked Jed.

'The opposite of a hard place?' I said.

'Hey, did you hear?' John addressed Jed and me. 'Feshwari and Wylie. They got sentenced last week. Wylie got four years, Feshwari twenty-two. We managed to get him on the money laundering charge as well.'

'Luke only got four?' I said.

'When he's finished his time, we're going to extradite him to Finland. Finns want him for a racketeering scam. Don't worry, both of them will spend a while trading cigarettes for laundry duty.'

'Fantastic,' I said.

'Hi, chaps,' said Nigel. 'Fack, this wedding cake is chewy, isn't it?'

'That's because you're eating your cravat, Nigel.'

We left shortly after Nigel discovered his father in the kitchen with his hand down his new bride's wedding dress. The Earl of Derby claimed he was helping her adjust her corset.

'Terrific wedding,' I sighed happily, resting my head on Jed's shoulder as he drove us home. 'Can you believe Chanelle's pregnant? She'll make a wonderful mother.'

'What are you thinking?' asked Jed. He picked up my hand and kissed it.

'Who, me? Nothing.'

'Nothing?'

'Not a thought in my head.'

little black dress

**brings you fantastic new books like these
every month - find out more at
www.littleblackdressbooks.com**

Why not link up with other devoted Little Black
Dress fans on our Facebook group? Simply type
Little Black Dress Books into Facebook to join up.

And if you want to be the first
to hear the latest news on all things
Little Black Dress, just send the details below to
littleblackdressmarketing@headline.co.uk
and we'll sign you up to our lovely email
newsletter (and we promise that we won't share
your information with anybody else!).*

Name: _____

Email Address: _____

Date of Birth: _____

Region/Country: _____

What's your favourite Little Black Dress book?

_____

How many Little Black Dress books have you read?_____

*You can be removed from the mailing list at any time

Pick up a *little black dress* – it's a girl thing.

IT MUST BE LOVE
Rachel Gibson
PB £4.99

Gabrielle Breedlove is the sexiest suspect that undercover cop Joe Shanahan has ever had the pleasure of tailing. But when he's assigned to pose as her boyfriend things start to get complicated.

She thinks he's stalking her. He thinks she's a crook. Surely, it must be love?

978 0 7553 3746 0

ONE NIGHT STAND
Julie Cohen
PB £4.99

When popular novelist Estelle Connor finds herself pregnant after an uncharacteristic one-night stand, she enlists the help of sexy neighbour Hugh to help look for the father. But will she find what she really needs?

One of the freshest and funniest voices in romantic fiction

978 0 7553 3483 4

You can buy any of these other
Little Black Dress titles from your
bookshop or *direct from the publisher*.

FREE P&P AND UK DELIVERY
(Overseas and Ireland £3.50 per book)

Leopard Rock	Tarras Wilding	£5.99
The Fidelity Project	Susan Conley	£5.99
See Jane Score	Rachel Gibson	£5.99
It Should Have Been Me	Phillipa Ashley	£5.99
Animal Instincts	Nell Dixon	£5.99
Dogs and Goddesses	Jennifer Crusie, Anne Stuart, Lani Diane Rich	£5.99
Sugar and Spice	Jules Stanbridge	£5.99
Italian for Beginners	Kristin Harmel	£5.99
The Girl Most Likely To . . .	Susan Donovan	£5.99
The Farmer Needs a Wife	Janet Gover	£5.99
Hide Your Eyes	Alison Gaylin	£5.99
Living Next Door to Alice	Marisa Mackle	£4.99
Today's Special	A.M. Goldsher	£4.99
Risky Business	Suzanne Macpherson	£4.99
Truly Madly Yours	Rachel Gibson	£4.99
Right Before Your Eyes	Ellen Shanman	£4.99
The Trophy Girl	Kate Lace	£4.99
Handbags and Homicide	Dorothy Howell	£4.99
The Rules of Gentility	Janet Mullany	£4.99
The Girlfriend Curse	Valerie Frankel	£4.99

TO ORDER SIMPLY CALL THIS NUMBER

01235 400 414

or visit our website: www.headline.co.uk

Prices and availability subject to change without notice.